TO FIGHT MY OWN BATTLES

Prologue

Tim fidgeted restlessly in his seat and smiled at his wife, sitting contentedly in the front passenger seat. "Not far now" he commented, more to distract himself from his feelings of growing panic than to impart any valuable information. He hoped that the tone of his voice had not relayed his inner turmoil. He was acutely aware of the tingling sweatiness if his palms, gripping the steering wheel with unaccustomed tightness and the feeling of constriction in his chest, causing him to breath fast and shallow, in turn making him feel slightly dizzy and generally unwell. How was it possible for what should have been a long distant memory to evoke such a physical response? Especially with the freedom and confidence imparted by the eight cylinders purring in front of him and a beautiful wife beside him. His mind drifted back to a time, nearly twenty years earlier, when he had first experienced this feeling.

Tim had taken an unexpectedly interesting job in advanced technology when he had left university and it had entailed extensive travel around the country working with clients to develop the company's products to their specific requirements. He greatly enjoyed his work as it was simultaneously intellectually stimulating and enabled him to work alone "in the field" without close supervision or control. Tim functioned best when left to his own devices and he achieved excellent results. An added bonus (in the eyes of a status conscious young man, possibly the most important thing) was that he was provided with a large and regularly renewed company car which imparted immediate visible evidence of his success wherever he went. One day, on the way back from an interesting day at the offices of a "blue chip" company, his mind already planning how to interpret the customers needs in terms of the high technology response that they were seeking, the motorway had come to a standstill due to a combination of roadworks and two accidents. Tim had taken the next exit and decided to navigate cross country rather than risk sitting bored in traffic for potentially more than an hour. He had a good sense of direction and of the geography of this part of England and he enjoyed driving so this was his natural response to the situation. Some time during the course of this new journey Tim began to feel unwell. His stomach felt tight, his skin was sweaty and he felt light headed. He hoped he wasn't catching the flu. When he got home he swallowed some paracetamol and had a large glass of gin to settle his stomach. Surprisingly he had started to feel better almost immediately and he was soon able to eat a microwaved frozen prawn curry and rice for two before heading out to the pub for a pint with the peaceable country folk of the village in which he lived.

It had not been until the middle of the next day that he had suddenly understood with a sickening certainty what had caused his feelings of the previous day.

Tim indicated, slowed, changed into second in anticipation of the steep hill and turned left, revving hard to increase speed on the long incline. The road narrowed more than he remembered and the hedgerows seemed to close in from both sides, threatening to scratch the car and increasing his feeling of discomfort and unease. He felt certain that there would be some dry-stone walling hidden within the profuse May growth, waiting to inflict serious damage should he make one false move. Could even the local lanes be accomplices in the plot to ensnare him in the web of fear once more?

Three minutes later he was driving along the village street, mixed rustic and grand stone buildings placed seemingly at random beside the narrow road, vivid green fields rising up the hill behind them. Tim struggled to remember where the road might widen so that he could park his car. He had never before considered the place in which he had spent five long years from the perspective of a driver and the problem momentarily distracted him from the maelstrom of feelings that seemed to assail him from every angle.

At last the street widened sufficiently to allow for a pavement on one side close to the village church and pub. Tim bumped the car up the curb and parked, straddling pavement and road, turned off the engine and unclipped his seatbelt. He could hear his heart beating wildly in his ears and he hoped he wasn't going to faint.

"It's miles from anywhere!" said Sarah "and *so beautiful*" she gasped.

With a feeling of weary heaviness and foreboding Tim forced himself out of the familiar security of his car into the familiar discomfort of the sun drenched High Street. Joining his wife on the pavement he heard the click of the doors locking and was aware of the simultaneous flash of the indicator lights. "Well, here it is" said Tim, starting to walk beside his beloved wife, a warm, secure, source of reassurance amongst the fears, insecurities and terrors that were now assailing him from every angle.

As much to prove to himself that this really was nothing more than a row of mixed historic stone buildings in a pretty rural setting Tim began to point out the different activities that happened behind the blank, black faced leaded light windows that squinted onto the street. "They're the kitchens, with the sanatorium above them – they must have known that most of what was produced in the kitchens would be poisonous so that there was quick access to medical help!" "That door goes into a long, dark passage that was supposed to be haunted." "I lived up there! In my last two terms here." "That's the original castle where the school first began. You can see how the village must have developed around it for safety and security and the fantastic views of potential attackers that the castle offered. It must have seen some exciting history over the centuries".

"You were so lucky to have been in a place like this! Every day would be an inspiration with these beautiful views and all the history and grandeur around you. I can't imagine that anyone would fail to do well in these surroundings".

"Exactly!" replied Tim, suddenly reacting angrily to what were obviously perfectly sensible and reasonable observations. "Waking up to ice on the inside of the windows, cold baths shared with other boys, lumpy porridge and warm, bromide flavoured tea for breakfast". And they're just the easy bits, he thought grimly to himself, shivering in response to the freezing fist that was gripping and twisting his entire insides.

The castle had developed over the centuries, first to ever larger and more defensive fortresses then, as the country moved from feudalism towards secure democracy, from the rather utilitarian needs of warlords to the desire for comfort and status of the ruling classes. By the middle of the nineteenth century it had evolved into a fully-fledged (If still crenulated) stately home. It was at this time that the owner had set up a small school for "the betterment of the sons of Christian gentlemen". The school had flourished and expanded, first filling the castle and then spilling over into village houses and shops, purchased as and when they became available. Thus the school now owned or otherwise controlled almost every building in the High Street and many more of the larger houses in the surrounding locality. Such haphazard expansion had resulted in a veritable rabbit warren of different floors, levels, and weird shaped rooms, linked together by outside paths and unexpected entrances. This in turn had caused a very complicated and largely unsupervised system of control and management in which, outside lesson times, the older boys had almost unfettered power over all that happened within the school.

The couple turned off the High Street and followed the public right of way that skirted the school grounds and headed towards the extensive and highly manicured playing fields. To the left, on what had been a sloping area of uncultivated pasture in Tim's day, used for many an arranged fight, for secretive smoking or drinking of dangerously large volumes of alcohol, now stood a huge oak and glass building, pretentiously sign posted as the Sports and Wellbeing suite. Through the plate glass Tim could see an Olympic sized swimming pool glistening seductively and, beyond, a room filled with the latest weight training equipment. Tim remembered, with dismay and discomfort undiminished by the passing of thirty years, the roughness of the blue painted concrete of the unheated outside pool in which he had been forced to swim length after length in the interests of "stamina training". No doubt this, along with the many other developments since his departure, had been funded by the inexorable increase in the school fees which were now, as in every other public school in the country, far beyond the means of even the professional classes like Tim. This trend had been just beginning in the mid nineteen seventies, first when the schools began to attract and then to actively recruit the sons of wealthy overseas families. Tim had seen the trickle and then flow of swarthy Arab boys, their parents paying double the usual fees that were justified by the bursar for the special facilities that would need to be provided for their special religious and cultural needs. These needs had, of course, never been met at all, the welcome extra income being syphoned off to build "show piece" new facilities in the school that would help to attract more wealthy foreign pupils. The Arabs, Tim reflected, would by now have been joined by the sons of Russian oligarchs, Asian business men and Chinese industrialists.

The couple stood looking across the striped green acres of manicured grass playing fields, the stately pavilion nestled amongst light green fronds of weeping willow, the brook shimmering placidly in the warm summer sun setting the whole picture postcard off to the most poetic effect.

"How could anyone not love this place? "mused Sarah. Tim was picturing the cold mud of the mid-winter rugby pitches, the swirling currents of the rain swollen brook running deep and treacherous and icy cold under the iron grey clouds heavy with snow. He shuddered again, his inner cold now enveloping his entire skin as well.

"let's go, we can still be in time for some lunch at the pub. I heard it used to be very good".

The menu was extensive and varied, the venue welcoming and the beer was excellent. Tim remembered old Mrs. Mundy who had been the land lady at the pub when Tim was a boy. She had once had a son at Barforth School so she had felt sympathetic to the needs of "those poor boys" and would regularly let a group of them enjoy the facilities of her hostelry from a private room at the back, safe from possible recognition by a Master. He doubted that any land lady these days would dare to risk her licence and reputation for the benefit of even a regular flow of local school boys. As the couple started to eat it became clear that the accolades for excellence, repeated both in many guide books and in local repute, was indeed well deserved. Tim began to feel more comfortable. The possibility of being able to enjoy the day for what it was, a visit to a stunning part of the country for a walk and a delicious meal, began to seem more plausible. And yet.........Every time the door opened for someone to come in Tim turned, startled, ready for trouble. Even the perception of movement in the car park beyond the window was enough to make him feel an urge to leave while he still could. Sarah scowled. "Please calm down. What is the matter? It's as if you are a criminal on the run, expecting to be arrested at any moment. I promise that there is nothing and no one to hurt or frighten you here now. Please try to relax and enjoy yourself. The whole point of coming here was to make you feel better, not to distress you more."

If only it really was that simple thought Tim, forcing a smile, trying to appear suitably reassured, unable to face the prospect of an argument.

Wednesday the third of September, 1975

Tim was sitting in the early autumn sunshine in the sun lounge trying to relax his growing nervousness and feeling of unease at the prospect of starting a whole new phase of his life. He had hoped that the warmth of the room and the calming beauty and scents of the plants around him would help to make him feel better but it hadn't really had much effect

"It's time to come and get ready Tim" his mother called from the sitting room doors. Reluctantly he stood up and went to join his parents in the hall. His mother was dressed in tweed and a mauve blouse and his father looked uncomfortable in a dark grey suit and highly polished black shoes. Tim stamped into his own new black shoes and stooped to tie the laces. When he stood up his mother proffered his new tweed jacket. It felt stiff and tight around the shoulders and suggested that, combined with his new white shirt, it may become uncomfortably itchy too.

Tim obediently took one end of his blue trunk with brass corners and lock and helped his father to carry it out to the car. The large estate easily swallowed it together with his wooden tuck box and tartan overnight case. Tim opened the door and climbed into the back seat, settling into the soft but slippery brown plastic seat behind his mother in the front passenger seat. He wondered glumly if there was any hope that the car wouldn't start. There was not. His father engaged gear, twirled the large car round in the paved court-yard and swung out on to the drive way with a satisfying crunch of gravel beneath the wheels and then out into the road.

They drove in miserable silence. Tim guessed that his father would rather have been at work and that it had been his mother, anxious to make "the right impression" who had persuaded him to take the afternoon off to make this journey. He looked out of the window as the familiar roads and land marks began to thin and make way for unknown towns and villages.

"I expect you're feeling a bit apprehensive." His mother broke the long silence. "It's obviously perfectly normal to feel like that dear. Just remember that you have passed your entrance exams very well and better than most of the other boys and that everyone else will be feeling the same as you are. You'll settle in in no time!"

"Yeah" replied Tim, trying to speak normally through the lump in his throat. "Please come and take me out soon".

"You know that it's much too far for us to come here just for a day out. We'll see you at half term when we come to the speech day. Just remember how proud we are of you and that we will be thinking of you all the time. I will write to you every week. Try to write to us often so we can share all the exciting things that you will be doing."

The car turned off the main road onto much smaller country lanes. They were following closely behind two Volvo Estates. "I expect they're new boys too" said Mum "I wonder which house they will be in." Remember, Tim, you're in School House. It's really important that you remember to tell people that and write it on your work and things like that. It's a big school and things will get lost if you don't."

Tim wondered, not for the first time, what it was that made his mother so tiresomely confident of her own ideas. How was it that she was always able to believe totally in what she thought to be the case and did not feel shy to share her thoughts with anyone else who would listen? He hoped that she wouldn't do or say anything to embarrass him now when it was so important not to appear in any way different to anybody else.

Father turned off the lane into the school main entrance. A large red sign proclaimed Barforth Senior School For Boys. Temporary signs directed cars to park along the lane that led to the playing fields. "It's not very considerate of them when they know that everyone is going to have to unload and carry heavy trunks all the way back up to the school" complained mother. "Obviously they can't fit everyone in the main car park" replied father reasonably.

Tim and his father carried the trunk towards the main school while mother walked confidently looking around her as if she owned all that she surveyed. They were directed to School House and the Junior Dormitory by more temporary signs. At last, after two flights of steep and narrow stairs and half a dozen heavy self-closing doors they reached their destination. It was a huge room, painted in light blue, with windows along three sides and a full two stories high, the vaulted ceiling being crisscrossed by a series of hefty beams and less hefty steel bars. Arranged around the room were some fifteen beds, each made up with dull grey-brown blankets. There were two other sets of parents, each with their own son, delivering similar trunks.

"I think the boys are supposed to choose which ever bed they fancy" one of the other mothers volunteered to Tim's parents. The three boys stared at each other in silence. Tim just selected the bed next to the other two boys, having no idea of any minor benefit that may exist between one position and another.

The third mother sat on her son's bed and started bouncing on it. "It's not exactly comfortable" she laughed. "Be careful or you will spoil all the hard work that someone put in to making all these beds" warned Tim's mother. "Oh good!" laughed the bouncing lady.

"I believe that we are all expected to go to meet the staff over a nice cup of tea" the first lady interjected, trying to divert a possibly difficult situation. The six parents and three recalcitrant boys started to leave the room just as another set of parents and son pushed through the heavy door at the far end of the long passage way. Three excited younger siblings ran and shouted their way ahead of the family.

"Hello! We're just on our way to tea! Just choose any bed you like and then come and join us. The boys need some nice cakes to cheer themselves up." The bouncing lady said as she passed the latest arrivals.

The group descended the stairs, passing another father and son struggling upwards with a trunk. His mother was following, burdened with a tuck box. As they followed yet more signs welcoming all parents and sons to The Headmaster's Tea, the three mothers started chatting and laughing together as if they were long lost friends, the fathers smiled sheepishly at one another as if they knew that they were expected to be talking but could think of nothing to say. Each of the boys walked in a kind of dispirited silence, forced together and yet alone in their nervousness.

In the vast, wood panelled dining hall there were already a large number of people, helping themselves to cups and saucers of tea and then trying to juggle a separate plate of cakes and sandwiches while eating and drinking. Some, like Tim's parents, stood in small groups of new acquaintances, trying to make cheerful and uncontroversial small talk to people about whom they knew nothing. Others stood as a single family, feeling awkward and unsure how what surely would be an emotional parting should be conducted, the discomfort of everyone in this contrived social gathering heightened by the omnipresence on every wall of imposing portraits of past Head Masters peering disdainfully down on the proceedings.

"Mr and Mrs Croy!" It's so nice to see you again. And Timothy! Welcome to Barforth!" A tall but stooped old man broke into the small group. Tim's father, who had been looking the other way, jumped with the surprise of the sudden address and slopped his tea into the saucer. Mrs Croy fired a warning stare at her husband as she thanked the Head Master for such a welcoming tea. He moved on with similar introductions to the rest of the small group.

When the Head Master had moved on to another group the bouncing lady's husband smiled at his wife. "We'd best be hitting the road love, if we're to get back to Leeds tonight." "yes! It's time we made a move too." Tim's father joined in. The parents made their farewells to one another as the group moved out of the grand dining room and then dispersed to say their private good byes. Tim and his parents walked past what seemed like hundreds of blank, unwelcoming windows and across the Head Master's Quadrangle. From there it was only a short walk along the private lane to their car.

"You know we're very proud of you dear" Mrs Croy told Tim, leaning forward to give him a quick peck on his cheek. Tim's nostrils filled with the familiar and comforting scent of her Eau de Cologne and he felt the burning of tears at the back of his eyes. Of-course he wasn't going to cry – men were not supposed to and he was considered to be very grown up now that he was at senior school. His father shook his hand, rather self-consciously, but said nothing. They got into the car, started the engine and began to move slowly along the lane, restricted by the Jaguars, Fords and Volvo estates that were parked along both sides. Tim stood watching the car and then its flashing brake lights recede into the distance as he took some calming deep breaths to compose himself. He felt suddenly very small and alone in this disorientatingly complicated and unfamiliar new world.

This was it. There was no way out. No choices to be made. As his mother often said it was up to him to fight his own battles. Trying hard to look calm, confident and cheerful Tim set off to find his way back to where he had seen the School House Junior Common Room in which, an hour earlier, he and his father had deposited his tuck box.

Pausing for barely a second for fear of his resolve abandoning him Tim turned the brass handle and opened the heavy door. Seated in a semi-circle of hard, upright wooden chairs were four boys. "Hello! I'm Croy" Tim introduced himself, adopting with well -practiced ease the use of his sir name. The other boys introduced themselves as Andrews, Eglington, Williams and Slater. Tim recognised Eglington as the son of the bouncing lady. He moved another chair from its' place at the kind of kitchen work top that surrounded two sides of the room and sat next to Andrews. He spoke with a noticeably northern accent.

Over the following half hour, as the conversation started, faded into uncomfortable silences and was then restarted with forced determination from one or other of the young men, the room filled until there were twelve. Some bright spark amongst them worked out that they were now all there. "Let's go and explore" suggested Williams. Everyone was glad to agree to the diversion and they set of, closely knit like a pack of hunting dogs, each individual keen not to stand out in any way, trying hard to blend in with the group as he tried to assess the other boys with whom he had been arbitrarily placed to live and work for the coming five years. For every one of them knew, either from experience at prep school or from some kind of instinct, that however he became placed in the social hierarchy during those first few days would play a fundamental role in the way his whole career in the school would develop.

The group walked paths, opened doors, climbed dark stairs, went into empty, but scruffily well used classrooms that smelt of feet and disinfectant. They found the library and the impressive language laboratory, whose interesting looking equipment they could only glimpse through tightly closed windows. The assembly hall impressed with a stage at each end and possibly a thousand small and uninviting chairs in the middle and, lastly, the toilet block where they all lined up at the urinal and pissed.

The boys found their way back to School House through the Head Masters' Quadrangle, which was now filling with returning boys. Tim was amazed at how big some of them looked. How could you tell if they were boys or teachers? He remembered the "Leavers Speech" on the last day at his prep school in which Mr. Drake had warned them that, while they had become used to being the oldest and most important boys at this school they would be the smallest and least important ones at their new schools.

Somehow the group decided to go to the dormitory. They sat on their beds chatting more freely and noisily now until a senior boy came in and told them that the dormitory was out of bounds until nine o clock at night unless special permission was sought and granted from a prefect. They trooped together down the narrow staircase. "He's bossy" grumbled Williams. "I don't like him already"." I think he's the Head of House," added Eglington "so you'd better get used to listening to what he says" "Hum!" came Williams's reply.

Hardly had they got back to the common room than they heard a thunderous clanging of a bell somewhere above them. The boys looked at each other, unsure about what it was that they were being summoned to. Another boy looked in. "That's the supper bell" he said and, without any introduction he went on his way. The boys headed off towards the grand dining hall. When they tried to go in from the main hall way, as they had three hours earlier with their parents, they were turned away by a very important looking young man who explained that Third Fourth and Fifth Form boys had to come in from the "the Bogs passage". This turned out to be exactly as the name suggested, a long, stone, basement passage and stairs that wound through the old toilet block.

There were sausages and baked beans for supper with bread, jam and tea to drink. Tim noted with approval that the portions were large and the supply of bread and jam unlimited. The School House boys sat themselves on a long table at the end of the hall, nearest the Bogs Passage.

Back in the Junior Common Room the boy's spirits seemed to have lifted, probably as a result of a full meal and the collective realisation that life at Barforth would probably not be so very different to the lives that they had lived in their previous schools.

The School Bell clanged again, bringing conversation and laughter to a ragged end. Voices from within the building and the grounds outside summoned them to Chapel. The School House Boys filed out of the Junior Common Room and joined the flow of pupils heading across the Head Master's Quadrangle towards Chapel. As they entered the arched wooden doors there was something of a scuffle as every boy paused to find his name on seating plan that was stuck to a black board on an easel that rather obstructed the entrance. Tim located his name, in the middle of the third row from the front, on the left. He followed the mass of boys pouring along the aisle until he reached his position and slid into the hard, dark wood pew which was slowly filling with other third form boys from different houses, bringing once again the chilly insecurity of being alone amongst strangers. A short, shabby grey haired man stood up at the front of the chapel. "Welcome back to another wonderful new school year, for which we all thank God. Our prayers reach out, tonight, to all our new boys who we welcome and may God help them! Let us start by joining together to sing hymn number twenty-three in the Modern Compilation book.

There was a rustling of six hundred books being lifted from pew back racks and flicked open to the correct page followed by more shuffling noises as six hundred boys rose to their feet. Tim wrinkled his nose in distaste at the musty, rather damp smell of the chapel which combined with the smell of floor polish and dust from the newly opened books made him feel as if he was going to sneeze. He flinched slightly as the organ boomed into life from somewhere high up behind him, and was taken by surprise at the deep roar of six hundred adult male voices starting to bellow out the words to hymn twenty-three. As he composed himself and began to join in the singing Tim realised that his surprise sprang merely from a subconscious expectation of the sound of his prep school assemblies with Mrs. Ball playing the piano and ninety shrill young voices singing.

Hardly had they all returned, one by one, to the Junior Common Room than they were called to a house meeting, to be held in the Junior Dormitory and they jostled their way up the two flights of stairs, the group swelling on the way to include the boys from the Senior Common room and from other rooms and studies that were spread around the wider house area and beyond. The Junior Dormitory was unrecognisable, every bed, window sill and chest of drawers draped with boys and young men, some chatting and laughing boisterously, glad to be reunited with good friends, others more morose, regretting their loss of freedom or fearing coming exams.

The Head of House, accompanied by a group of other senior boys, came into the room and everyone fell silent. Mr. Linford, the House Master, came in and looked nervously around the room, appearing to be almost startled to see so many people there. He welcomed the new boys to the house and then talked briefly about the expectations of behaviour and the daily routines of school. He left the room.

The Head of House introduced himself as Simon Moor. He started talking about the different categories of prefect, recognised by the colour and pattern of tie that they wore. School prefects had power throughout the school, House prefects had similar authority but only within their own house. He, the Head of House, was a School Prefect and had authority over all the house prefects. Together the prefects were in charge of most things that happened outside the classrooms. It was made clear that they had to be obeyed at all times.

There followed lots of information about the rules of the house, how things were to be done and what was expected of the Third Formers. Each of them would be allocated as the individual fag of one of the Sixth Form boys. A list of names would be put up in the morning. The duties of a fag were basically to do whatever their Sixth Former told them to do. Everyone would also be allocated tasks as a "School Fag" which was how all the administrative day to day tasks were done around the school. The lists for these would go up on the Head Master's Notice Board in a week or so. Anybody who was caught contravening the rules or who disobeyed a prefect would be punished by a variety of methods, largely at the discretion of the prefect concerned.

"Right, meeting over!" announced Simon Moor. "Third Formers have to go to bed now because it's nine O'clock so get yourselves ready. Lights out at nine thirty".

The dormitory emptied quickly, the older boys returning to their own rooms, leaving the Third Formers alone in their new surroundings. Slowly they began to unpack their overnight cases, shuffling off to brush their teeth in the large communal washroom at the end of the long passage, returning and changing into pyjamas, surprisingly everyone had similar striped sets, mostly in blue with just the occasional daring green or orange to add interest to the scene. Tim was glad that his were blue, conforming reassuringly with the safety of the majority. They sat around on their unfamiliar, creaky metal beds, chatting in small groups or exploring the immediate area. Climbing up to check the top of the curtained wardrobe, searching the drawers for any items of interest left by past occupants. The wondered aloud how the ancient gas fire, hung precariously on the wall above the door, could be lit and if it would do any good to the temperature of their sleeping level.

The door opened and in strode a tall, fair haired young man. The boys understood from his tie that he was one of the School Prefects. He introduced himself as James Long. Tim was surprised to hear him use his Christian name.

"Right, it's lights out time. That means no more talking. I'm on duty this evening and I will be up and down the passage seeing to the other two dorms so I can hear you if you do talk and you will probably be punished if you are caught." He looked round at them all, seemingly making a mental picture of each of them. "Because this is the first night of the school year I suggest you don't try to sleep too quickly." He added mysteriously as he clicked off the light and closed the door behind him.

The obedient silence lasted barely long enough for Long to have reached the end of the passage way. "What did he mean don't go to sleep too fast?" Tim recognised Andrews's voice. "Well obviously they don't want us to sleep yet" Tim guessed that that was Williams. "But *why*?" insisted Andrews. Nobody seemed to know and the whispered conversations moved on to other things that they could discuss with more certainty.

The sounds of talking, stampings backwards and forwards along the passage and the slamming of doors became more continuous as the older boys began to make their way to bed. Occasionally Long's voice could be heard exhorting better behaviour.

Then the rhythm of the cacophony of sounds changed, seeming to be funnelled up the passage way, getting closer and closer. The door burst open, the light blazed on and all the boys in the house filled the room once more. Some were still fully dressed in school uniform, some wore dressing gowns and others carried bath towels folded over their arms. They all stood now in the centre of the dorm, the third formers sitting up in their beds, wondering what this unexpected turn of events meant. Moor stood up on a chest of drawers and addressed them. "School House has a tradition that has to be maintained by every third former on his first night. You all need to climb up here and get hold of the beams up there." He gestured up at the barn like roof space "then you all need to keep swinging round the room as many times as you can or until I tell you to come down. Whatever happens you **must remain silent**. If you fall off or touch the floor or beds with your feet you will be made to do something else that you won't enjoy. Everyone understand?"

None of the Third Formers said anything. Tim, who was quite short in stature and had never been much gifted with athletic prowess, felt his heart pounding with fear and dread. This is when he might make a fool of himself, open himself up to being singled out as weak or somebody who could be made fun of. It didn't seem fair that some silly game like this should have the potential to undo all his efforts to blend in with the group to which he had been assigned.

Slowly, self-consciously, fearfully, the young boys rose from the security of their hard beds and clambered, under the gleeful, challenging scrutiny of fifty pairs of eyes, onto the chest of drawers that were clustered in the centre of the dormitory and then reached up to pull themselves onto the lowest of the steel bars. Hanging thus they began to follow each other in a circuit around the ceiling, changing level between bars and beams. Tim began to feel reassured once more. Despite his size he had always been strong and had exceptionally large reserves of stamina. He was confident that he could continue with this process for as long as it took.

After they had all completed the second circuit, as if by some signal, the lashings began. At first they were infrequent but well aimed arriving with a whistling hiss followed by a stinging slap as the wet towel or dressing gown cord made contact with the dangling and helpless thirteen year old body of a Third Former. Tim didn't comprehend what the sounds were until he was struck on the left leg with a painful slash. The boys continued their silent circuit of the ceiling, each desperate neither to be the first to fall nor the one who broke the silence. The lashings continued, quickening in pace, frequency and fury until it seemed that all fifty of the tormentors were flicking, whipping and slashing their make shift weapons together, again and again. Tim was hit twice, simultaneously, once with a very wet towel that splashed his pyjamas with cold as well as burning his skin with pain. Still the boys circumnavigated the vaulted roof space unable to escape the hissing venom of wet fabric that was flying up at them from their senior house mates.

"Enough!" Moor's voice called in a stage whisper. The lashing weaponry dropped, silent and flaccid beside each boy. The room emptied. The Third Formers remained, hanging but stationery, stoically awaiting instruction. "You can get down now." Moor sounded calm and gentle now." Well done all of you! I think you will be a very successful year for this house. Now you need to get back to bed and try to sleep. You will have loads of things to do tomorrow."

The boys were all off the beams and bars now, painfully, cautiously, finding their way back to bed. "Good night!" Moor clicked off the light and left. There was a stunned, tense silence. "Shit!" someone exclaimed. "I didn't think that was going to end." Eglington added. "Some bastard put something sharp in his towel. I'm bleeding." Williams said. "Yeah I'm bleeding too." Volunteered another voice. Murmurs of support, complaint, discontent, moved around the dark dormitory until, one by one, the boys drifted off into exhausted sleep.

Thursday, fourth of September 1975

Tim was roused, suddenly, from deep dreamless sleep by a scraping, rasping sound directly behind his bed followed immediately by the demanding clanging of the School Bell. Sunlight was flooding through the thin blue curtains and the startled tousled heads of young boys were starting to sit up in their creaky grey clads beds. Each of them experienced the momentary bewildering disorientation of waking up in unfamiliar surroundings to face unknown new challenges.

Norton, who was the dorm senior and a house prefect, sat up and instructed everyone that they had to get up, washed and dressed within twenty minutes in order to be in time for breakfast. The boys scurried down the long passage to the washrooms, brushing teeth and splashing water over their faces. There was a notice on the pin board on the washroom wall giving times of different activities that had to be accomplished during the course of the day. The tasks appeared simple enough but the names of unfamiliar people and places added an element of complexity to the new boys' ability to comprehend exactly what they had to do, where they had to do it and with whom. They could always come back to refer to the list!

When they were all ready they traipsed together along the wooden passage, down the two flights of steep stairs and out into the September sunshine, with just a hint of Autumn nip in the air. They followed the path past the many tall buildings and round the ivy clad outside of the Dining Hall to join the long, hungry queue that was already snaking towards the outer end of the Bogs Passage. After an interminable and increasingly chilly wait beside dripping taps and then balanced on concrete stairs they found themselves in the warm dining hall, already full of boys. The took a tray each and were served with bacon and tinned tomatoes. They helped themselves to a selection of cereals and slices of toast and then assembled at the same long table that they had occupied at supper. This would become their default table for the whole year. Some Third Form boys from other houses joined them at their meal. Tim recognised one of them from having sat next to him in chapel.

After breakfast the boys hung around in the Junior Common Room for half an hour before the clanging of the School Bell summoned them once more to morning chapel. Tim found himself standing to sing, kneeling to pray and sitting restlessly listening to readings from the Bible in a disinterested state of complete normality as if he had been at the school for years already. He reflected that, apart from the volume and quality of the singing, this was little different from his prep school so he really had been performing the same rituals for years!

Directly after chapel the School House boys headed back to the Junior Dormitory to meet Miss Coulson for unpacking. She introduced herself as the Domestic Matron and immediately set about instructing the boys about how many shirts and socks they should keep in the drawers and how they should be looked after. She made them line up and follow her, like so many ducklings, to see where the Sewing Room was, how they could knock on a hatch to ask for things and where they were to deposit their dirty laundry in sacks labelled Pants, Shirts, Rugby Shorts. Since they were School House this was to be done before breakfast on a Saturday. Any later and they wouldn't have any clean clothes by the middle of the following week "And then you'll find out what for!" Unpacking completed, the boys were instructed to carry or drag their bulky but now light trunks across the school to the field outside to toilets under the Assembly Hall. From there they would be stored in the cellar.

The third formers returned briefly to the Junior Common Room for break, during which they shared a packet of ginger nuts that Tim retrieved from his tuck box. When the School Bell clanged again it was time to go to their first lesson where they would meet the other boys with whom they would be sharing a class for the coming year. Tim was in form 3B, neither in the top class, which was reserved solely for academic scholars who were to be fast tracked to take their "O" levels in two years instead of three, nor in the bottom class which was for the less able boys. As he had always been, he told himself, nothing special just middling. Andrews and Slater from School House were with Tim in 3B and they set off together in search of Maths Room 2, as written on the timetable. They joined a group of other boys in the old-fashioned classroom with twenty ancient wooden desks, complete with lift up lids and built in inkwells, all thoroughly gnarled and darkened from generations of poking with compass points, carving of names and spilt ink. Everyone sat down and waited in slightly uncomfortable silence for the maths master to come in.

"That's impressively quiet! Well done!" the master announced his entrance. He was old, very tall and thin and wore thick rimmed glasses. Tim thought he looked exactly as a maths master should look. The lesson was spent distributing and naming text and exercise books and being told how Mathematics was the key to success in all walks of future life. Tim's mind began to wander, looking out of the window he watched a Sixth Form boy boiling a kettle and making a mug of tea in his study in another house, across the road from the maths room. He thought how nice and free this school was after the confines of his prep school.

An electric bell heralded the end of that lesson and the class trooped downstairs to the Chemistry laboratory. It looked just like the lab at Tim's old school, except bigger and with more bottles of chemicals lined up on the desks. It smelt of burning and gas. The teacher turned out to be a very small, wizened looking lady with a very quiet voice. She talked about how exciting Chemistry could be and then handed out several sheets of questions for the boys to answer "Just so that I can find out what you do know and what you don't know". Tim discovered that he didn't understand much on the sheet and came to the conclusion that he would probably not be very successful at chemistry. The bell rang again for the end of the lesson, immediately followed by the clanging of the School Bell summoning the school to lunch.

Lunch was an elastic affair which lasted for just over an hour and a half during which boys were free to wonder in, serve themselves, eat and depart at their leisured convenience. Many other activities for individuals and small groups were fitted in to this time which meant that there would be individual music lessons, house meetings, team meetings occasional whole class punishments or individual tutor meetings happening at the same time. As with everything in the school, information was publicised on a series of notice boards situated outside the Dining Hall, The Head Master's Notice Board, Rugby Board, Sports

Board, Rowing Board, Urgent Board and various small, specialist boards including one titled Sister's Sanatorium on which Tim would never once see a single notice throughout his five years at Barforth.

As they finished lunch the School House boys reassembled in the School Junior Common Room, talking about their first encounters with different teachers, comparing anecdotes and gathering information to help them prepare for future academic experiences. Shortly Moor came into the room to collect them for a "new boys briefing" with the Head Boy and School Prefects in the Gym.

One hundred and twenty Third Formers sat uncomfortably crowded together on some low benches facing a group of some fifteen young men in the wide striped ties that signified School Prefect status. One of them introduced himself as Michael Yeldom, Head Boy. There followed half an hour of information and advice. The need to check the various notice boards regularly throughout the day. When the Tuck Shop opened, the soon to be published School Fag duties, the expectation that each boy should be responsible for being in the right place at the right time to do what was expected of him. A list of some of the punishments available for use by School Prefects including "drills" in which a boy would have to run three times around the entire school perimeter, a distance of about three miles, before breakfast, beatings, which could still, in the mid-seventies, be administered by senior pupils on junior pupils and other, unspecified punishments "which we might think of at any given time". Were there any questions?

One boy wanted to know if they needed permission to go out of school into town. They were told that they had to ask their House Master and that they must wear school uniform. Another asked if they could use the games fields in their free time. They could, of course, but they could not use the main field, with the big pavilion on it as this was reserved for the First Fifteen Rugby team and the First Eleven Cricketers together with a select few Athletic groups. And Tennis, added one of the School Prefects. "OK" Yeldom said "That's the end of this meeting. You need to go and get changed into your swimming kit and meet up at the pool in ten minutes, ready for your swimming test with Mr. Price."

The School House boys trooped out of the Gym, round the edge of the Head Master's Quadrangle and through the small door that led into the School House Junior Changing Rooms. Amidst excited chatter and banter they freed themselves from their stiff, itchy new uniform tweed jackets and constricting ties and were soon clad in their dark blue uniform swimming trunks. Brightened by a gaudy selection of brightly patterned beach towels the School House Boys spilled out of the side door once more, meandered across the Quadrangle and then a short distance down the private school lane before turning off onto the Swimming Pool Terrace. All the Third Form boys were assembling there and very soon a School Prefect began to collect them into their House groups. A stocky, red faced man strode onto the terrace and addressed them all with an unexpectedly loud voice. Each boy was to swim two full lengths, without stopping, using any stroke he liked. They would do it house by house and he would call individual names from his list so that he could record pass or fail accurately. "Obviously there's no room for any misunderstanding of such simple instruction so let's start with Bridge House."

Six boys from Bridge house were summoned to the pool edge, jumped in and began to splash their way across the pool. The process continued, six boys at a time, house by house, everyone seeming to pass the test one way or another. Standing bored in their swimming trunks with a beach towel draped over their shoulders the waiting boys began to feel the under chill of the September afternoon. They talked intermittently, tried to look interestedly at the never ending splashing lines in the pool and grumbled about the ants that were creeping over their bare toes as they stood on the rough concrete paving stones. School

House was second from last. Tim heard his name, chucked his towel on the paving stones behind him and went to the edge of the pool with Andrews, Eglington and Williams. "Go!" fired Mr. Price's harsh voice. The boys jumped in. Tim's breath was sucked out of him by the freezing cold of the unheated pool. Shocked he began dutifully to thrash his arms and legs and thus to move along his lane towards the far distant end of the pool. He could hear the others striving similarly. Someone was ahead of him but he was pretty sure that the other two were behind him. Tim touched the far end with his finger tips and turned for the home length. The cold was eating into his bones now, causing his muscles to ache and his movements to become more cumbersome as his sensation numbed. For the second time in twenty four hours Tim had reason to be grateful for his larger than average reserves of stamina. Resolutely he pushed himself onward, realising with relief that he was over half way back now. To his surprise one of the other boys came into focus, only just ahead of him now, obviously similarly slowed by the cold. This fired an unfamiliar urge to compete and Tim employed his last remaining strength to try to power forward, to pass the other boy, to demonstrate his determination to his house mates. At last! Tim's fingers grasped the hand rail at the return end of the pool. So cold were they that he had difficulty closing his fingers round the rail to help pull himself up out of the pool. Somehow, amidst a torrent of dripping water he found himself standing once more on the rough concrete paving slabs of the Swimming Pool Terrace. "That's a very convincing pass. Well done Croy!" he heard Mr Price comment as he sought the modest comfort of his beach towel and, wrapping it round as much of his body as he could, he headed alone back to the house to change.

Tim dried himself quickly and was attempting to revive his circulation by rubbing himself vigorously with his towel as the other boys began to return, shivering and shocked, to dress and prepare for whatever was to come their way next.

None of the School House Boys could remember what they were supposed to be doing now so they all headed up to the wash room to check the list on the notice board.

They were surprised to see their names typed on a new list indicating to which prefect they had been allocated as a fag. Tim was fagging for Long, who lived in Top Study Two. They turned their collective attention to the First Day Timetable and discovered that they were to report immediately after swimming to the Music School for Choir testing. After that was tea and then some free time during which they were expected to met their prefect to be told what he expected from his fag. There would follow supper, prep and bed.

The group of boys, still subdued by their icy chill within, headed off in search of the Music School. Eglington said that he thought it was in the same building as the Sewing Room where they had been taken that morning by Miss Coulson. Since nobody else had a better idea of where they were supposed to be going they were happy to follow him. They wound their way once more past the grim faced buildings, down steps, round the Dining Hall and then along the narrow path that circumnavigated first the Old Boggs and then the sewing Room, finally reaching the Music School, the main door of which was propped open with a fire extinguisher, the red floored classroom beyond full of shivering Third Formers.

The boys were being called, one by one, again in House order, to sing to one or other of the two Music masters. The cold crowd of boys milled around the empty room, grumbling in small groups about the coldness of the pool, why Third Form boys were not allowed hot baths and how you were supposed to be able to do a singing test for the choir when your bollocks had just been frozen off. After what seemed like an eternity, during which every tiny source of possible interest had been explored, discarded and then tested again in the forlorn hope that some small potential amusement may have been overlooked Tim was called upstairs to Room Two. A tall, thin, man looking silly in a suit and red spotty bow tie was sitting at a piano. "Stand just there, nice and straight" he fussed. "When I play a scale on my piano I want you to replicate it to "la"" Tim stood as he had been told. The man played a few notes. Tim tried to copy them to la. "No, no, no" fussed the Music master "Try these." He played and Tim tried again. He wasn't interested in Music, certainly did not want to have all the extra hassle of being in the choir and had been regularly told that he was "tone deaf" by his disappointed, piano playing mother, his piano teacher at prep school (though Tim had asked his mother to allow him to continue with piano lessons as they usually happened in a Latin lesson which Tim was glad to miss and the old lady who taught it had an endless supply of chocolate coated dates which she kept in a screwed up paper bag in her powder scented handbag and which she would proffer as a reward at the slightest hint of success in the playing of middle C scales) and the school singing mistress. "No, no, NO!" the man stormed, suddenly scarlet faced. "You have no notion of the pain you've inflicted on my ears this afternoon. Please **never** darken the door of my classroom again." Tim would indeed never go upstairs in the Music School again.

Afternoon tea, available for half an hour between games time and afternoon lessons, consisted of an urn of warm tea and as much bread butter and jam as a boy cared to eat. On this occasion, after the initial disappointment that there were none of the splendid array of cakes and pastries that had been on show to impress parents the previous afternoon, the Third Formers were hungry but more interested in the possibility that warm tea, if drunk in sufficient quantities, may ameliorate the lasting effects of the unheated swimming pool. Back in the Junior Common Room boys began to wonder off to seek their Prefect and find out what expectations awaited them. Tim headed up the two flights of stairs and through the wash room, past the long dormitory passage and instead through a door at the far end which opened on to a short, wide passage, with a row of six blue doors on one side, opposite a grimy table with two gas rings on it and a sink full of dirty mugs beside it. Tim tapped a little nervously on the door of Top Study Two. "Come" commanded Long's voice from within. Tim pushed open the door and stood in a small but comfortably carpeted room. Along one wall was a low bed and against the other was built a desk and book shelves. Long turned in his seat to face Tim. "Ah, Croy! You're my fag. Well you're quite lucky to have me because I don't ask a lot of you. I want you to make my bed each day, in break time and, on Mondays, Wednesdays and Saturdays you can bring me my loaf of bread from the kitchens at break time. And on a Sunday morning you can polish my shoes before Chapel. I might ask you to do something else sometimes but in general that's about it really." "OK" replied Tim and remained standing in the door way, uncertain what he was expected to do now. "You can go now" Long turned away again and started fiddling with his record player. Tim left the room and closed the door. He returned to the common room to join a discussion about what other boys had been asked to do. Williams was stating boldly that he certainly was not going to wash up his prefect's dirty mugs and saucepans. He wasn't a slave and who did the boy think he was anyway? Just because he was four years older. Slater had to clean shoes *before breakfast,* **every** *day*. "well, if he wants his shoes *that* clean he's obviously a poof. You'd better watch your back!" advised Williams with a mischievous glint in his eye. "What do you think they'd do if we didn't do something" mused Eglington. "Give you a drill, most likely." Shrugged Andrews.

Supper came soon enough, heralded, as ever, by the clanging of the School Bell. Another clanging an hour later warned of five minutes to get ready for Prep. The School House Boys found a pile of Bandered sheets with a lengthy French test to be completed in the first ninety minutes of prep and to be handed in, **named,** to the prefect on duty. Gloomily each boy took a stapled collection of sheets and found themselves a pen and ruler. Moor entered the room. "Right, shut up and make sure you've got everything you need. No talking or moving once the second bell goes until eight thirty. Don't disturb me with stupid questions or I'll make you wish you hadn't." The bell rang again and the room descended into silence. As time elapsed and work began to be completed, or at least dismissed as "impossible" the sounds of fidgeting, chairs scraping on the plastic tiled floor or occasional coughing, sometimes replied by another boys forced cough of increasingly unlikely severity, started to alter the quality of the "silence". At last the bell rang for the end of First Prep and the start of Second Prep. "OK, give me your papers." Moor demanded. "Normally now you would either be doing your second prep or you could go to club and society meeting. Nothing's happening tonight so you'll have to stay here and read something. Don't irritate me." The boys tried their best to occupy themselves for a further silent half hour by reading or, increasingly, by passing scribbled messages and insults to one another on torn off scraps of paper. Tim suffered a wrathful stare from Moor when he was unable to stifle his mirth as he read a particularly crude depiction of the prefect who wanted beautifully polished shoes every day.

At last the bell sounded for the end of Second Prep and bed for Third Formers. Moor left the room and the boys descended with howls of laughter on a picture drawn expertly by Williams, of the kind of things that *that* prefect may be imagined to do in his shiny shoes. None of them were exactly edifying. At length the boys decided that they probably ought to go up to the dorm before any prefect had reason to exercise his unreasonable power over them. Their first full day at Barforth was coming to it's end.

Saturday September 6th 1975

On Saturdays the morning chapel service was extended to incorporate a hymn practice in an effort to ensure suitably impressive singing in the forthcoming Sunday service to which many parents could always be expected to come. The Third Formers had all been disappointed and then outraged to discover that the lengthened chapel time did not reduce the following lesson by the corresponding amount of time but rather the lost time was made up simply by deducting it from morning break.

After the normal chapel service was finished the Reverend Pullman and all the staff left for some welcome coffee time in the staff room. The Music master whose ears Tim had assaulted on Thursday afternoon pranced to the front of the Chapel. Today he was sporting a green velvet bow tie. For the next twenty minutes he sang the first line of various hymns, or sometimes selected the parts "That so many people get wrong, for some reason" and expected the school to repeat it. He used his favourite "No,no,**no**" again and again, the pain and disappointment visibly hurting him each time that the school failed in some way to satisfy his sensitive ears. Tim and the other Third Formers became increasingly bored and restless, crammed far to close together in their hard pews. Saturday mornings were evidently not going to be a time to look forward to!

The first half of the afternoon was dedicated to Rugby trials. The Third Formers were all to gather on Lower Fields, the least good playing fields in the extensive selection available to Barforth School. Nobody seemed to be at all certain of the location of Lower Fields until Eglington took it upon himself to go to ask Moor. He returned to the Junior Changing Room announcing the he *thought* he understood where they had to go and that it was a very long way away. The School House Boys set off across the Headmaster's Quadrangle smartly dressed in new blue shorts and blue and white striped Rugby shirts, clopping noisily on the asphalt with their studded Rugby boots. They were joined by the boys from neighbouring Baker House, glad to have found people who seemed to know where they were supposed to be going.

Lower Fields really were a long way away. All the way to the end of the private lane, climb over a five bar gate into a field of tussocky grass and cow pats, splosh under a tunnel beneath the railway line in which water collected together with more cow dung and soil to make a stinking six inch deep slurry which threatened to spill over the top and thus into rugby boots and finally out to Lower Fields, two roughly mown Rugby pitches surrounded on one side by the railway track and on the other three sides by a gentle meander of the river.

The boys joined a large group who were already gathered around three masters with sacks of Rugby balls and a stack of red and white striped police cones. Tim wondered which of the masters had stolen them and from where. Two or three more house groups of Third Formers arrived at irregular intervals, apologising for being late on account of getting lost on the way. After waiting a further fifteen minutes for the final house to arrive, without success, Mr. Price decided to start. He split boys up into groups of similar size and set them different tasks, each a basic component of the whole game, to practice. The three masters were running between groups with clipboards, assessing, noting and occasionally blowing a whistle or bellowing and instruction. Tim recognised the short, fat History master, dressed now in shorts and a yellow and black striped Rugby shirt that made him look for all the world like a giant bumble bee. As the afternoon wore on each group undertook each task as the boys became more tired and less interested. The last group of boys had arrived an hour late, to be subjected to a tirade of verbal humiliation by Mr. Price.

When they had squelched their weary way back through the tunnel and finally arrived in the School House Junior Changing Room Moor was waiting for them. "Thought I ought to come to make sure you all understood about washing properly after games. As you can see now, you can get quite dirty. I've helped you out today by running the baths for you but you'll have to sort them out for your selves from now on." The boys rid themselves of their muddied and wet Rugby kit, wrapped themselves in their brightly coloured beach towels and filed barefoot up the concrete stairs to the "four aside" bathroom. As the name suggested it consisted of a large room, with concrete floor, along two sides of which were installed four bath tubs, an added nicety being that the room doubled as a passage way that connected two parts of School House, thus ensuring a regular flow of boys passing through so that there was no hope whatsoever of any kind of privacy. "Two to a bath – you'll need to sit sideways, obviously, to fit you both in. Use plenty of soap and be quick, though because they're cold you probably won't want to hang around for long!" Tim found himself sharing a tub with Williams, each boy manoeuvring himself gingerly into the freezing water, positioning himself as far from the other as possible and resting the back of his knees on the rim of the tub, his lower legs and feet hanging uselessly outside the bath. How on Earth was one supposed to get the dirtiest part of oneself clean when you couldn't get it in the water? They managed as best they could, splashing most of the bathwater onto the floor in the process, anxious not to prolong the miserable experience and aware of the sounds from the Senior Changing Room beneath them indicating that the Fourth Formers were ready to run their hot, but still shared baths. It would not be until the Fifth Form that they would be able to enjoy individual hot baths. Each incremental privilege was greatly anticipated and keenly protected from those who were too junior to be entitled to it.

    Tea time was spent, as would become usual, trying to drink sufficient warm tea from the urn to counteract the deep-seated chill from the cold bath. All Third Formers were then expected to congregate in the Assembly Hall to be informed of their appointed role as a School Fag.

    The boys milled around the hall until all the School Prefects arrived. The Head Boy called for quiet and started reading lists of boys' names who were to be directed by different School

Prefects. Most boys were being put into "gangs" that would be directed by their allocated School Prefect to undertake various menial tasks around the school like moving chairs, setting up desks in the hall at exam time, standing at strategic points around the school all afternoon to act as guides if required when visiting schools were expected for matches. Tim was allocated to the young man in charge of "special duties". This group went to sit on the stage, away from the general clamour of the busy room to discuss their individual roles. One was to report to the Sargent Major every break time to distribute post around the school, another had the daily chore of unlocking the classroom doors. Tim and another boy were to be "Brook Ball Boys" which would entail retrieving any rugby ball that was accidently kicked or thrown into the brook that surrounded the First Fifteen Rugby pitch during Saturday afternoon matches. Two were required because the brook frontage was long and a speedy response was essential. They were to be on the playing field ready for work by two 'o clock each Saturday and would be free to go as soon as the match ended.

When the School Fag meeting was over everyone was free for the rest of the day. The School House Boys hung around in the Junior Common Room, reading, talking or doing nothing at all. Some drifted off to one or other of the television rooms or to the library. Tim spent a short time in the library flicking through a newspaper and then headed back towards the School House. He took the short cut through the Four Asides and, as he was passing the Senior Common Room he met a red haired, thick set, freckled boy who he knew to be a Fifth Former. He was standing beside a trunk. "I'm late taking this back. Could you help me carry it to the cellar? It's much easier with two." Tim was always happy to help and, having nothing particular to do, readily agreed. "I'd better just check that it's empty" said the boy, lifting the lid. Tim felt a sudden push from behind, half lifting him off his feet and tipping him into the trunk. "What's going on?" But the boy's pudgy hand pushed Tim hard into the trunk and the heavy lid shut over him. Tim couldn't quite understand what was happening, so taken by surprise had he been, but as the total darkness surrounded him and he heard the clunk of two catches being snapped closed outside, he knew that he was not in a good place.

Tim felt his new prison being heaved around. Though he was small for his age the confines of the trunk enveloped Tim tightly and he could not uncrumple himself or move in any direction to get lass uncomfortable. He felt the trunk being tipped up to stand on its end, which meant that Tim was standing on his head. With a lurch, Tim felt the trunk start to move, tumbling over and over with increasing speed and violence. Tim's knees, elbows and head were banged and bumped against the hard sides of the trunk again and again and again. The rumbling, crashing, scraping sounds were amplified and contained within the confines of the big box adding further to Tim's disorientation and discomfort. With a final shuddering scraping sound the trunk came to a standstill. In the ensuing silence Tim could hear his heart pounding and his breathing heavy with fear. He strained his ears for any sound that might indicate where he was or the vicinity of anybody whose attention he had any chance of attracting.

Crammed into such a small space Tim began to feel hot and to sweat. His breathing was becoming difficult and the claustrophobia began to mount. He knew that he couldn't have been there for more than a very few minutes, though he had no way of knowing exactly how many. He wasn't certain where he was but thought it was likely to be at the bottom of the stairs near the Junior Common Room. If that was the case then somebody would find him soon enough because it was a well used route. Tim lay still, trying not to breath too fast. After some minutes encapsulated in darkness and unable to change his position to any beneficial extent Tim heard several sets of heavy foot steps stamping down the stairs. "What silly tosser would leave that like that" said a muffled voice. Mustering all his energy Tim tried to kick and bang and shout. It was difficult, in the confined space, to move his legs or arms enough to make a very loud sound on the sides of the trunk and his breathlessness made his voice rather feeble too. "Shit! There's some poor sod inside it" came the muffled voice. The trunk rolled over once more, the catches were released and, with a rush of cool refreshing air and light that made Tim blink, the lid was raised. Three older boys, none of whom Tim recognised, were standing looking down at him. "Are you alright?" "How long you been in there?" Tim took some deep breaths. He had never been so aware of the simple joy of breathing. "I'm OK" said Tim, trying to heave himself out of the trunk. He stood unsteadily, feeling shaken and unexpectedly dizzy. "It's OK man" A fair haired and rather tall boy extended his hand and helped him out. "I think you need to sit for a bit. Do you know which bastard did this to you?" Tim described his assailant. "Lucas!" came a chorus of voices.

Tim, recovering rapidly from his ordeal, thanked his rescuers who, despite his protestations, insisted that he should go up to the Senior Common Room with them and have some coffee. Later, as he sat with them gratefully enjoying a hot mug of sweet instant coffee, the boys started to talk about other nasty incidents that had happened to them or their friends and Tim began to relax and to enjoy the company of these Fourth Formers who were definitely not at all intimidating as he had imagined they may be.

When the clanging bell summoned them to supper Tim went to the Dining Hall with his new friends. Again Tim thanked them for their help and their coffee and went on his way. As he collected his food, pushing the tray along the slippery rails, and went to sit with the other Third Formers Tim reflected that he would have to keep out of the way of that boy Lucas.

The Hierachy

As the first days merged into the first weeks the School House Boys settled into the school routines and began to understand each other's personalities and form sub groups in response to them. Like granules of sugar being sorted into size and shape by a series of sieves, the boys were finding friends and foes, similarities and differences, shared interests and irritating characteristics. The four academic scholars became a natural group, as they were on an accelerated two-year route to their "O" levels and consequently were doing different, more advanced work than the others so were rather forced to seek one another's assistance with work related matters. A couple of the boys were keen and successful Rugby players, and Williams earned himself a reputation for over excitability and exuberance which often resulted in clashes with the authority of the prefects. Slater was a rather sneaky, underhand boy who was always glad to stir up trouble if he could and began to align himself to Williams, probably because he would have liked to be as noticeable as him but lacked both his quick whit and audacity. Tim tended to watch and wait on the side lines, always friendly but definitely peace loving, happy to join in most things that might be going on but rarely enthused by anything. If you were to have asked any other boy for their opinion of Tim you would most likely have been told that he was the calmest of the group and that he didn't like getting involved in the many silly little squabbles and disputes that inevitably punctuate the daily life of a small group of boys who live in constant close proximity to one another.

One evening, as the boys were getting ready for bed, Williams suddenly jumped onto the bed at the end of the dormitory and proceeded to jump from one bed to another all around the large room. A few boys were already in bed and protested at having another boy suddenly jump heavily onto them. Eglington sprang out of bed with unexpected alacrity and rugby tackled Williams as he landed on the next bed but one. "What did you do that for?" he demanded when he had regained his composure after the sudden interruption to his fun. "What did *you* do that for? Eglington jutted his jaw into Williams's face, pushing for what he considered to be a suitable apology. "I didn't do anything to you". "You just jumped onto my stomach and it hurt. You never seem to think of anybody but yourself and I, for one, am getting pissed off with you".

Slater, delighted as always to see conflict and an opportunity to add fuel to the fire, sidled up to the angry pair with a crooked smile on his face. "You didn't see him finishing off your biscuits in the common room the other day?" He addressed Eglington. "You bastard! You know that it wasn't me." Williams flared up, full of the righteous indignation that every teenage boy has bubbling close to the surface of his feelings. "Well now you're going to have to *prove* it wasn't you." Sneered Slater, ambling back to his bed, happy to have done his nasty work so easily and to such good effect. Eglington turned back to Williams. "Was it you? Because I did notice that they had all gone and someone stuffed a dirty sock into the packet to make it look as though it was still half full." "No" Williams was shaking his head. "I didn't even know you had any biscuits – you never offered me any anyway." "Why would I offer you any when you're such a prat?" Unwilling to take so public an insult without retaliation Williams grabbed Eglington by his arm and thrust a hefty punch into his stomach. "Fight, fight, fight" several other boys began to chant as a crowd formed around the two angry boys.

Before the situation had a chance to escalate the House Prefect who was on duty that night came into put out the lights. He waited, his finger poised over the light switch until the boys had all shuffled back to their beds. He turned out the lights and, with the customary warning not to let him hear any talking, he shut the door and clumped off along the passage to sort out the next group of boys heading to their dormitory. A couple of minutes later the scuffle between Eglington and Williams flared up again, all hushed whispers and creaking floor boards under the cover of darkness. Soon other boys were drawn into the dispute which began to highlight other frustrations that had been building up between different boys and, spreading like a wild fire, the darkened dormitory was soon heaving with wrestling bodies on beds and under beds, all the time the noise level rose, increment by increment, until it became a veritable storm.

"Your busted!" The lights blazed on and Moor, looking red and furious, was standing tall in the doorway, his eyes roving from dishevelled bed to overturned chair and heaps of bedding tangled on the floor. "What the fuck's been going on in here? You're supposed to be going to sleep. OK! All up and out to the washroom. In silence. Now."

The Third Formers, some relaxed having burned out their pent-up anger, others still glowering at one another because they had not finished sorting out their differences to their satisfaction, but all sheepish, somehow ashamed and guilty at being caught like this by the Head of House, trooped out in a silent line down the long passage to the glaring lights of the washroom. Older boys, in various states of undress, were brushing teeth and applying lotions to their faces in hopeful efforts to reduce the crop of spots that plague most teenagers.

Moor, already cool and calm again, addressed the Third Formers. "Wait here in silence and don't move. I will be back in a minute". He headed into the short "Top Study" passage way and could be seen through the window in the fire door knocking at the first study door. When he returned he was carrying sheets of paper. He instructed the boys to go to stand facing the long wall opposite the wash basins. When they had done so and he had moved them around so that they were far enough apart from each other to preclude any physical contact he handed each sullen boy a sheet of paper. "Nice easy punishment! All you have to do is stand up straight and still and hold the paper against the wall with your nose for half an hour. If anyone lets their paper drop I will reset the clock."

Time passed slowly. The "easy" punishment was anything but easy. The requirement to keep the sheet of paper pressed firmly against the wall to stop it falling ensured that each boy had to stand both straight and still which made their shoulders and calves ache with the unaccustomed strain of sustained stillness. Tim could feel older boys looking and smirking at them as they passed through the washroom on their way to bed. A couple of House prefects came to stand in the now empty room to chat to Moor. "They'll learn how to behave". We've all been there before". "They've gotta learn exactly who they are and where they belong, cocky little sods".

At last the thirty minutes was up. "OK, give me your piece of paper and go to bed and get to sleep. I'm going to stay around here for a while and I will be waiting to catch you if you make a sound. If that happens you will really wish it hadn't". The Third formers, now very tired and completely subdued, handed Moor their paper and slunk back to their dormitory, collecting what they could locate of their muddled bedding from the floor of the dark room and winding themselves up uncomfortably in it for the night.

A couple of nights later a different prefect came to supervise the Junior Common Room prep. "Oh Tom, those shoes *do* look lovely and clean" called Williams, signalling to all the other boys that this was the prefect to whom Slater was fag. "Yes! They are nice aren't they" replied Brice. "Brice really likes to look *beautiful*" laughed Slater. "He even makes me polish his pen every morning". "*Polish his pen!* Well we all know what he does with his pen all night". Announced Williams, causing a general sniggering around the common room. "OK now it's time to settle down. There goes the first bell. Make sure you've got everything you need for prep before the next bell rings because I won't let you get anything after that". The boys grumbled as they collected pencil cases, Latin translations, Maths books and slide rules for the following ninety minutes of work. A semblance of silence descended on the room as the second bell sounded but, as the minutes passed a gradual pushing of boundaries began. Slater dropped a tin box of geometry tools on the floor with a loud, metallic clatter and then apologised with excessive politeness to Brice, provoking stifled sniggers from most of the other boys. Andrews farted loudly, unleashing a howl of laughter from everyone. An excess of clicking of biros, scraping of pencil sharpeners and slapping of rulers with unnecessary force onto desk tops continued throughout most of prep. Huband, attempting to control a building pressure of laughter, suffered a loud but genuine bout of coughing, a contagion that reverberated round the room as other boys succumbed to similar discomfort. Brice became irritated and started to sigh loudly at each new interruption. This encouraged further "accidental" noises until he snapped. "That's enough! You're all being so *silly* I've got lots of serious work to do and I'm pretty sure you all have too". "We all think *you're* pretty!" Andrews interjected to an explosion of laughter and jeering. Brice turned a shade of red so fierce that the boys could almost feel the heat. "Now you're all punished! Nobody can go to clubs at eight thirty. You can all stay here and write me one hundred lines in your best hand writing. And I *will* count them".

When the eight thirty bell clanged Brice handed each sulky Third Former a piece of paper with the caption "I must do exactly what a House Prefect tells me to do". The boys settled down to copy it one hundred times but poor Brice had forever lost control of the group.

A few days later, after lights out, somebody suddenly lifted and pushed Tim and his mattress onto the floor. Momentarily stunned by the unexpectedness of the heavy impact with the floorboards, Tim looked up to make out the silhouette of Slater standing on the other side of his bed frame. "What was that for?" "Well I know you're not going to fight back so I thought it would be fun" taunted Slater. "You really shouldn't be so sure of that" Tim's voice was so thick with malice that even Slater faltered. "It's only a joke" he sniffled, clearly feeling that he may, indeed, have pushed too far this time and not at all certain of what Croy may be capable of.

Tim lay on the floor, his heavy, lumpy wadding stuffed mattress still on top of him breathing deeply as he had once been taught to do in these circumstances. When he had composed himself he extricated himself from under his bedding and stood up. He sensed that all the other boys were keen to see what would happen next and he was sorely tempted to lay into Slater until he begged for mercy. This was his chance to assert himself and gain good standing in the developing hierarchy. But years of training and practice controlled him. He knew that the consequences of acting in anger could be frighteningly serious and that it was better to let things go, never mind the personal loss of face. "Pick my mattress up and put it back, if you think you're so strong". To his eternal surprise something in Tim's voice evidently imparted sufficient fear in Slater that he obeyed meekly and went back to his own bed. Tim began to make his bed once more in the dark. The door opened and the light came on. Brice stood there. "What are you doing? I heard you from down in the washroom". "I'm making my bed" "I can see that. Don't cheek me. Why?" Tim was not going to get another boy into trouble, however strong the provocation, and especially not with a poof like Brice. I just had to make my bed. It's not doing anyone any harm". "I heard a noise like a herd of elephants". "I didn't make any noise, I'm just making my bed". "No one argues with me Croy! Right you've got a drill tomorrow morning at seven. Report to my study then, changed into your Rugby kit and I'll teach you why nobody talks to me like that". The lights went out and the door closed. Tim got into bed, silently furious. "You're a real bastard Slater" Andrews whispered into the darkness. "Yeah, you could at least of owned up" Eglington agreed. These unexpected words of unity and support began to appease Tim and his mind turned to a time more than four years earlier in his prep school.

Since first arriving at the school at eight years old the twelve boys in Tim's year had been bullied and oppressed by a tall, lanky eleven year old boy called Murphy. Daily he would corner a boy and extorsion sweets and other school boy prizes, champion conkers, a water pistol disguised as a pen, if they failed to comply he would happily give them a bloody nose or a wrist burn from his elastic belt. One day, early in his second year, Tim had gone to the toilets in break and found himself cornered by Murphy who was lurking just outside the outdoor entrance. He stood blocking the door as Tim prepared to go back outside. "What have we got for me today, Rabbit?" he smirked. "I haven't got anything and if I did you wouldn't be getting it" "We'll see about that" Murphy, standing on the door step, blocking Tim's exit, leant forward and grabbed Tim's wrist. Tim, nine years old now, was not going to put up with this anymore. When he had talked to his mother about bullies she had told him that it was very important to stand up for himself and that she would always stand up for him if he did. In an almost reflexive response Tim kicked Murphy in the balls. Stunned by the combined pain, shock and outrage Murphy took a step backwards and, being on the door step, he had fallen backwards on his head onto the stone paving of the stable courtyard with a sickening thud. Still shaking with mixed fear and anger Tim stood on the step looking down in disbelief at the motionless boy, a trickle of blood oozing from under his head.

"Oh shit! What's going on?" the young Australian student helper exclaimed, running to the stricken boy. "Help! Quick!" he bellowed, bringing two further masters onto the scene. "What happened Croy?" Demanded Mr. Tonge, the French master. "I don't know sir" "You *must* know something" "Yes sir. No sir. I don't know sir" Tim stammered. Matron rushed up at that moment. "Don't move him. I think we need an ambulance. Get me some warm water". Her calm, insistent instructions brought forth a flurry of activity and Tim stood, still motionless, overlooked for the time being.

After Murphy had been carried away on a stretcher to the waiting ambulance Mr. Tonge came to take Tim to the French room to talk. Tim Liked Mr. Tonge, always calm, authoritative and, above all, fair and understanding of the plight of young prep school boys. "So" he began, sitting beside Tim at a table "Murphy came and threatened you". "Yes sir" "And then?" "I pushed him sir but he was standing on the step and he fell down sir". Tim bit his lip, trying not to cry. Mr. Tonge put his arm reassuringly round Tim's shoulder. His jacket smelled of pipe smoke. "I know all about Murphy. I'm sure it was just a nasty accident. Now I have to take you to see the Mr. Drake. Try not to be frightened. Just tell him exactly what you told me".

Tim was left waiting, facing the wood panelled wall of the dark passage way that led to the Head Masters Study. He could hear Mr. Tonge talking to the Mr. Drake and, beyond, he could hear the rhythmic clatter of the secretary typing in her office.

Mr. Tonge came and took Tim into the Head Master's Study. It was comfortably furnished with deep pile carpet, a huge leather topped desk and some impressive antique chairs. "Tell me what has happened" The Headmaster said in his deep and loud voice that seemed to fill the large room. Tim told the story.

"Well, Croy, you can't hurt people the way you did. I know that he's bigger than you but what you did is very serious **you could have killed him".** the Head Master suddenly bellowed. "You are a young boy so this time I will deal with you but, if you do something like this when you are older it will be the police that have to deal with you. *You could be sent to jail for this kind of thing*". "Bad temper and violence are very dangerous things and you have to learn to control yourself. I am going to punish you for this incident and I've arranged for Matron to give you some special lessons in self control to help you not to get into trouble again. Do you understand what I'm saying to you?" "Yes sir" Tim, who had been trying hard not to cry for more than an hour now, suddenly felt tears streaming down his cheeks. "But it's not fair sir! Murphy's horrible. He bullies everyone all the time and nobody punishes *him*". "That is my concern, not yours. Stand up". Tim Stood up. The Head Master produced a well-worn looking gym shoe from a drawer in his desk and proceeded to beat Tim six times with it.

For the rest of the Autumn term Tim attended lessons weekly with Matron in which she taught him to think before he spoke. To take deep breaths before he reacted. To walk away when he felt angry with somebody. Never, never, never make physical contact with anyone again. Tim learned his lesson well. Murphy never came near Tim again.

Tim drifted off to sleep, still smarting from the injustice of his punishment but quite pleased at having somehow made Slater do his will and by the support of the two other boys.

As soon as Tim was wakened by the clanging of the School Bell he rushed down to the junior changing room, pulled on his Rugby kit and gym shoes and reported to Brice in his study. "I'll be watching you from my window, here. Remember it's three times round the circuit. Report to me when you've finished". Brice seemed cheerful and not at all nasty, as he had the night before. Tim headed obediently down stairs, crossed the Head Master's Quadrangle and began jogging up the hill, down the other side of the hill, along the village street and then round twice more. By the time he was reporting back to Brice his throat was sore and his voice hoarse from the frosty air. "Go and have a bath and don't be late for breakfast. Well done!" Tim splashed himself with cold water, alone in the Four a Sides and made it to breakfast in time. He felt unexpectedly exhilarated by the experiences of the past ten hours.

Rejected!

The incident in the dormitory between Slater and Tim

had, in the end, damaged the status of both boys. Slater had made public, by his own hand, exactly what a bully and coward he was and every boy in School House Third form understood that he was a boy to be despised and avoided. Slater's assertion that Tim never fought back had also been noted and remembered by everyone and, despite Tim's successful verbal control of Slater, they all now knew that they could behave towards Tim as they pleased and get away with, at worst, a tongue lashing. Tim became something of a target on whom any boy could take out his frustrations with life. His tuck would often be taken, Rugby shorts would go missing and when somebody lost his text book he felt free to help himself to Tim's.

Life for Tim became filled with little annoyances from the moment he woke up to the time that the boys eventually fell asleep. No single incident was ever very significant in itself but the cumulative effect was to gradually wear Tim's resilience down. His reaction to this situation was to opt out as much as possible from situations in which he could be targeted. He was fortunate to be both strong willed and self-confident and to be very content with his own company. Above all Tim understood without a shadow of doubt that he must not allow his temper to control his behaviour.

Tim started to avoid the Junior Common Room during periods of free time. Instead he would sit in the library and read the newspaper or one of the magazines or, if the weather was not wet, he would sit, huddled, on a bench by the wall of the Head Master's Quadrangle under the protective cover of darkness, thinking his own thoughts which were beyond the reach of even the most disruptive boy. Tim began to see lessons as a time of respite from the constant sniping of other boys and even Chapel became a place of refuge, although he would not have gone so far as to claim that he enjoyed it for he did not.

On Saturday afternoons, after Rugby and on Sundays after morning chapel Tim would often go for very long walks. Occasionally he would get permission from Mr. Linford to walk into the nearby town where he would look in shops, thinking about the merits or demerits of different radio cassette players that he may ask for for Christmas or he might go into Smiths and read car magazines on the shelves or look at LP records of currently popular groups. More often he would go walking through the local countryside, selecting different foot paths that would lead him to quaint villages or interesting local land marks. Tim spent many hours minutely exploring the woods on the far side of the Rugby field brook or the banks of the big river where he liked to watch the bird life and to search for interesting plants or traces of wild animals. At these times Tim was completely content and time would pass without incident.

Wednesday afternoons were probably the worst part of the school week from Tim's perspective. These afternoons were dedicated to the activities of the Combined Cadet Force, overseen by the a short, fat and definitely very unfit bully of a man called Sargent Major Dixon. His was the responsibility to assign each boy to a section, Army, Navy or Royal Air Force. The boys were expected to dress up in the full battle dress of their section and then to line up in their section on the Head Masters Quadrangle. There Sargent Major would bawl instructions and hurl insults at the boys. "Company. Company, get on parade!" "By the left, quick march." "You're supposed to be marching, not bally dancing". "You're a bloody ugly duckling not a cadet".

After an hour or so of this drill practice the different sections would be sent to undertake various tasks of varying impossibility when they would be subjected to further humiliation and bullying from this little man from the East End of London who was so shockingly at odds with the upper class self importance of the rest of the school community.

Tim resented the evident inadequacy of the Sargent Major and the way in which he was allowed to exert such malicious power over boys whose parents were paying substantially for them to attend Barforth. It was very evident, in the minds of most boys, that Sargent Major hated what he believed to be the over privileged classes and that he had taken it upon himself to wage a one-man crusade against their children. He seemed to spend the whole week deliberately planning and setting up activities that would cause the cadets the maximum pain, fear or simple inconvenience by way of punishment for the position in society that had been given to them by nothing more than an accident of birth.

There was the assault course, consisting of a series of difficult or dangerous obstructions that the hapless boys had to traverse, as a group, within an unreasonably short period of time. The twelve foot high wall of splintery railway sleepers that had to be mounted and then jumped off by the whole group, climbing on each others shoulders, balancing on the top to pull up the last remaining boys, slipping and gripping, their hands and bums filling with sharp splinters. The muddy, water filled ditch, topped with low hanging and rusty shards of barbed wire under which they had to crawl, submerged, eyes closed and breath held against the muddy and stagnant water. The shaky rope ladders that had to be climbed to access the rough rope over head walk way, high in the trees, that had to be negotiated hanging by the hands. Nobody could survive the assault course unscathed and most were unable to complete it in the allotted time, eliciting a barrage of rough and scathing verbal from the Sargent Major, followed by more drill practice by way of retribution.

Another possibility was to be forced to construct either a raft or a bridge out of impossibly inadequate supplies in unreasonably short time via which the whole group were expected to cross the Rugby Pitch Brook. Inevitably every boy would return cold, soaked and dejected, only to be shouted at to go get into the water and salvage every piece of junk with which they had been supplied and return it to the Quarter Master's Stores without delay.

Tim saw Sargent Major Dixon as another level of officially sanctioned bullying.

Tim's self-imposed isolation from his peers had not gone totally unnoticed by the school staff. One lunchtime as Tim was dutifully checking the notice boards he came upon a folded sheet of paper with his name written in fountain pen ink lodged in the "criss-cross" notice board titled Chapel. Tim removed it and took it with him to the library.

Dear Tim,

Please come to see the Reverend Pullman in the Chapel Office after games today.

Tim wondered what ever the Reverend Pullman could want with him. And how strange it felt to see himself addressed by his Christian name from within this manly world of Sir names only. He was not very impressed by the man who, as well as overseeing all Chapel services and running the Christian Union also taught Scripture lessons to most classes in the school, including Tim's. The Reverend Pullman failed to achieve much respect from any of the boys either through being strict or through being an inspirational teacher and he was further hampered in the popularity stakes by teaching a subject that many felt to be of little importance in the grand scheme of "O" and "A" levels and the subsequent attainment of a place in a good university.

After Tim had cleaned himself up from a muddy game of Rugby in his cold bath shared by an equally muddy Third Former he set off, armed with his letter of invitation, to locate the Chapel Office. He knocked smartly on the heavy, arched, wooden door within the vestibule of the Chapel and was surprised as it swung silently open. The Reverend Pullman looked up from a wide desk littered with chaotic looking piles of paper and boys exercise books. He smiled. "Tim! You got my note and you found your way here with impressive punctuality. Sit down". Tim sat. "Tim I just thought it would be nice to get to know you a bit more, outside the classroom. How are you settling in to Barforth?" "It's OK sir" "Good. Are you making some nice friends and finding lots of interesting things to do in your free time?"

"I'm OK sir". "Well to be frank, Tim, I've heard some concerns from people that you might be finding some things a bit difficult and that you may be feeling a bit lonely."

Tim was surprised at the direction that the conversation was taking and saw something of an invitation to seek help with his less than ideal social situation. He wondered if he should, *could* talk openly to this Master and if, since he had been asked a direct question, it would still be seen as sneaking on his peers to do so.

"Are you feeling lonely Tim?" the Reverend Pullman persisted. "Well sir, I am a bit sir. You see I don't like fighting much, I don't think it's right sir, so I seem to get picked on a lot sir because the other boys know that I won't retaliate sir."

"Mmmmmm I can see that that could be a bit of a problem but I must say I am really impressed by your good Christian attitude. Why don't you start attending the Christian Union meetings on a Tuesday evening during second prep? I think you'd find a lot of nice friends there."

"I don't think that's really my kind of thing sir. I don't like praying out loud or singing those modern hymns and I don't really know much about the kind of things that you do there sir."

" Well why don't you just give it a try Tim? And, in the meantime I shall pray for you so that God will help you to make the most of the wonderful Christian atmosphere of Barforth."

Tim felt let down and disappointed that his courageous effort to seek the help that he had understood he was being offered had been met with the mere offer of prayers and an invitation to the Christian Union with no concrete actions whatsoever. He sat in front of the Reverend Pullman's desk, in miserable, deflated silence.

"Is there anything else you'd like to share with me? You know that I'm always here waiting to talk to you if you do need anything."

"Yes sir. Thankyou sir."

"It's been so nice to talk to you and get to know you a bit better. You'd better go now because first bell has already rung and I'd hate to get you into trouble for being late to lessons."

"Yes sir. Thankyou sir. Bye sir" And Tim took his leave, hurrying to gather his things from the Junior Common Room and get to the Physics laboratory before the second bell clanged.

The School Fag

The Third Saturday of term saw the first First Fifteen Rugby match against a rival school to be hosted "at home". Tim was to experience his first School Fag duty as "Ball Boy – Brook." Because he was not at all certain of exactly what was expected of him or how best to prepare for whatever task lay ahead he asked Long when he went to his study that morning at break to deliver his bread and milk supplies and to make his bed. "I've got to do my School Fag job for the first time today. I'm Brook Ball Boy. Can you give me any advice about what I need to do?" Long turned to him from his desk, holding a steaming mug of coffee. "Shit! You've got a nasty job there Croy." Long's face was the picture of concern for his young House Fag. Tim had already realised that he had been assigned to a decent sort of Prefect who, despite being so much his senior, really did seem to be almost on Tim's side. "The good things about it are that there are two of you doing it so you won't be all alone and that it only goes on until the end of this term. If you keep quiet you probably won't have to do any more School Fagging in the next two terms." Long looked at his coffee mug, seemingly transfixed by the steam that twirled upwards from within it. "Just make sure that you take a towel with you for when you get out of the water because it's a long walk back up to school when you're soaking wet and cold. There's not much point in taking dry clothes down with you because you won't be able to get dry properly so it wouldn't help much. Obviously, wear your Rugby kit and don't get into position until the game starts. Oh and don't wait for someone to tell you that you can get out at the end because they won't. Just get out and get back to School." Tim listened with appreciation because he sensed that Long was speaking sincerely.

Soon after lunch Tim changed into his Rugby kit and, carrying his red and orange beach towel round his neck like an overgrown scarf, he headed down the private lane to the First's playing field. He met Alex, his fellow Brook Ball Boy beside the pavilion and together they waited for the First Fifteen to arrive on the pitch. "It looks bloody cold doesn't it" Tim's accomplice said, screwing up his nose in discomfort at the prospect of what both boys knew lay ahead of them for the next two hours. "Yeah" Tim agreed, adding nothing further to the conversation for what more could be added?

The young men of the First Fifteen and their rival team came striding, like a small army, onto the pitch. A cheer went up from the rows of supporters lining the far side of the field. Mr. Price came to talk to Alex and Tim. "Ok boys You need to be ready in the water as soon as the whistle goes. One of you to the left of the pavilion and the other to the right. Now you won't be able to see the game from down there but you must try to concentrate on the sounds of the game so that you can anticipate when the ball might land in the brook. Then just get it as fast as you can and throw it up to one of the team who will be on the bank. Half time is only ten minutes. You can get out then if you want to but, to be honest, that will probably only make you get colder. Understand?" The two boys nodded. "Ok, you'd better find your way into the brook now then because I'm going to get the game started."

Tim stood on the steep and unwelcoming bank of the

brook, looking down into the deep brown water with gold tinged gravel and streamers of green weed on the bottom. He really didn't want to immerse himself in it at all but he supposed that he had no choice. Putting a steadying hand on the cut grass of the playing field Tim eased himself into the gently flowing water. He felt his gym shoes fill with cold water, soaking into his socks. With a deep breath he let go of the bank and launched himself fully into the brook. The water came up to his waist, the benign current causing it to ripple around his body. Tim stood still in the middle of his section of the brook, feeling self-conscious and rather at a loss as to what he should do now. Ahead of him he could see Alex standing similarly uncomfortably up to his waist in water. The minutes ticked by and Tim began to feel very bored and increasingly cold. The water was percolating up his rugby shirt almost as high as his shoulders and, exposed to the cool air around him this section of his body became considerably colder than that which was immersed in water.

Suddenly the cheering and shouting on the pitch reached a crescendo and the brown leather Rugby ball landed with a heavy splosh in the brook, midway between Tim and Alex. Both boys waded towards it as it bobbed half submerged in the current. Tim was the first to reach it, but it had already become lodged against the far bank of the brook, entangled in a clump of slimy and prickly brambles. Alex joined Tim and together they fumbled to extricate the ball, trying unsuccessfully to avoid scratching their fingers on the brambles which they discovered, too late, were mixed with stinging nettles whose sting seemed to have been fortified by the water and the lateness of the season. "Get the fuck on with it will you?" One of the First Fifteen shouted irritably from the safety of the bank. At last the ball was free and Alex chucked it up towards the bank and the waiting player. The two boys waded back to their positions to await further developments. The ball did not come their way again so both boys idled away the remaining hour trying to keep themselves slightly less cold by wading up and down, blowing into their hands or thinking about the warm tea that they would soon be able to drink in the Dining Hall.

This would become the pattern of Tim's Saturday afternoons for the rest of the Autumn term. One Saturday, in mid-November, when the weather had been largely wet and stormy for most of the week, It had been widely expected that the match would have to be cancelled for fear of ruining the pitch due to it's wetness. However on the Friday afternoon the grey skies cleared to the cold blue of winter high pressure. There was a sharp overnight frost and at Saturday break time it was announced that the match would, after all, be played.

Two O'clock found Alex and Tim standing dutifully beside the pavilion ready to perform their now familiar task. The brook was full almost to the top of its' banks, the water swirling fast and almost spilling over onto the playing field. Tim looked at the unexpectedly unfamiliar waterscape and felt a prickle of fear. "It doesn't look good." Alex spoke Tim's thoughts. The boys peered into the deep, fast flowing water, opaque with mud and debris washed from the surrounding fields and woods. They could not see the gravelly bottom of the brook and this rather disorientated them. They heard the whistle blow and the roar of support as the game began. Resigned to their task Alex and Tim moved along the bank to their customary stations and eased themselves into the raging brook. Tim was taken aback to find the muddy water was up to his shoulders, the force of the current making it a struggle even to stand up securely. A piece of branch lodged against him momentarily, startling the young man. The roar of the crowd alerted him to the ball which sploshed into the water not far from Alex. Tim assumed that he would get it and then realised belatedly that the current was such that the ball was bobbing rapidly towards him and that Alex, lurching bravely through the brook, had no hope of reaching it. Tim stepped forward to intercept the ball and, misjudging the effects of the force of flowing water on his balance, lost his footing, lurched forward and was momentarily submerged. Crying out with the shock, Tim's mouth and nose filled with water and he emerged choking and spluttering. Somehow he had grasped and held the slippery wet leather ball and he threw it up to the waiting player. It took Tim fully ten minutes to start breathing normally. The sub zero air temperature took it's toll on the two unfortunate Brook Ball Boys who were soon shaking and shivering violently and unstoppably. The ball ended up in the Brook twice more that game and, as their fingers became paralysed with the interminable cold both boys became less and less effective at grasping the ball and throwing it to the waiting players. They endured some very angry and unjustified shouted abuse which simply added to their abject misery.

At last the game came to an end. Muddy players and chilly spectators vacated the playing field in quick time, keen to enjoy a hearty match tea of toad in the hole and baked beans for the players or a cup of warm tea for the spectating boys. Alex waded to meet Tim in the brook. Exhausted they tried to hoist themselves out of the water but their customary hand holds were submerged and invisible and the banks had become a soggy, slippery assault course in their own right. Tim pushed Alex upwards towards the safety of dry land and, for a wobbling second Alex appeared to have made it successfully but then the clump of grass that he had been pulling himself up on became uprooted from the water-logged bank and the boy fell backwards into the water. Coughing and cursing Alex regained his poise after emerging from below the water. "You'd of thought Mr. Price might have bothered to help us get out of this shit" he cursed, his voice sounding shaky with what may have been tears or cold. "Come on". Tim took charge, sounding much more optimistic than he felt. "I'm going to try getting out over there, and then I'll pull you up". Tim grasped the bare branch of an over hanging weeping willow tree as tightly as his immobile fingers would let him. It was no good. He simply couldn't hold on tight enough to hoist himself up. Driven on by mounting fear

Tim hurled himself as hard as the resistance of the water would allow against the bank and the tree roots. Painfully and incredibly slowly he eased himself up and onto the safety of the bank. Tim drew breath, turned to face the brook once more and, as he had once seen somebody doing on a film when the hero was rescuing a child from a frozen lake, he laid down on his stomach and reached down into the water so that Alex could pull on his hands to help himself out. Shivering and terrified the boys lay together on the bank, too exhausted to stand up, let alone find their towels and get themselves back to school. Alex, sobbing unashamedly now, hugged Tim. "I think you probably saved my life". Tim shook his head, unable to speak as he too found himself crying. They were only thirteen.

Somehow back at school and having washed and warmed himself up as best he could in a second-hand cold bath Tim went to the Dining Hall to get his warm tea but he was too late and the tea urn had been cleared away. He could hear the kitchen staff working in the warm kitchens preparing supper. Cold, disappointed and disgusted Tim slunk off to the library where he sat almost hugging a radiator and reading the Motor Magazine. He was still shivering and struggling to concentrate on his reading when his mouth began watering copiously. He realised miserably that he was going to be sick. Tim got up and hurried out of the room and out to the Head Masters Quadrangle. He staggered to the corner beside the Library wall, lent forward and vomited violently and noisily twice. When he had finished and stood up straight again Tim found that he was feeling instantly better. Evidently the brook water had not been good for him. Now feeling embarrassed Tim hoped nobody had seen him. He headed to the New Toilet Block to clean himself up and drink some fresh water from the drinking fountain. Returning to the Library he reclaimed his chair and magazine and read comfortably until the School Bell summoned him to supper. Tim was still shivering when it was time for bed.

End Of Term

As the days grew shorter, darker and greyer the time began to go faster. End of Term Exams came all too quickly so that most boys had not prepared adequately for them. Tim had always quite enjoyed exams, though he obviously would not have admitted as much to his peers. For Tim they were a welcome change from normal lessons because he didn't need to worry about being suddenly verbally questioned by a master which always made him feel embarrassed at having to talk in front of his class mates, whether or not he got the answer right. Another advantage for Tim was that he had always performed better in exams than in normal class work with the result that he never felt worried by the prospect of exams as so many people do. In the lessons after exams the masters spent time going through the things that boys had not understood and then resorted to time filling activities that were designed to minimise any intervention or marking for the masters who were busily occupied with writing end of term reports. The boys began to feel increasingly cheerful and carefree and spirits throughout the school were high.

Tim, along with every other boy in the school, was summoned to a meeting with his Tutor, Mr. Jones, his Maths master. Tim was by no means an able mathematician and he neither much liked nor respected the teaching skills of Mr. Jones. He had the distinct feeling that Mr. Jones did not rate him at all highly either. Tim skulked on the "Maths landing" outside Mr. Jones's classroom, waiting for him to finish with the boy who was having his meeting before him. The boy, who Tim did not know, came out and pulled a face at Tim, indicating in the Barforth Boys language that the meeting had been a real chore, this preparing Tim for what was to come. Taking the deep breath of one who is resigned to his fete Tim pushed open the door and closed it behind him. "Hello sir!" "Hello Croy. Sit down". Mr. Jones was sitting, tall thin and yet somehow crumpled at his spindly and dilapidated teacher's desk and Tim wondered if the desk had become like the master or vice versa. He had heard his mother say that dog owners often came to resemble their dogs. Tim sat uncomfortably in front of the desk. Mr. Jones's breath smelt heavily of cigarette smoke. "How do you think you've got on for your first term?" "OK I suppose sir. "Yes I think that's probably about it. OK. But I and most of the other Masters who teach you believe that you could do a lot better than just OK if you were really to try a bit harder in class rather than waiting until exams come around. We'd like to see you doing more extracurricular activities too, nobody is quite sure what you do in your free time?" "Yes sir. I mean I do do things sir but nobody notices me doing them I suppose". "Do you want to tell me anything Croy?" "No sir". "Well have a nice holiday and I'll see you next term". "Yes sir. Thankyou sir. Bye sir".

Sunday evening saw an elongated Chapel for the annual carol service. An hour and a half is a long time for teenage boys to be confined to uncomfortable pews and forced to remain silent. The Music masters, both sporting bow ties on this festive occasion pranced about conducting the choir who were singing complicated hymns and psalms, often in Latin, in an attempt to demonstrate the excellence of the Music School and the highly academic status of Barforth School in general. For many of the boys these performances occasioned poorly suppressed mirth, camouflaged by bouts of coughing, incurring angry glares from the Head Master directed mainly towards the more junior boys near the front of the chapel. There were long and dignified bible readings from the Chaplain, the Head Master, the Senior Master, the Head Boy and "a younger boy". Tim supposed that they used the same service, printed on a piece of stiff card with a token holly leaf boarder on the front, each year so were unable to be more specific about exactly who would be reading. The enjoyable bits of the service were the widely known traditional Christmas carols, sung lustily and loudly by the congregation to the thunderous accompaniment of the organ. At last the school spilled out of the Chapel and surged towards the Dining hall to enjoy a bonus mince pie and warm tea.

On Monday it was Christmas Dinner. The Barforth tradition was for the Third Formers to dress in their Sunday suits and white shirts and serve the rest of the boys and staff throughout the meal. Long was laughing with Tim while he was making his bed that morning. "You'll be rushed off your feet, serving food, pouring wine to us prefects and the staff and cleaning up all our mess. And we *make a mess!* "Tim wasn't too concerned. He remembered the previous year when he had been a prefect at the top of his prep school that the masters had served the boys. It seemed a perfectly reasonable and light hearted thing to do at this time of year. "Tomorrow will be the last time you have to make this bed" Long continued. "You and I are moving to School Study One next term". Tim knew that School Study One was the big study occupied by the Head of House. He quickly deducted that, as rumour had had it, Long had been appointed to the top position now that Moor was leaving having completed his Oxbridge exams. Tim felt an unexpected surge of pride to know that he knew for sure what others were only guessing at and that he would be House Fag to the Head of House as if something of Longs superior status might rub off on him. "Well done, Long. I'm really pleased for you. You definitely deserve that. "Thanks Croy. But don't tell anyone yet – it has to be officially announced on the Head Master's Notice Board tomorrow." Tim grinned and nodded. "Course not".

Christmas lunch *was* hard work for the Third Formers. There was a very formal and traditional three course Christmas Dinner, necessitating the young suited boys to scuttle hither and thither between the servery and the Dining Hall and up to High Table where the most senior boys and staff sat and were served wine with their meal. The boys had been given a half hour training session with the kitchen manager who they all knew only as "the gnome" on how to serve from the correct side, where to put side dishes and how to pour wine without slopping it. Tim was not sure that any of the Third Formers had really listened or understood but who would care or notice anyway? At last it was finished, everyone had departed the Dining Hall and the Third Formers were left to clear tables, sweep the floor and prepare for their own meal. There was much grumbling about the rumour that was circulating that they would only be given the leftovers that had been scraped off plates to eat. Ofcourse they need not have concerned themselves with that and they were soon enjoying freshly cut turkey and crispy potatoes and Christmas pudding of their own. Having been working so hard and having built up such an apatite there was a rowdy and euphoric atmosphere amongst the young boys.

Break time on Tuesday morning heralded the end of lessons for the term. Boys from throughout the school began to descend like locusts onto the lawn beside the Assembly Hall cellar where all their trunks had been deposited by the two School Porters. Finding their own trunk amongst the six hundred or so there was a time consuming process because almost all of them were near identical dark blue with brass corners. They were stacked up to four high in a completely random order and covered a huge area of the lawn. The stacks of four trunks were as tall as Tim which rather hindered his efforts to locate his own, his name being printed on the lid and thus either covered by other trunks or too high for him to see. Gradually, as time passed and boys removed their trunks, the chaotic scene of six hundred boys searching six hundred trunks began to appear less daunting. Tim had agreed to cooperate with Andrews so that between them they could more easily carry their trunks and those of the prefects to whom they were fag back to School House and up the two flights of stairs to dormitories or studies. It seemed to the two friends that Bohemian Rhapsody was blaring from a radio behind every window in the school.

The rest of the day involved hasty stuffing of armfuls of belongings into blue trunks, much swapping and bargaining between boys of unwanted items discovered at the back of lockers and the excited tipping of crumpled paper, stale biscuits, filled exercise books and the other detritus of junk that had built up on desks, in lockers and stuffed into odd corners during the sixteen weeks of term onto common room and dormitory floors. Calls of "Quiz" and replies of "Ego", signifying offers and acceptance of items being exchanged between boys vied with the latest "Top Twenty" hits on radios or LP albums blaring from high status stereo systems in senior boys' studies to create a continuous cacophony of noise throughout the school and, by definition, most of the village too.

After lights out in the dormitory that night the Third Formers ran amuck. Pillow fights between boys combined to become a mass, dormitory wide pillow fight which somehow spilled down the long passage to involve the two more senior dormitories. The prefects were nowhere to be seen and were evidently either else where or too busy with their own end of term entertainment to bother to respond. In due course the mass fun petered out to a natural conclusion and the boys sorted themselves and their pillows, some no longer containing much in the way of stuffing, out and returned to their allotted dormitories. In the darkness of their room the Third Formers had a little more business of their own to complete. Eglington crept up to Slater's bed and thwacked him with his pillow. "Piss off" Slater grizzled, "We've finished now and I have a headache". "You're certainly finished" replied Eglington as he was joined first by Williams then Andrews and then, all at once, the rest of the dormitory all of whom had been goaded and irritated by Slater throughout the term and each of whom had good reason to want to give him a good pounding with their pillow. Tim, caught up in the general end of term spirit, decided that a pillow fight did not really constitute a real fight and entered willingly and whole heartedly into the mass beating of Slater. Everybody, with the exception of Slater, slept deeply and contentedly until they were awakened by the School Bell joyfully ringing in the end of term.

After breakfast Boys moved their heavy trunks from dormitories and studies to the grass verge beside the Private Lane and then the school piled into Chapel for some final words of Christian wisdom from the Reverend Pullman and to bellow out the hymn "God be with you till we meet again". The boys milled out onto the Head Master's Quadrangle, friends thumping each other on the shoulders good naturedly, some shaking hands with some of the masters, before walking down the Private Lane to wait with their trunk for collection by their parents.

As Tim sat in the cold, frosty, early morning December air he reflected upon his first term at Barforth and surprised himself as he realised that it had passed unexpectedly fast and that he had actually quite enjoyed most of it. His musing was interrupted as he saw his mother's big white estate car snaking its' way towards him, avoiding boys, trunks and other large cars on it's way. Tim was going home!

Boat Club

The start of the Spring term saw a big change for Tim. Towards the end of the Autumn term the Third Formers had been asked to select the sport that they wanted to do during the Spring and Summer terms. Either Hockey and Cricket in the Spring and Summer terms respectively or Rowing for both terms. Tim had opted for Rowing, more because he knew that he didn't like Cricket than because of any expectation that he would much like rowing. At least he believed that he would spend his time doing something whereas during interminable games of prep school Cricket Tim had either spent afternoon after afternoon doing nothing while he waited for his turn to go in to bat or he had simply stood in the sun in some far distant fielding position doing nothing more than ambling to the opposite side of the pitch at the end of each "over".

On the first afternoon of term the Third Formers who had selected Rowing were summoned to the Assembly Hall to be "briefed and selected" and introduced to the Boat Club. When everyone had been ticked off on the list by Mr. Linford who was Master in charge of the Boat Club, He addressed them all briefly, welcoming them to the Boat Club and introducing them to various senior boys who were of importance within it. They would all go to see the Boat Club and something mysteriously described as "The Tank" so that they would know their way around from then on. The boys were instructed to form a line in height order, the tallest, as always, in the front and the shortest at the back. Tim, knowing that he must be one of the shortest, immediately felt that he was starting from a position of disadvantage simply because he was short. This had happened to him so many times in his school career, for school photographs, prep school boxing lessons or to be selected for a part in the school play, that he resigned himself to being handed some inferior role within the Boat Club. He supposed that there was nothing that he could do about it and he prepared himself for more years of boredom being bossed around by those who considered themselves superior to him merely because of their size.

The Captain of the Boat Club started walking up and down the assembled line of boys, moving some from place to place until he was satisfied that they were in the correct order. Starting from the back of the line he singled out the shortest seven boys and separated them into a different group. Having turned out to be the second shortest boy Tim was in this group. The small boys stood around, most of them feeling that they were probably about to be humiliated in some way, as, like Tim, they all had been regularly in the past, purely because of their size.

A Senior boy, who Tim did not recognise, came over to the group and introduced himself as Toby Phillips. Tim immediately liked the way in which he used his Christian name, making the boys feel that he was not planning to oppress or humiliate them simply because he was their senior. Toby explained that they had been selected because of their size because, if it was alright by them, they were going to receive special training to become "coxes". "I don't suppose many of you know what a cox is but he is the most important person in every crew. He steers the boat, plans the best way to get around corners and gives commands to the oarsmen. I was cox to the First Eight until the end of last summer but now I'm too big so I will be coaching you this year. I bet you didn't realise what an advantage being small can be!" There was a ripple of laughter from the group, relieved from the gloom of an expected bad start to their newly adopted sport. "Come on then! I'm going to take you round the club separately, on an exclusive tour" laughed Toby. The boys followed him out of the Assembly Hall. His evident enthusiasm was infectious.

The Boat Club was based on the bank of the river, about a mile and a half walk from school. The small group marched cheerfully along the Private Lane, darted across the busy main road and headed down a gravel track to a range of long, low buildings fronted by a kind of floating pontoon from which the boats were launched. Toby took the boys into one of the buildings which was filled with metal racks on which were resting many long, thin boats of highly varnished wood. They looked like delicate instruments of great beauty. He showed them proudly the best boat, named Brokley Jones, after the previous, now retired, Master in charge of the Boat Club. "This is the one that I used to cox the First Eight in. We won every race except one in it!" he told them with the warmth of pride clear in his voice. "Look over here, these are the oar racks. The oarsmen are responsible for these but the Cox has to dry down the boat before it is left on the rack, so that it is at it's best for the next outing". The group moved on to see the next shed that contained more boats and oars and then on to the third one in which boats and equipment was repaired and maintained. Toby led them down onto the pontoon, which moved a little unnervingly beneath their feet as they stood and looked at the deep, clear water of the river. Toby took them for a walk in each direction along the river bank, pointing out the landmarks by which they would be expected to navigate – Parson's Pond, The Tree,

Tom Fool's Turn, Snaky Bends.

They headed back towards the school before diverting from the Private Lane up a muddy track to" The Tank". This proved, disappointingly, not to be the tracked army vehicle that most of the boys had pictured but a large concrete swimming pool like structure, half filled with water and with two lines of eight wheeled rowing seats on tracks, each with a rigger set in the side. "This is where you will learn to row at first, before you are ready to go on the river." It's quite difficult but much safer than trying things out in a real boat", explained Toby. "OK, that's it for today. Keep your eye on the Boat Club Notice Board for instructions and I will meet you up here tomorrow for your first lesson. See you then!" The trainee coxes set off back to school, excited at what lay ahead and feeling optimistic after all.

Next afternoon the novice coxes met Toby at The Tank. Everyone was told to collect an oar from a covered rack and Toby explained and demonstrated how to secure them by means of a brass screw fixing called a gaiter. Each boy took a polished wooden seat and learnt how to slide the seat up and down the runners while moving the oars in the air. They practiced the technique of twisting the handle of their oar to "feather" the blade while it was in the air to minimise the air resistance of the moving boat and then twisting it again in time to push the blade at right angles into the water so as to maximise the power of their stroke through the water. When they started to actually put the oars in the water everyone was shocked at how hard they had to pull to move the oar through the water. "That's because the Tank can't move." Explained Toby "When you get into a real boat it will feel completely different and you will find that the oar moves through the water very fast by itself which can be really dangerous if you lose concentration."

After some more practice at getting the motions of rowing correct Toby gave each boy a sheet of paper on which was printed the standard basic commands that a Cox is expected to use in different situations. They were to learn these by heart and he would test them on Friday. Each boy then took it in turn to call out the command to start and stop rowing "Come forward. Are you ready? Row!" and "Easy all!" Toby stationed himself at the far end of the Tank to test the volume and projection of the voice of each boy. "Speak louder and *look at me* so that your voice carries over the heads of your crew. Remember that there are **eight** oarsmen who all need to hear your commands above the sounds of the boat and the water and, in a race, the cheering of the crowds". Tim felt rather self-conscious standing and shouting at his peers but he made himself do it because that was to be his job. Somehow Toby inspired in him a wish to do well.

On Saturday afternoon the five trainee coxes who had successfully passed the test of commands on Friday met Toby at the boat house. This was to be their first experience of rowing in a real boat on real water. Each boy was to take it in turn to cox the boat, discovering for the first time the feel of steering a boat via the two ropes that operated the rudder and of commanding the crew in the right way to control the boat. Toby took them to a disappointingly battered looking boat that seemed much shorter than the ones that they had admired on their first visit to the Boat Club. "This is a Four, not an Eight, because obviously there are only four of you to row and, being half the length, it will be much easier for you to manoeuvre. It's called a clinker because it is made of overlapping planks of wood, we're going to use this to start with because shells are much harder to balance and a lot easier to brake so the clinkers are the best ones to learn in". Toby showed them how to stand beside the boat on the rack and then slide it into their hands, two of the boys having to duck under it to get hold of the far side of the boat as it moved off the support of the rack. Tim was to have the first turn at coxing so he was supposed to issue commands to his crew to carry the boat safely down to the river and float it on the water. Suddenly feeling nervous at the responsibility of the task and the awareness that he had not fully understood how the commands that he had learnt related to the motions of getting the boat launched his mouth became dry and his voice croaky. Under the reassuring eyes of Toby Tim tried again and managed to speak loudly and with enough assurance to get the crew to carry the clinker safely down to the pontoon and then to turn it upright and sit it gently in the water. Tim then squatted down to hold the boat against the pontoon while the four oarsmen went to collect their oars. "Well done Croy!" Toby squatted beside him "I remember how I felt the first time I did this. Remember that you will make mistakes when you first try to steer the boat – everybody does. Just try not to panic, you *can't* really do much damage whatever you end up doing".

Toby instructed the nervously excited crew to row up as far as Parson's Pond and then turn around and come back, at which time the coxes would change position. Tim had to push the boat firmly away from the pontoon at the same time as getting himself into the hard, cramped coxs' seat. He dipped his hands into the water on each side of the boat, feeling for the wooden hand grips on the steering ropes.

"Come forward. Are you ready? Row" Tim called. The sound of casters rolling up runners, oars being turned and the ragged splash as each oarsman pushed his blade into the water filled the air. The boat seemed to shudder slightly and then it was moving. "Get into the middle of the river Croy" Toby called from the bank. Tim pulled too hard on the rope and the boat swung almost horizontal across the river. Surprised he over compensated, causing the rudder behind him to make weird sploshing sounds. The boat seemed to tip towards his left, causing two oarsmen to have their blades lifted clean out of the water. "Don't worry! You're doing fine" Encouraged Toby. Tim remembered the advice to just relax his grip on the rudder ropes and to let the boat do its' own thing. Sure enough the boat straightened out and righted itself. As the oarsmen started to find some kind of rhythm and the boat began to cut through the water more smoothly Tim began to relax. In surprisingly short time Tim recognised the approach of Parson's Pond. "Easy all!" he commanded and the crew stopped rowing. The momentum and the current combined to bring the boat into the "pond" where they were to turn around. Tim looked up to Toby on the bank, seeking confirmation. "Go on then. Get it turned around". "Carry on stroke side. Back her down bow side" Tim instructed, pulling on the rudder. The boat began to turn but Tim had not bargained for the power of the current in Parson's Pond and, seemingly without warning, the bow of the boat was stuck in the soft mud of the river bank. "Crew take two firm strokes together" Toby took command from the bank. You need to get off the bank or the bow will snap off. A stab of terror shot through Tim's spine. Please don't let me crash the boat on my first time coxing, Tim thought to himself. He didn't. The boat was freed and the manoeuvre was completed without further incident. It took longer to get back to the pontoon because they were rowing against the flow of the river and the inexperienced oarsmen had to fight with their oars to get them to slice through the water. Toby was waiting on the pontoon to catch the clinker as Tim steered it too sharply towards it. Tim got out and swapped seats with the next boy. As they moved off for the second time Tim was surprised at how much more easily his oar moved through the water than it had done in the Tank. He remembered that Toby had told them that that would be the case. The process of rowing up to Parson's Pond and back was repeated three more times until each boy had had his turn at coxing the boat. The boys then learned how to extricate the boat safely from the water and carry it up to balance it on trestles while they washed it with a hose and dried it with slimy leathers before returning it to it's rack in the boat house.

After another week of training to row and to cox each of the novice coxes were allocated to a crew of their own novice oarsmen from the Third Form who had been training separately. For the remainder of the term every boy would be regularly moved between crews to slowly develop each crew to be as well matched in size, strength and ability as possible so that by the Summer term the school would be able to enter them into races with other schools in serious Under Fifteen competitions at Regattas around the county.

The Hurt

One afternoon, after tea, Tim was rummaging in his locker in the Junior Common Room filling his bag with the books that he needed for the afternoon's lessons. He remembered that he had left his English reading book in the dormitory. Tim climbed the stairs, two at a time, keen to retrieve his book and be ready when the first bell went. He was only popping in to the dorm to grab his book and would not be there even for a minute so he reasoned to himself that it was not worth disturbing a prefect to ask permission.

Tim picked up his book from the blue windowsill where he had left it and was turning to leave when Lucas appeared in the open doorway. "I hope you've got permission to be in the dorm". He sneered. "Of course not. I only came to get my book for English. I'm not exactly staying here". "Boys who don't get permission find themselves in trouble" There was a malicious edge to Lucas's voice. He shut the door and strode across the room towards Tim. He screwed his plump, freckled face into a sickly smile. "But don't worry. I'm a good guy and you're a very nice boy so this can stay between us". Lucas was very close to Tim now. He could smell his bad breath and see beads of sweat on his forehead. Tim sensed danger but could do little by means of escape as he had his back to the wall and was enclosed by a bed on each side of him. Lucas's thick set and tall form was blocking his path out between the beds.

Lucas grabbed Tim's wrist roughly and held it in a tight grip. His hand was moist and sticky with sweat. Tim wrinkled his nose in distaste. Although he felt afraid he couldn't help feeling disgusted by this fat bully of a boy. Lucas lunged forward and kissed Tim, all wet and slobbery with his fowl smelling breath. Tim pushed him away and tried to dodge his head out of the way but Lucas had a firm hold of Tim's wrist. "No! You're a beautiful boy and you came up here to find me because you wanted it. That's why you didn't ask permission." Lucas leaned his tall, heavy body against Tim, toppling him onto a bed. Tim tried to lift himself off the bed but was pushed back onto the hard, lumpy school mattress by the full weight of Lucas. The breath was squeezed out of him by the force of the impact. Tim became rigid and motionless with fear. He would have shouted for help but his face was buried in the pillow and, anyway, at this time of day there would be nobody within ear shot.

Tim felt his trousers being ripped off and seconds later a searing, tearing pain enveloped his entire body. He heard roaring in his ears and struggled for breath, his nose and mouth being forced into the unyielding pillow by the pressure of Lucas's head and shoulders. He was sure that he was going to die.

Suddenly the weight of Lucas lifted off him Tim turned his head and drew rasping, desperate breath after desperate breath in a subconscious determination to survive. "You *are* a lovely lad. We must do it again. Soon". Lucas taunted. Then, as suddenly as he had appeared, he was gone.

Tim lay deadly still, still fighting for his breath. The burning pain inside him nearly overwhelmed him. Now that he could breath Tim began to wish that he *had* died. Death must be better that what he now had to live with.

At length Tim changed position, curling himself into the foetal position. He realised that he was not on his bed but on Eglington's. He felt guilty. Guilty for being on someone else's bed and guilty for having somehow defiled it. He knew he ought to move onto his own bed, barely two feet away, but he hurt so much that he could not. The School Bell clanged to summon the school to their lessons. Tim thought how strange it was to hear the rasping sound of the mechanism that passed along the wall behind his bed at this time of day. He had only ever heard it every morning, easing the boys out of sleep before the clanging bell shook them fully awake. Tim could hear boys clopping along and talking two stories below him on their way to classrooms throughout the school. He knew that his Third Form mates would be heading that way to their English lesson. Tim made no effort to join them. Five minutes later the second bell sounded. Tim was now officially late. Tim made no attempt to move. He could not move. The golden rays of the sinking sun sent elongating shadows across the room and then the room darkened. Tim just lay there. The physical pain was terrible but his emotional turmoil was paralysing. He didn't know how to move forward from this moment. What to do with himself. He never wanted to see anyone or do anything again.

The door opened and the light glared on. Tim cringed, willing the bed simply to envelope him and make him invisible. Mr. Linford stood there. "Here you are Croy! What are you doing? I've been searching for you everywhere". "I'm not feeling well sir" Tim thought quickly. "Well you can't just stay here". Explained Mr. Linford, his voice now sounding gentler. "Nobody knew where you were so we were worried". "You do *look* ill, Croy. You'd better go to the san." "Yes sir. Can I go later, when I feel a bit better sir?" "No, I think you'd better go now". "Yes sir".

Since Mr. Linford showed no sign of leaving him alone Tim eased himself off the bed and stood up unsteadily. He stumbled slightly. "Are you OK? Do you need me to come with you?" the concern was heavy in Mr. Linford's voice now. "No sir. I'll be OK sir. Sorry sir".

Tim dragged himself slowly down the two flights of stairs, along the wide path towards the Dining Hall and up an unfamiliar flight of concrete steps to the Sanatorium. A smell of disinfectant and ether assailed his nostrils as he approached the surgery. There was a bell push with a notice beside it telling visitors to ring if the surgery was closed. Tim rang. Sister appeared, tall, grey hair and wearing a blue uniform. "yes dear?" I've been sent to see you by sir" "Oh, why dear?" "I was sick" Tim lied. "Hmm, you *do look* a bit peaky. Let me take your temperature." She took a glass thermometer out of a glass of pink water and stuck it under Tim's tongue. "No, you haven't got a temperature" she said, frowning at the thermometer as if she some how blamed it for having disturbed her evening. "I'll give you an aspirin and you can go and rest in your dormitory until prep. I don't suppose you want to eat supper if you've been sick dear". Tim dutifully swallowed his aspirin and headed back to School House Junior Dormitory and the comfort of his own bed.

The aspirin did little to help to make the pain recede but Tim made himself go to prep, not wanting to attract any more attention to himself. Mr. Linford looked in to the Junior Common Room in the middle of prep and asked Tim if he was feeling better. "Yes sir. Thankyou sir".

By the time the School Bell clanged to signify second prep Tim could bear no more. He put his things away and headed upstairs to seek permission from a prefect to go to bed early.

As Tim entered the washroom Long entered it from the other door that led from the Top Studies. "Can I have permission to go to bed early please?" Tim asked. "Yes, sure, are you OK?" "I was sick." Tim lied for the second time in as many hours.

Slowly, painfully, trying to minimise the amount that he bent down, Tim brushed his teeth and changed into his pyjamas. There were blood stains in his briefs which Tim screwed into a tight ball and put into his laundry bag. On an impulse he thought better of that idea, retrieved them and pushed them deep into the rubbish bin in the washroom.

Tim had just got into his bed, leaving the dormitory light on because it would not now be long before the other Third Formers came up to bed and he didn't really want to be alone in the dark anyway. He didn't know what he wanted any more. He just wanted to get away from himself and everything that had happened to him in the last five hours. He only wanted everything to be made alright again. Somehow he knew that it never would be.

The door opened, making Tim jump, alarmed, startled from his thoughts. Long came in carrying a steaming mug. "Sit up Croy! I brought you this". Tim sat up obediently, surprised. "You looked so rough I thought this might help to make you feel better. It's very cold up here" Long handed Tim the mug of steaming hot chocolate. It *did* smell very good and Tim realised that he hadn't eaten since lunch and that he was very hungry. "Thanks" he said, taking the mug gratefully. Suddenly Tim was overwhelmed by a wave of emotion, as if this small act of kindness between a senior boy and his fag, a master and servant, had opened the flood gates of feelings that Tim had been suppressing for five long, lonely, hours. He screwed his eyes tightly shut against the stinging prickling of tears but to no avail.

Confused and terribly ashamed Tim felt the hot tears cascading down his cheeks. How could he start crying now when Long was being so kind to him? It just didn't make sense. "Don't cry man! I know it feels horrible when you're not well and you're all alone but I'm sure you'll feel better in the morning." Long sat on the bed and put his arm round Tim, in a gesture of support. "I'm not queer or anything, I promise. But I feel like you need to be comforted". The unknowing use of the expression "queer" and the rawness of the terror that it brought to Tim's heart caused Tim to start to shake with uncontrollable sobbing. Long, being above all a kind young man, held Tim tightly until he began to calm down. "Come on man! Drink that nice chocolate. It will make you feel better" Long exhorted Tim. Tim began to drink. To his surprise it did help him to calm down.

Long departed and, by the time the other Third Formers began to struggle into the dorm to get ready for bed Tim had composed himself and really was feeling slightly better from the warming, nourishing effect of Long's hot chocolate. "Are you alright Croy?" Andrews enquired. "Sir was well pissed off with you for not turning up for English. Did he report you to old Linford?" "Yeah he came looking for me and he was obviously going to give me a good bollocking but he could see I wasn't feeling well so he let me off and made me go to the san instead". "She obviously made you better straight away since you were in prep". Tim surprised himself with his usual broad grin as he remembered that part of the story. "Well you know how they say that if you break your leg or if you loose your voice she will only ever give you an aspirin? Well *she gave me an aspirin* and told me that I would feel much better if I went and got on with my prep. And it was *Latin!*" Both boys began to laugh at the perceived inadequacy of Sister and the unlikely medicinal effects of a Latin prep.

The customary whispered conversation around the dormitory that night centred around Tim's experience of the widely derided sanatorium. He was the first of the School House Third Formers to have sampled the care and sympathy of Sister and everyone wanted to hear about it and to add their views on how and why she never did the right thing by ailing boys. The conversation gradually petered out as one by one the boys fell asleep. Tim did not sleep. He lay awake, surrounded by his peers and yet quite alone, his brain analysing and reliving the terrifying events of the evening. Every time he heard the springs of a bed creak as it's sleeping inhabitant moved Tim would start into full, frightened wakefulness, certain that someone was coming in to get him again.

I can't deal with this.

The morning after his assault Tim had been in immense pain which had hindered him in everything that he had had to do throughout the day. Walking up and down endless flights of stairs between dormitory and Junior Common Room, up to the Biology lab, back down to Maths and then up again to English where the Master reprimanded him harshly in front of the class for missing his lesson yesterday without permission. Tim's face reddened with mixed humiliation and rage at the injustice of it. Simply sitting for lengthy periods on hard seats in Chapel and classes was painful. When games time came and Tim found himself in the cramped cox's seat, having his back jolted against the hard wooden back of the boat with every inexperienced stroke of his crew's oars in the water, he thought he might scream with the rejuvenated pain of each bash. He managed to bite his lip and control himself, even putting on a good show of shouting loud, clear and correct commands through the entire outing, bringing praise from Toby who was following the boat on the bank. "You're a natural Croy. You've really got it now!"

The hours began to stretch uncomfortably into days. By the second day the physical discomfort had greatly receded to the extent that it no longer dominated Tim's every move. Tim found himself feeling a constant need to be with other people all of the time, never mind if he really enjoyed the company or not. Every minute when he was not safely ensconced in a classroom or the Boat Club Tim made certain that he was in the Junior Common Room or with a crowd of boys in the Dining Hall or changing room or dormitory. The fear of finding himself alone and potentially vulnerable became all consuming for him. For the first time in his living memory Tim found his own company and solitude very uncomfortable indeed. This feeling became, of itself, deeply unsettling for Tim because he didn't understand it and was not comfortable with the new situation which he had imposed on himself.

Tim found that he could not stop himself from reliving the events of that afternoon. If he hadn't left his book in the dormitory that morning then it would never have happened. Maybe if he had done the honest thing and asked permission to go and get it somebody would have been visible so that Lucas would not have been able to be prowling around as he had been. Tim became increasingly certain that, however he looked at events, it was obviously his fault. He had not been honest. Maybe he had said or done something to attract Lucas to him.

He had been careless, forgetting his book like that in the rush to get to breakfast. Or had he been too worried about getting into trouble for turning up to his English lesson without his reading book? Tim knew that some people thought he was too good, too careful and that he was too afraid to take risks.

The constant circulation of the same set of thoughts, throughout his wakeful hours was wearing him down. Twice in lessons he was shouted at by an angry Master for day dreaming and failing to listen to questions. At night in the dormitory Tim dreaded the time when everyone else would be asleep, deserting him to lonely thoughts and terrifying images that span repeatedly through his tormented head. Sometimes Tim would hug himself and weep silently, unable to sleep and having no idea how he could recover from this. He could not believe how alone he could feel amongst so many people from whom, only a week earlier, he had often longed for tranquillity and independence.

Slowly, but with absolute certainty, Tim came to the conclusion that he could never recover from this. That, indeed, he did not want to *have* to recover from this. It just wasn't fair and he couldn't do it.

On Saturday, after games, Tim went to see Mr. Linford to ask permission to walk into town. He also asked to take one pound out of his House Bank account. Mr. Linford obliged on both counts and Tim set off on his mission.

The town was unexceptional, flanking the river that had once powered water mills that brought it prosperity from spinning and weaving the wool from the local farms and now dissected by two major roads which made it both congested for cars and difficult to get around on foot. None of these things mattered to the Barforth boys, whose interest in visiting the town centred on the shops that enabled them to replenish their supplies of tuck or illicit cigarettes or alcohol.

Tim was interested in none of these things. Taking a deep

breath he walked into the small branch of Boots, approached the pharmacist counter and looked for what he wanted. "Can I help you love?" the white coated girl asked him kindly. "My mums got 'flu and asked me to get her some aspirin on my way home from school" Tim told her, the lie tripping easily off his lips. "Do you want twelve or twenty-four?" Tim had not been prepared for this complication to the transaction. He thought momentarily and decided that, since he had no idea how much such things cost, it was safer to go for the cheaper option. Twelve, please". "that's thirty-seven pence please". Tim handed her his one pound note and took the change and the slim packet of medicine in it's crisp paper bag. Tim went into Woolworths next door and cheered himself up by buying a large bag of "Pick and Mix" for fifty pence. He stuffed them in his jacket pocket and ate them all on the way back to school.

That night, after lights out and the subsequent cheerful Third Form banter about Tom Brice and his shiny shoes, whether Slater, his fag, was becoming like him and how wealthy Mr. Linford may be. "He's a House Master, Head of the Boat Club, Head of Maths and he isn't married" Williams had pointed out. Tim, feeling more light-hearted than he had done for days, had joined in with gusto. "And look at his cars. He's got that huge new Triumph estate and that little Honda too". Later Tim lay sleepless as usual waiting now with a sense of purpose for the heavy silence that he knew indicated that all the other boys were safely asleep and that all the senior boys had finished in the washroom.

Tim eased himself silently out of bed, felt in the pocket of his jacket, hanging on the back of his bedside chair, and retrieved his Boots paper bag. Clutching it in his left hand, Tim crept across the dark dormitory, gently opened and closed the dormitory door and walked carefully down the long passage to the washroom. There he pushed the first of the aspirin out of its' foil pouch and crunched it. He repeated the process with the remaining eleven pills, crunching them stoically and washing them down with water from the tap, cupped in his hand. Putting the empty foil back in its' box in the Boots paper bag, Tim headed back up the long passage way and to his dormitory. He put the empty, incriminating Boots bag back in his jacket pocket. Tim intended that somebody should find it there. Tim got back into his bed and lay back on his pillow, confident that he would wake up dead. Tim had heard his mother once before talking of how dangerous it was to take more than two aspirins at a time so twelve was certain to be fatal. They would wonder why he had done it. He imagined that the police would come, that there would be lots of trouble and that "they" would find out what had happened and feel sorry. Amid thoughts of such perpetual, total relief from his torment Tim drifted off into deep, untroubled and much needed sleep.

The School Bell mechanism rasped noisily behind Tim's bed, heralding the clanging of the bell waking the school, an hour later than usual, for Sunday breakfast. Tim sat up in bed as usual, wondering why he felt slightly surprised, as if something was somehow wrong. Then he remembered. He wasn't supposed to *be* waking up at all. A wave of disappointment, followed rapidly by an all enveloping blanket of despair swept over him. He was so useless he couldn't even manage to kill himself successfully. Tim knew now with devastating certainty that he was destined to go on suffering for ever and ever.

To Hell With It!

It rained all day the following Tuesday. Icy cold, grey sheets of heavy, persistent, all pervading drizzle. The wetness seemed to envelope the entire school, both inside and outside and to dampen the mood of boys and masters alike. Wet weather accentuated the subtleties of status differentiation between the age groups because Sixth Form boys were allowed to use umbrellas to keep themselves dry as they moved around the school while more junior pupils had to manage as well as they could by wrapping their jackets round themselves tightly and running for it. During games time Tim had huddled forlornly in the tiny coxes seat at the back of the clinker, his blue tracksuit becoming darker and wetter by the moment while his hands, dipping in the river as he operated the steering ropes, became colder, number and progressively less effective at controlling the boat.

After supper Tim huddled as close as he could to the tall buildings along the terrace, seeking what little shelter from the rain that they offered. Intending to shorten the time spent outside he entered School House via the changing rooms and cut through the Four by Fours to the top of the stairs beside the Senior Common room. He was on the point of descending the stairs to the Junior Common Room when Lucas stepped in front of him with a sickly sneer on his fat, freckled face. "I've been looking for you Croy, my beautiful boy" he crooned. Tim was rooted to the spot by the sudden terror that gripped him. He knew that he had missed the moment of opportunity to run for safety.

Still sneering, taunting, terrifying Tim, Lucas leant towards him and gripped his wrist. Tim's stomach lurched with recognition of the feel of his pudgy hand, damp with sweat. In an instant Tim knew that he was not going to suffer the attentions of Lucas without putting up a strong resistance. Without thought or planning Tim lunged forwards and sank his teeth into Lucas's bare arm. "You little bastard!" Lucas screeched, recoiling in pain and shock. At the instant that Lucas recoiled, in a second of imbalance, Tim launched his full weight forward in the biggest push that he could muster and Lucas staggered, lost his balance completely and hit the wooden floor with a solid thud. He lay still for a second, on his side, no doubt shocked at the unpredicted turn of events.

Something simply snapped inside Tim. Four years of carefully nurtured self-control were thrown asunder. A kind of blind rage seemed to cover Tim's eyes, somehow isolating, separating him from what he was going to do.

Tim kicked Lucas in the chest, hard. He heard his heavy Doctor Martins make satisfying contact with Lucas's solid body. He kicked again and again and again, in an increasing frenzy, pushing his heavy toes into his ribs, his nose, his balls. Tim needed to inflict as much lasting pain on his tormentor as he had had inflicted on him.

Behind him, quite beyond his awareness, a small, stunned, silent crowd of Fourth and Fifth Formers had gathered in the doorway of the Senior Common Room.

A strong pair of arms encircled Tim's chest, pulling him beyond reach of Lucas. "That's enough now Croy. You can't go on like that". Norton, a tall, fair haired Oarsman from the Fourth Form restrained Tim, his steady, reasoned voice breaking through Tim's trance like state and bringing the fight to an end.

Tim looked at Lucas, seeing him as if for the first time. He lay still on the floor boards. Blood oozing from his arm and flowing freely from his nose. He felt neither pity nor remorse. The crowd of boys still stood motionless, waiting to see what would happen now.

Lucas sat up groggily, somehow got to his feet, leaning heavily on the wall, regaining a little balance. Blood dripped from his nose, soaking into the unpolished wooden floor boards. Lucas walked unsteadily towards the Four by Fours. The gathering of boys heard what sounded like a sob as he disappeared from view.

Norton released Tim from his strong grip. Tim, still breathing heavily but now icily calm, simply walked away, down the stairs to the Junior Common Room to prepare for prep. He could hear the crowd of older boys beginning to speculate about how, why and what had been happening. Tim knew that he would be in trouble sooner or later but he really didn't care. He felt euphoric, as if a massive burden had been lifted from him.

News spreads quickly within the close-knit community of a boarding school and it wasn't long before Williams came in and, giving Tim a strange look, went and had a murmured conversation with Andrews and Eglington. Tim knew that they were talking about him, speculating about how and why and what might happen to him now. Slater came shouting into the room "Croy beat up Lucas really badly. He had to go to hospital". Everyone turned to stare at Tim. "Did you really thrash *Lucas*?" Eglington asked in an almost reverent tone of voice. Tim nodded. "Yes". "Well he certainly needed it" observed Huband. "Everyone hates him and he makes life hell for everyone in the school". Outside in the early evening darkness Tim distinctly saw a group of faces peering in through the window, looking for evidence of the fight about which boys were talking excitedly. The School bell clanged it's warning of the impending start of prep and the School House boys scurried around retrieving the books that they needed from their lockers. Brice swept into the room to supervise prep and the usual disparaging snigger rippled around the room. Throughout prep there was a kind of unsettled, excited, edgy atmosphere as if everyone was waiting for something expected but unspecified to happen.

When the bell sounded for the second half of prep Brice called Tim over to him and told him that Long wanted him to go to his study. Since this was not unexpected and because he was a daily visitor to Long's study anyway, Tim did not feel at all concerned as he mounted the two flights of stairs to Long's room. He tapped on the door and pushed it gently open as he had done so many times before. Long was sitting at his desk frowning. "Come in Croy" he growled "What's been going on? Half the House saw you laying in to Lucas. Kicking him all over when he was down on the floor. That's a disgusting way of behaving and we don't do that here". Long almost spat the last few words out, as if the words themselves were disgusting. For the first time Tim felt a pang of regret. Not for what he had done to Lucas, who deserved it all and a lot more besides, but because he felt that he had, in some way, let Long, who had always been so good to Tim, down. He looked down at his feet and said nothing. There was a long silence. "Lucas had to be taken to hospital Croy. He's got two broken ribs, a broken nose and serious bruising. I just can't get my head around what you've done". Tim stared dejectedly at the floor but said nothing. He had nothing to say. "I probably ought to take you to Mr. Linford to let him deal with this. It's very serious. But for some reason Lucas made me promise not to get Mr. Linford involved so it's down to me". Long rose up slowly, almost wearily, from his chair. He went over to the open cupboard in which hung his suit, coats, spare jacket. He rummaged in the dark recesses at the back and retrieved a yellow brown cane. Long looked at it, held in his hand almost as if it was poisonous. "I never thought I'd actually have to use this" Long spoke almost to himself. With a deep breath Long came towards Tim, who was bracing himself, holding his body rigid and clenching his teeth ready for the inevitable pain. Long beat Tim, six times, hard, equally paced strokes of his Head of House cane. "Now go" Tim went. Long was left standing alone in his study, probably more distressed by the events of the previous five minutes than was Tim.

Tim returned to the Junior Common Room and sat stiffly and with considerable discomfort, reading for the remainder of prep. When the bell went the School House boys crowded round Tim. "What happened?" "What did Long Say" "Are you going to old Linford?" Tim grinned, rather enjoying the attention and the fact that he had jumped head and shoulders above anyone else in terms of the severity of his punishment. "No" He paused for maximum effect. "He caned me. Six of the best!" "Shit! I wouldn't have thought he'd do that. Not really". Slater looked truly appalled. "I hope you told him that he's a bastard" Williams interjected "Because that's not fair. Lucas deserved what you did and we all know it." Tim felt really quite touched by the genuine support that his friends, and even his old enemy Slater, were showing for him.

At break the next morning Tim felt a little awkward at the prospect of delivering Long's milk and bread rations to his study. He wasn't sure what he should say or do. He decided to behave as usual and act as if nothing had happened. He liked and respected Long and still felt disappointed in himself for letting him down.

Tim tapped on the door and let himself in without waiting to be invited. Long was sitting, contemplating his hands which were clasped together almost as if he was praying. He put the rations on Long's table and turned to start making his bed. Long continued to sit in silence which made Tim feel uncomfortable. Long turned in his chair to look at Tim. "Sit down Croy" he commanded, unexpectedly gently. "We need to talk and you *must* be honest with me Croy." Long took a visible deep breath. "I had to beat you last night, Croy, because you did wrong and lots of people saw you doing it and I can't let people think that they can just go round fighting like that. Especially not the way you did it. But I know that it's not like you to do that. Something doesn't feel right about the whole thing. I was talking to Tom Brice about it last night, trying to make sense of things, and he reminded me of a couple of things that happened last year." He fidgeted in his seat "Then I woke up in the night and things suddenly seemed to fit together". Long was twisting his fingers together in agitation. He took a deep breath and looked Tim firmly in the eyes." "Lucas has been bullying you, hasn't he? I heard about him locking you in a trunk last term". Tim nodded. "And now he's done something much worse that just bullying you". Long's face was blushing now and Tim felt his own face reddening. "Last week, when you wanted to go to bed early. You hadn't been sick, had you Croy? Lucas had done something really, really bad to you" Tim hung his head. He couldn't answer. He didn't need to. Long didn't need him to answer. Both boys knew the truth. There was a long silence during which they were both wondering what should be done next.

"Tim. It *is* Tim, isn't it?" Tim nodded. Long spoke softly.

"I am so sorry. It's not enough but I am sorry" It was Tim's turn to look Long in the eyes. "You don't have to be sorry. You haven't done anything wrong. You've been really decent to me Long. And I'm really sorry for letting you down".

"Let's have some coffee!" Long skilfully changed the atmosphere. They were sitting with their steaming mugs, prefect and his fag, somehow united in an unlikely but genuine friendship that spanned the four years and aeon of seniority between them. "Everyone's talking about what you did last night Croy and I think you'll find that lots of things will be better for you now. Lucas has caused loads of people problems and we've all been kind of wanting somebody to do what you did." Tim felt a deep feeling of calm and wellbeing filling his soul. He had not felt so optimistic about his life before.

New Beginning

Tim discovered that his reputation had, indeed, changed beyond recognition overnight. With this change came an unexpected reordering of the hierarchy amongst the School House Third Formers, very much in Tim's favour. No longer did he find himself at the wrong end of rough and selfish little acts or left out of group activities. Slater suddenly and very unsubtly started seeking Tim out as a friend, in his sniffly, obsequious way, keen to be seen to be very much "in" with one who was so brave and tough. Williams, always the boisterous joker, began to include Tim in his schemes and Tim found, much to his surprise, that he rather enjoyed the action. It complemented his sense of humour well and gave him a new perspective on school life. Huband, tall, rugby playing, socially skilled, who had appeared from the first week to be a future leader, started treating Tim not only as an equal but with considerable respect. A few weeks after the fight Huband confided in Tim that Lucas had been bullying him repeatedly since their second day at Barforth and that he had lived in daily dread of meeting him.

Some of the older boys who had had to live in close proximity to Lucas's nastiness throughout their time at the school and who had watched the fight now held Tim in high esteem and would often ask him in to the Senior Common Room for a mug of tea or coffee, a very valuable and greatly appreciated privilege for a Third Former. Most of the Prefects, who probably knew more about the story and the background to it, now valued Tim as a trustworthy and stable voice of reason in affairs of discipline amongst the younger boys.

Around the wider school word had spread that Tim was a boy who, though he appeared mild mannered enough, it was very unwise to push. Trouble makers gave him a respectfully wide berth while others began to actively seek out his company. In effect the fighting incident had given him a reputation for being one who would stand up for himself against anybody and had made his existence known to everybody.

Lucas himself was not faring so well. Beyond his physical injuries he had suffered irreparable damage to his powerbase of fear. Many of his peers had seen the fight and, while not approving of Tim's unconventional and, in school boy terms, unfair methodology, had realised that Lucas need no longer pose a threat. They had understood from the fact that Lucas did not even try to seek any kind of retribution from Tim that he had more to hide than to gain from such a course of action and the rumour mill had quickly built "facts" out of little bits of information that tarred him with a very undesirable and surprisingly accurate image that he would never be able to live down. He spent his time glowering and sulking, avoiding other boys and being shunned by them in equal measure. Neither Tim nor Lucas would ever know it but Long, with the help of other senior boys, had thoroughly primed the informal system of checks and controls that permeate throughout every level in closed communities like boarding schools and prisons to make certain that Lucas's every move would be scrutinised, reported and, if need be, punished for the rest of his time at Barforth.

The last weeks of the Easter Term at Barforth were always busy with a series of traditional inter house competitions and Tim and the Third Formers threw themselves into the spirit of these events whole heartedly. First came the House Singing Competition. A couple of weeks of regular secret house meetings in which the senior boys decided on a suitable song and then got their house to unite around performing it culminated in a Saturday night in the Assembly Hall in which each house would perform to the best of their ability and would be judged by a panel of external judges who had been invited by the Music School. The event was light hearted and boisterous, the musical content fairly low key but the entertainment value first rate.

James Long had decided that School House should sing "The English Are Best", a rowdy and rather jingoistic song that lent itself well to the loud and tuneless efforts of sixty teenage boys. Tom Brice who, rather fittingly, had been a member of the School Choir and was studying Music for A level, fussed and became upset at every practice because of the boys' inability to sing in tune but, despite his heroic efforts and considerable repertoire of methods, was powerless to alter the course of events. On the night of the competition the School House boys shuffled themselves into position on stage, feeling rather self-conscious standing above and in front of the entire school, and shouted out their song with immense spirit and enthusiasm but rather less skill and melody. For as long as anybody could remember School House had failed to make a good showing in the House Singing Competition and the Easter Term of nineteen seventy six proved to be no exception.

The last weeks of term, by which point the weather was supposed to be becoming less wintry, The Inter House Boat Races were scheduled to take place. This event demanded each house to put forward two "fours", one under sixteen crew and one senior crew, to compete between houses in each age group until the final two crews in each group competed for the winning title. The effect of these heats, fought daily during games time, was that all normal Boat Club activity was suspended while boys lined the river bank shouting support for either their own House or their preferred House in the current heat. Because Mr. Linford, School House Master, was also Master in charge of the Boat Club it was somehow expected that School House should do well in this competition and, indeed, this regularly proved to be the case. The School House Third Formers were highly excited at the prospect of being part of a winning House and were loud and exuberant in their support from the river bank.

Making Long's bed each morning Tim would ask about his hopes and expectations for the school House crews. Long, a Hockey and Cricket player himself, had ceded leadership of this competition to Norton, who was Stroke to the School House under sixteen crew. It was clear to everyone concerned that School House had a very sparse showing for the senior race this year and all their hopes were pinned on the under sixteens. "It sometimes happens like that, I suppose" Long mused. "It's just that in my year and the year after me most of the boys in School House chose not to join the Boat Club so we've hardly got enough boys between both Sixth Forms to fill one boat. I know Mr. Linford's sick as a parrot about it but there's nothing anyone can do now. You're in the Boat Club, aren't you?" Tim confirmed that he was, but that he was learning to cox rather than actually row. "We've had to use a cox from Hillside for our senior boat – so he's likely to do a bad job for us just to try to get an advantage for his house. But we haven't got anybody who knows how to cox in School House sixth form so we didn't have a choice". Both boys fell silent, in shared despondency about the chances of School House Seniors. "Norton's pretty good though, isn't he?" Tim broke the silence. "Yeah, he will probably be in the Under Sixteen A's this summer. Mr. Linford says he's got the potential to go all the way to stroke the First Eight next year." "So you think we might win the under sixteens?" "I don't really know. I can see when our crew wins against another house, obviously, but I don't know how to judge them in general. Mr. Linford just smiles and won't make any predictions when we ask him."

School House Seniors were eliminated in the quarter finals, disappointing despite the widely help predictions of such an outcome. The under sixteens fought their way through to the finals. The whole school lined the river bank, two or three boys deep to watch the two crews in the senior race, followed by the under sixteens. Jakes won the senior race, something they had not achieved since before the Second World War. There would be much celebration in that house that evening, Mrs. Harding, the House Masters wife, was well known throughout the school for her ability to make a brilliant party for the Jakes boys at every opportunity. Because of her efforts Jakes was far and away the best loved and most envied house in the school.

The under sixteens race was close. The Hillside crew took the lead, School House somehow seeming to get forced too close to the bank to avoid clashing oars and thus earning a penalty. At Parson's Pond School House edged ahead by a bows' length and, despite valiant efforts from the Hillside crew and their cox shouting himself hoarse, by the time the finishing line was in sight School House were leading by almost a full length. Spectators from both houses surged along the bank to see the end of the race first hand and, as the result became clear the whoops of joy from School House could be heard all the way back at school. While in no way as homely or lavish as the celebrations at Jakes, School House would be well supplied with take away Kentucky Fried Chicken, chips and bottles of Coke, brought back from town in the back of Mr. Linford's Triumph.

Days later the Spring term came to a ragged end, with none of the formal occasions to mark it that the Christmas term, by its' very nature, always offers. Trunks were sought on the field beside the Assembly Hall Cellars, dragged back to dormitories and studies and untidily stuffed with cloths and assorted possessions. In no time Tim found himself tunelessly belting out "God be with you 'til we meet again" in the final chapel service and then sitting on his trunk in the chilly March morning half way down the private lane. He was surprised by the unexpected arrival of his mother driving a brand new big, blue, futuristic Citroen estate car.

I Won't Go Back!

Mr. Croy was a man of action and imagination. A successful design engineer with clients around the world he believed in the need to develop independence and maturity in his children. This holiday he had in mind a project for Tim that was both very necessary and would teach him new skills and self-reliance. On the first Friday evening Mr. Croy arrived home from work with a satisfied smile on his face. He summoned Tim to the barn which the family now used as a garage for their cars and an extra large garden shed and workshop. In the loft of this barn Mr. Croy had a large storage area and an office. He spent a lot of time there, away from the demands of his family and free to do things exactly as he liked to do them.

Opening the boot of his Ford Granada estate with a flourish he showed Tim his latest purchase. A large, shiny chain saw. Together father and son removed it from the car and read through the instruction booklet that was attached to the handle of the machine with string. Mr. Croy demonstrated to Tim how to measure and mix the correct proportion of oil and petrol for the two-stroke engine and then, excitedly, he pulled sharply on the starting cord. At the second attempt the engine crackled into life. Picking up the unwieldy machine Mr. Croy squeezed the trigger throttle control making the little engine rev furiously and causing the cutting chain to speed round and round, the barn filling with blue smoke. Both men loved the smell of petrol and exhaust smoke and they shared a moment of silent, masculine pleasure.

On Saturday morning, over breakfast, Mr. Croy set out the grand plan to Tim. They were going to work together to fell the three tall trees that had succumbed to Dutch Elm Disease. During the week, while his father was at work, Tim would be trusted with the chain saw to cut the felled trees into logs which he would then be expected to split into suitably sized pieces and stack in the wood shed for use in the following winter. Tim, liking machines and savouring the prospect of physical work was delighted. Together they collected the new saw, some long, thick ropes and some strange, steel wedges that Mr. Croy fetched from his store room. Tim watched as his father showed him how to tie a noose in one end of a rope and then threw it up to a solid looking branch half way up the tree. Tim pulled the other end of the rope, tightening it round the branch. They discussed the safest direction in which to make the tree fall and then Mr. Croy started the saw and cut a deep V in the side of the trunk that they had decided the tree needed to fall. Moving to the opposite side he began to cut the tree. Having started the process Mr. Croy indicated to Tim that he should have a go with the machine. Gingerly Tim took it from his father and squeezed the throttle. He was surprised at the force with which the machine kicked back at him and it was all that the small boy could do to hold it steady. As he got used to the feel of the saw Tim began to enjoy the sight of white wood chips flying out behind the saw as it sank deeper into the wood. When he had got about two thirds of the way through the tree trunk Mr. Croy indicated that he should stop. Tim removed the saw and killed the engine. Father and son moved to the other side of the tree and, holding the rope tightly, a suitably safe distance from the tree, they began to pull, a series of sharp, firm tugs that made the branches shake. There was a sharp crack. A kind of creaking, groaning sound during which the lofty tree began to very gently lean towards them and then, suddenly, gravity did it's work and the tree fell with a whooshing, clattering sound of twigs and branches flying through the air and crumpling onto the hard ground. Both men were excited by the destructive success of their mornings work and they went inside for lunch in high spirits. In the afternoon they felled a second tree, barely finishing the task before dusk fell.

Daily in the next week Tim cut the old trees into large logs and then, using the metal wedges, split each log into four triangular sections and took them in the wheel barrow to stack them neatly in the wood shed. He derived a strange and unexpected satisfaction from seeing the fruits of his labour piling up into a store of future comfort at the same time as the scene of destruction on the front lawn gradually became a mere memory.

Tim woke with a start. He moved cautiously, expecting his body to be racked with pain. It wasn't. He was, however drenched in sweat. He shivered, filled with fear and dread. Where was Lucas? He must be lurking, hiding, waiting for Tim to drop his guard once more so that he could pounce on him and over power him again. Slowly Tim realised that he was at home, in his own bedroom, amid the safe familiarity of his desk and book case and the shelf on which were displayed his collection of sea shells. It was dark, it must be past midnight. The big old house was silent, even the dogs must be asleep downstairs in the utility room. Of-course Lucas was not, could not, be there. It had been just a terrible dream or maybe a nightmare. Tim shivered again, his saturated pyjamas clinging coldly to his body. Very quietly Tim got up and took off his pyjamas, hanging them on the radiator so that they would get dry by the time he woke up in the morning. He didn't want his mother interrogating him about how or why they were so wet. He knew that he could never explain to her the horrors of his school experience. He got back into bed, naked, and curled himself into the foetal position. He still felt very scared. He wondered if he would ever be able to clear his mind of the attack. Why had Lucas had to choose him? It was just so unfair. Unable to rid himself of his terrifying memories, alone and desolate in the small hours of the morning, he began to cry silently.

Similar dreams disturbed Tim on two further occasions as the end of the holidays approached with the inevitable return to school.

At Sunday lunch, roast chicken, roast potatoes, peas, carrots, gravy and stuffing, Tim's favourite, followed by lemon cheesecake, a newly fashionable desert, Mr. Croy brought up the subject of Tim's return to school. "You know that you will have end of year exams this term, don't you Tim? They are very important because they will decide which set you are in for each subject for the next two years while you get ready for your "O" levels. So I do expect you to work hard for them this time, not like the Christmas term ones". Tim's eyes glazed over. He didn't want to think about school at all, especially as he had reached the conclusion that he simply would not be going back there. How *could* anyone expect him to go back after what had happened to him? Tim's logic had failed to register the small matter that nobody knew what had happened to him. "Are you listening Tim?" his mother challenged him, seeing clearly that he was not. "I'm not sure that you appreciate how very fortunate you are to go to such a super school".

That last sentence simply hit too many raw nerves for Tim to bear. How could *anyone* think he was fortunate to have had Lucas attack him like that? And how could it be that a school that allowed that sort of thing to happen could be described as super? He felt the prickling sting of tears at the back of his eyes. He certainly didn't want to be seen to cry, especially not in front of his sister and grandmother so he pushed his chair back with a scraping sound as its' legs dragged over the wooden floor, stomped out of the room slamming the door behind him and ran upstairs to his bedroom. Burying his head between his two pillows Tim cried himself dry.

By the time Mrs, Croy came to find him Tim was fully composed once more. "What ever's the matter darling?" "I don't want to go back to Barforth. I *hate* it. I haven't got any friends, the masters are horrible and I can't do any of the work." Tim blurted out everything that he could think of. Everything, that is, except the one fact that might have caused his mother to take seriously his state of mind.

"I know that it must be difficult being away from home dear but it's a very important step towards growing up. We've already seen how much more responsible you are becoming and we're very proud of you. You've done a brilliant job cutting up those trees, you've really impressed your father by how much you've matured. As I say, you have to learn to stand on your own two feet and a good boarding school offers you the best opportunity to do that". "But I really need you help sometimes when I don't understand my work when I try to do it in prep". Tim tried another tack, playing to the concern for his academic progress that his father had raised at lunch time. "Well you need to go and talk to the masters for that kind of help. That's what they're there for dear." Tim pictured the school outside lesson times, devoid of masters who were all cosily ensconced in the pub or the staff room while the prefects took charge of the school. "It really doesn't work like that mum". "I'm sure it *does*. Other boys must get help. You obviously just haven't found the right time to get it Tim". Tim smiled a smile of resignation and followed his mother downstairs to eat the bowl of cheesecake that she had saved for him.

On Monday evening Tim had to carry his trunk downstairs and put it in the car with his father as his mother would be driving him back to Barforth the next afternoon before Mr. Croy came home from work. Tim spent Tuesday morning moping around the house gloomily, playing in the garden with the dogs, and feeling increasingly hopeless. After lunch, which Tim was scarcely able to eat, so tied up in knots of fear was his stomach, Tim tried again to persuade his mother that it would be better for everyone if he did not return to Barforth. "You always said that I should tell you if I didn't want to go there because it would save you a lot of money" Tim reminded her. "Well I *have* said that before but Life is never as simple as it seems dear. You would never *get on* if you just went down the road like everyone else around here. They don't have the best teachers or good facilities in state schools and they would never take as much interest in you there as they do at Barforth." The idea that the Barforth masters took much interest in Tim grated with him but he could tell from the note of triumphant finality in his mothers' voice that there was no more room for discussion about the matter.

Tim had little to say on the long journey back to Barforth. His heart became heavier with every mile that past and he could manage little more than one word replies to each attempt that his mother made to engage him in conversation. It was almost a relief for both of them when they reached their destination. Mrs. Croy helped Tim take his trunk into School House Junior Dormitory. "I'm starting to know my way around this place myself!" She commented cheerfully. Upon entering the room, its familiar smell of feet and floor polish assailing his nostrils once again, Tim had felt physically sick from the sudden vivid memory of what had happened to him there barely two months earlier. Following his mother back downstairs to collect his tuck box Tim began to want nothing more than to make his farewells and get it over with. His mother was right. He evidently would have to stand on his own two feet and the sooner he faced that fact the better it would be for him.

Mrs. Croy and her son stood awkwardly beside the car. Her mothers' instinct told her that something wasn't right but she could not understand what it could be. She knew that Tim was a sensitive boy and that he did tend to over react to situations in which he did not feel comfortable. She supposed that that was what he was doing now. And, of course, he was a teenager now, with all the emotional instability that that meant. Obviously this would all "blow over" soon enough. "Remember to work as hard as you can and do *try* to enjoy some of the great things that you can do here dear. You know we all love you very much and we're very proud of you". Tim felt a boyish embarrassment as she pecked his cheek and then she was starting the car and he was waving good bye.

Tim did feel better almost as soon as the finality of the parting was over. He sauntered back to the Junior Common Room and was soon absorbed in animated conversation about the things that they had or had not done during the holidays with the other Third Formers as they returned one by one for the Summer Term.

Success!

On the first afternoon at the Boat Club that Summer term Toby Philips gathered the remaining five Third Form trainee coxes together, sitting on the trunk of a fallen tree on the river bank just above Snaky Bends. "The next couple of weeks are going to be very busy for us. I want to get you all trained to the highest standards so that you will be ready to cox any crew that might need you. You've got to move from the idea that you are just learning and can make mistakes to believing that you are the best and can help your crew to win races." Tim had always found Toby's way of speaking very exciting and motivating and this explicit demand for something extra struck a particular chord with him.

Toby issued each boy with a double-sided printed sheet of the general competition rules for racing eights and the specific duties and expectations of a cox. These were to be learnt and implemented in their daily coxing as quickly as possible. Toby would be watching closely to see who was doing things well and would test them randomly and without warning from time to time, when he felt like it. For the first two weeks or so the boys would be moved randomly between different boats and different crews and they would sometimes be asked to cox more senior and experienced crews so that Toby could get a better picture of their progress. On Tuesday and Friday evenings they were to have a private training session in the gym in second prep so that they could get fit themselves and gain an understanding of the level of dedication that was required of anyone who wanted to be a success in the Boat Club.

Looking at his sheet, Tim thought that he already knew most of its' contents. He was less confident or enthused by the prospect of the compulsory evening gym sessions, never having been especially good at the kind of activities that went on in gyms and not really seeing himself as a serious contender in the sporting life of school who should reasonably be expected to give up his free time (In which, he had to admit, he never had anything else planned) to suffer what was likely to be pain and humiliation. It was only for two weeks he reminded himself, thus holding back from verbalising his sour thoughts. Tim was loyal to Toby and did not really want to challenge his authority or judgement.

There followed a very hectic fortnight for the young coxes. Every day they would look at the Boat Club notice board on their way out of the Dining Hall after lunch to see which crew they were to cox that day, at what time they were scheduled to be "on the water" and to try to work out the age and ability of the boys that they would be commanding. The good thing for the coxes was that they quickly developed a feeling of independence and self sufficiency together with a feel for the way in which different boats could handle very differently in similar circumstances and how the individuals that made up an "eight" could bring to bear very different dynamics amongst a crew. Less good was the constant feeling of being unsettled, not belonging, never having the chance to develop relationships or to become truly part of a crew.

The twice weekly gym sessions were hard work. Toby was very demanding and strict, far from the relaxed and laid back young man that Tim had previously seen

him as being. Toby trained with and amongst his young charges and, as all great leadership manuals advise, he never asked the boys to do anything that he was not demonstrably able to do himself. " As a cox you will have to lead these training sessions for your crew yourself and you can't make boys who may be older and more senior than you do things if you can't do them yourself" he exhorted them as they stamped up and down benches in "step ups" or broke their backs in "sit ups" or stretched their arms as they swung across beams or climbed up ropes. While none of the coxes would have admitted to enjoying these sessions, they did at least serve to develop the feelings of comradeship that their constant shuffling between crews denied them. They would regularly have to weigh themselves before a session, Toby carefully recording each boys weight on a chart.

One afternoon, when Tim steered "his" boat into the side of the pontoon after an hour and a half of perfecting racing starts and finishes with the crew, he found Mr. Linford and Toby standing in serious looking conversation. Tim watched them continue to talk as he squatted holding the boat while the oarsmen disembarked and put away their oars. Tim commanded them to lift the boat out of the water and carry it back to the Boat House where it was the cox's duty to wash it down with the hose and then dry it off with a soggy leather cloth. When he emerged twenty minutes later, squinting in the bright sunshine as his eyes adjusted from the half darkness of the dingily lit boat house, he was surprised to hear Toby calling him over to join him and Mr. Linford on the pontoon. "How's it going Croy?" Mr. Linford addressed Tim. "OK sir, I think" "Toby and I have been watching you and we think it's going OK too" "Thank you sir!" "We were just saying that it may be a good idea for you to learn to scull so that you can get a finer feel for balance and the way in which currents affect a boat". "Yes sir. I'm not sure that I'd be much good at that though sir". "That's why you need to learn. Toby's ready to give you a lesson right now if you like". Tim realised that this was the kind of "offer" that a Third Former at Barforth did not have the option to refuse! "Ok sir. Thankyou sir." "Great! Strike while the iron's hot!" and Mr. Linford strode off to his workshop leaving Toby and Tim standing on the pontoon.

"A scull is just a kind of shrunken, one seater eight" Toby explained to Tim as they walked together to the smaller Boat

House to fetch their oars and sculls. They took their oars first, placing them close to the river's edge of the pontoon. "It feels very kind of flimsy and unstable at first. The trick is to always keep your paddles flat on the surface of the water when you're not actually rowing. That way it will always stay nicely balanced and level". Tim listened, noting the wisdom borne of experience of the older boy. He wondered why they had singled him out to undertake this additional training. Really Tim would rather it had been somebody else. "You can carry a scull to the river by yourself" Just feel how light it is". Tim discovered that a scull was indeed light but never the less found it very awkward and ungainly to carry safely and lower into the water. The two boys fastened their oars into the gaiters, the river side oar laying with its' blade flat on the water. Tim watched Toby ease himself confidently into his scull and then tried to do likewise. He felt the small vessel tip disconcertingly as he got in and he feared that he would capsize before he had even taken his first stroke. "Push yourself away from the pontoon and get both blades flat on the surface" Toby instructed, knowing how Tim would be feeling. With trepidation Tim pushed off and did as he had been instructed. To his surprise the scull sat straight and steady in the water, gently drifting on the current of the river.

"Ok, we're going to take a few strokes, just gently, to get a feel for it. Try to keep close to me so that I don't have to shout too loud". Tim slid his seat forward, afraid of upsetting the balance of his boat. He turned both oars through ninety degrees and plunged each blade into the water, not too deep, and pulled then gently towards him as he slid back on his seat, as he had learnt to do in the clinker "four" a few months before. He was surprised both at how light everything felt and that the scull moved smoothly and without listing in either direction. Maybe he *could* master this after all.

Tim and his mentor spent half an hour on the water, Toby offering advice and encouragement and Tim rapidly building his confidence. The sun was shining, the light green of Spring foliage surrounded them and the river flowed placidly. It was a beautiful place to be.

Over the coming weeks Toby and Tim would scull together regularly, sometimes immediately after the scheduled outing in an eight, occasionally on a Saturday or Sunday afternoon as a kind of relaxing activity to get them out of school. Tim began to feel as if he had been sculling for years.

There began to be much excited talk and speculation amongst the Third Form members of the Boat Club about selections for crews and who would or would not make it into the A or B crew. Tim didn't take much part in this frenzy of speculation as he was not an oarsman and had not considered the possibility that coxes also were part of the selection process. He had noticed that Toby was now regularly to be seen with Mr. Linford in his motor launch, following closely one or another of the Novice Eights, pointing and talking about the merits of different individuals.

Then, as the Third Formers came out of lunch to look at the Boat Club notice board one afternoon, they found all their names jumbled up in a mass, none of them assigned as they had come to expect, into a specific position within a particular crew. Instead there was a typed note telling them that they were to report, changed for rowing, to the Old Hall straight after last lesson. This must be when they would find out the results of the long process of testing and selecting. Tim did not feel anything of the anticipation of the other boys because he still assumed that it did not directly involve or affect him.

As they assembled in the Old Hall it became clear that there were also some Fourth Form oarsmen there too. Toby explained that Mr. Linford would be announcing all the crews from the Under Fifteen A's downwards. This would be the beginning of some boys' successful careers in the Boat Club so it was a very important time for them all.

Mr Linford entered the room, accompanied by Snodley Pemberton, the Captain of the Boat Club. He signalled for Toby to join them. The boys hushed expectantly. Mr. Linford spoke a few words about how difficult the selection process was and that nothing was ever set in stone and how, if you had not been selected for something that you had hoped for it was probably because you had not been learning for long enough so you mustn't stop trying. He then began to announce which boys were to be in which crews, starting from the lower ones. As each crew was announced they would head off to the Boat Club to start training together for the first time. Tim realised, at last, that coxes were being allocated to crews. He waited patiently to be sent to join a crew on its' way to the river, just hoping that he was not going to find himself left out after everyone had been allocated. That kind of humiliation had happened to him several times before, at prep school. The room became emptier and emptier. At last Mr. Linford began to announce the Under Fifteen A's. Eglington and Huband from School House were in. "And the cox for the Under Fifteen A's is Tim Croy". There was clapping and cheering from those remaining in the room. Tim felt light headed and slightly confused by this sudden and totally unexpected turn of events. He had never been selected for anything before in his school career. He could feel himself starting to blush, suddenly shy and unsure of himself under the focus of everybody's attention. He walked uncertainly over to join his new crew. Mr, Linford and Snodley Pemberton started congratulating them all on their success and talking of a strict training regime from this point onwards.

As they left the room together, on their way to the river, Toby caught up with Tim and thumped him affectionately on his shoulders. That was a surprise for you, wasn't it?" "Yes". Replied Tim simply. "I've known that it was the likely decision for about a week, you definitely deserve it. It's been really hard not to tell you. I feel so proud of you!"

As he walked with his new crew from school to the

Boat Club Tim could still barely comprehend the recent turn of events. Was this really happening to him? How had he got into this situation? Was it a mistake? A joke? Would he really be good enough for the task? Tim had never, hadn't even ever hoped, to be any kind of sporting success and yet, without having made any particular effort, here he was coxing the Under Fifteens "A" crew. He felt as if he was walking not on the Private Lane but on air. At the Boat Club the proud Under Fifteens "A" crew positioned themselves beside the rack that contained what was to be their Eight. The David Tribble seemed like a very special boat to every boy there that afternoon, imparting in them a warm glow of pride as lustrous as its' deeply shining wooden hull and its' newly painted blue riggers. Together they took hold of the sides of their boat, under the command of Tim, and carried it reverently down to the pontoon. They spent the next hour putting the boat and themselves through their paces, getting a feel for the boat and beginning to develop the empathy with one another that would enable the nine of them to work as one.

Next morning when Tim arrived to make Longs' bed, he found a steaming mug of coffee waiting for him. Long shook his hand, then hugged him momentarily. "Well done Tim" Tim was taken aback by the use of his Christian name but also pleased, indicating as it did an unexpected degree of closeness and friendship. "It's a really big achievement. Mr. Linford is on cloud nine, having three School House boys in the Under Fifteens A, it means we won't have another terrible season like this one was for a long time."" Thanks". Said Tim simply, beginning to slurp on his hot coffee. He didn't think that he had ever felt so pleased with himself before in his life.

The days extended into weeks and Tim and the crew threw themselves into proving that they deserved their place in the top boat. They trained daily, coached from the bank by Toby and, sometimes, from his motor launch, by Mr. Linford. Tim did not much enjoy such times, not because he didn't appreciate the training from Mr. Linford but because the motor launch created such powerful bow waves that Tim had difficulty controlling the swaying Eight so felt that he must look inadequate for the task. Twice a week they would spend an hour in the gym in second prep circuit training. At first Toby lead the sessions but, as Tim became more confident in his role Toby melted away and Tim took full responsibility, shouting instructions breathlessly as he tried also to be thoroughly active in every exercise. The boys would go to bed on those evenings tingling and exhausted from an hour of solid slog.

The Saturday before half term was a kind of deadline towards which the crew was hurtling, seemingly with increasing speed. They were entered into their first inter school regatta. As the time got closer the boys worked harder and felt the tension of anticipation rising. Tim began to worry that he had never actually had to cox in a public competition before and was afraid that he would make some terrible mistake that would ruin the race for everyone. He lay awake on the Wednesday night, trying to rehearse the commands and to remember the official rules that he had learnt months earlier, when they had all seemed like just another set of things that he had to learn for no particular reason. He resolved to visit Toby the next day to seek his guidance and reassurance. Tim didn't know where Toby's study was and spent nearly fifteen minutes wondering round unfamiliar parts of the school searching for "Hillside Room 11". He knocked quietly at the door, suddenly feeling rather shy and uncertain of himself. Maybe Toby would not like being disturbed by a Third Former. "Yeah" came the reply. Tim pushed the door open and stood surveying a comfortable looking bed sitting room. It seemed that the belief that School House had the worst studies might be true, he reflected, comparing this room to the Top Studies with which he was familiar. "Tim! I thought you'd never come to see me. I was starting to feel that you're too important for me now!" "No, never. I just know that you're very busy with A levels now and anyway I didn't know where this place was." "I'm not *that* busy and I need a break sometimes". "Tea or coffee?" Toby put his kettle on and got two mugs ready. "So I'm guessing you're feeling the pressure for Saturday" Toby saved Tim from having to broach his concerns. "Yes. I just keep thinking that I will cock up somehow or that I'll forget what I should say or crash the boat or something." "That's normal, I think. I felt like that before every race I ever did. That's how I kind of knew why you'd come". "Thanks. I feel like you really understand how it is because I know you've done it all before". "Just remember that you've been selected to do this after watching you for ages and seeing you pass test after test. We all know that you are the best man for the job and that you will be fine". The boys drank their coffee, enjoying each others company and the strength of understanding between them that required no talking to share.

Saturday, like every day during the long, hot summer of nineteen seventy six, dawned bright and sunny. Twenty seven boys, the First Eight, Under sixteen A's and Under fifteen A's assembled after breakfast in the Head Masters Quadrangle, Changed into their smartly pressed rowing kit, to await the arrival of the coach. A selection of sundry boys, dressed in school uniform, turned up to fill the coach and support their school throughout the day. Mr. Linford taught the Under Fifteens how to check that the boats on the trailer were fixed securely for the journey and how to raise and lower the jockey wheel to attach the trailer to the tow bar of his Triumph estate car.

The venue for this regatta was a large lake, not far from Oxford. It seemed to Tim that the whole place was awash with boys and boats, each school had a designated area in which to unload and reassemble their boats and in which to gather to prepare for whichever race was due to take place next. There were lots of school minibuses and boat trailers, interspersed with large cars and the occasional Labrador. There was a feeling of suppressed excitement, of everyone playing their part in the event as calmly and efficiently as possible.

The Barforth boys set about unloading trestles and riggers, bolting together sections of boat and carefully fitting riggers. Mr. Linford moved confidently amongst the young men, checking and pointing out things that were not tight enough and reminding them all of what was expected of them. Despite the growing heat of the day Tim felt a shiver of dread and excitement. There was no escaping now.

The Tannoy system called for four Under Fifteen crews to bring their boats to the water. Tim knew that Barforth would be called in the next group. His crew began to hang around beside their boat, each boy feeling tense in his own private world, each keen to appear cool and relaxed. "Would Gainswell, Sommerton, Barforth and The Heights Under Fifteens bring their boats to the pontoon please". At last! This was It!

The four crews lowered their boats into the gently lapping water of the lake. Each crew covertly eying up the opposition, none at all sure what to expect. The four boats were pushed away from the pontoon and the coxes manoeuvred their boat into the designated lane. "Come forward to row!" the Tannoy reverberated across the water. "I'll ask you once". "are you ready?" "Row!" The race was on. With a jerk Tim felt the David Tribble launch through the water, gathering pace with every stroke of her oars. He could hear the occasional splosh of an oar hitting a wave on the surface of the water. He focussed on keeping between the buoys that separated the competing boats from each other with just enough space to prevent their oars clashing. "In! out! In! out! In! out!" Tim began to shout, pacing his crew, projecting his voice clearly above the heads of his crew so that even Bow could hear him against the headwind that had built up. They were level with a boat to their left. Tim had no idea which school it was but he did know that they had to pass them. "Stride it out!" he called, indicating that he wanted every oarsman to give a little bit more than he thought he could. "Our bow's ahead!" he encouraged "in! out! In! out!" Slowly, oarsman by oarsman, David Tribble pulled ahead of their competitor.

"We're gaining! Yes! Stride-It-Out!" Tim implored, encouraged, cajoled his crew. "Let's get a full length between us" "In! Out! In! Out!" Out of the corner of his eye Tim could see a boat to their right coming into line with them. Tim set his sights on passing that one too. He knew that the finishing line could not be far away now and he sensed that his crew may have given everything that they could give already. He wasn't sure that he should push them any further. They were his friends. But then it was his job to get the best from them. Every last ounce, Toby had described it. "Stride-It-Out" he commanded once more. He could see Huband at Stroke, his face contorted in pain and effort, force himself to up the pace of the oarsmen behind him one last increment. The David Tribble nosed towards the other boat, their bow levelling with the stern, then with the stroke. Then, suddenly it was all over. They were past the finish. "Easy all!" Tim brought his crew to a timely rest. Their blades feathered, each boy took deep breaths, tried to gather their thoughts and control their shaking, exhausted bodies. They had come second. They would not be in the final. The disappointment made each of them feel heavier and more tired than they would have believed possible. Carry on Stroke side, back her down Bow side" Tim commanded his crew to turn the boat round to row gently, despondently, back to the pontoon and the encouraging welcome from the Barforth contingent.

Having been encouraged and congratulated for a "very strong showing" by Mr. Linford the boys set about dismantling David Tribble and putting it back on the trailer. The Under Sixteens were soon disqualified too so everyone was free to shout support for the First Eight who had got through to the final. To hoots of delight the Barforth boys watched as Brockley Jones nosed ahead of their competitor to win the regatta. Later Tim watched in awe as the crew grabbed their cox, still dressed in his special white braded blazer and trousers, and good naturedly threw him into the lake. The boys all cheered as he came sploshing out of the water waving his fists in the air.

The return journey was a joyful one, everybody delighted and proud that Barforth was bringing home the cup. The next morning, in breakfast, the meal was interrupted half way through by the shout "Barforth Boat Club!". The First Eight marched in triumphantly, their cox sitting on the shoulders of their Stroke, brandishing the cup. After a circuit of the Dining Hall, accompanied by the banging of six hundred spoons on six hundred cereal bowls, the cox placed the cup on a shelf high up on the far wall of the Dining Hall. This was a traditional Barforth ceremony that would become a familiar feature of Summer Term Sunday Mornings.

Two weeks after half term the Under Fifteen A's entered their second regatta. This time it took place on a river, rather wider than the River Bar, in Lincolnshire. Toby had called Tim to his study to poor over a kind of diagram of the river, depicting the course of the race and the different lanes. They talked about the problems and benefits of each lane and the likely strength of currents in different bends of the course. Tim tried hard to visualise, understand and remember the information so that he could derive maximum benefit for his crew on the day. Toby had told them often that it was the cox's ability to make use of the natural features of a course that could win or lose a race. Tim knew that Toby had raced this course on several occasions so he had valuable "inside knowledge" to impart and he determined to make the most of it.

The usual busy sight greeted Barforth upon arrival in Lincolnshire. Like a well oiled machine the crews unloaded and assembled their boats. They gathered excitedly around Mr. Linford who had acquired a programme of events indicating which crew would be rowing against which in the first round. Barforth Under Fifteens were to meet Sommerton once more, to whom they had lost so narrowly last time. Tim and his crew determined resolutely that they would not let that happen this time.

On the water Tim ordered his crew to move the boat into position for the starting orders. The race was being managed from a motor launch this time, which bobbed, its' engine idling, level with the start line. "Come forward to row". "I'll ask you once." Are you ready?" "Row!" Tim felt the familiar shudder as the David Tribble was heaved into motion by his determined young crew. They were in a middle lane so Tim focussed his efforts on steering a straight course through the lane to keep as far from competing blades and cross waves as possible. "In! Out! In! Out! In! Out!" Tim paced his crew. He knew that they were in the lead almost from the start. He had seen one of the other boats come to a sudden stop after one of the oarsmen "caught a crab" causing him to lose his grip on his oar and to be nearly pushed out of the boat by the force of the handle swinging out of control back at his chest. "Stride it out!" Tim commanded as they passed the half way point. "We're out in front!" he encouraged his crew. "In! Out! In! Out! Don't slack off now!" Tim could hear the conflicting roars of the spectators at the finish line now, calling their schools' crew to give it all they had. He saw the line of red buoys indicating the finish. They were past. Barforth had won! They would be in the final race! "Easy all!" Tim brought his crew to a halt and David Tribble slowed to a standstill beneath them. The breathless crew dropped their feathered oars onto the water and rested. "Yes!" Huband shouted, raising his fist in a victory salute. The rest of the crew followed suit.

With their boat out of the water and safely balanced on trestles Mr. Linford and the other crews gathered round them congratulating and advising the young crew. "There's a bottle of energy drink for each of you in the boot of the car. Drink that now but don't eat anything yet because the final will be upon you before you know it". The advice was sound. Almost before the boys had got their breathing back to a normal pace they were being summoned back to the water for the Under Fifteens final. They were against a school called Chilton End.

Tim positioned David Tribble in the outside left hand lane as instructed. "Come forward to row!" "I'll ask you once". "Are you ready?" "Row!" The now familiar command rang out over the water from the burbling motor launch. The oarsmen almost pounced on the water with their cleanly squared blades, slicing smoothly in and out, loosing no power in making splashes. Tim concentrated on positioning his boat as close to the inside of each corner as he dared in an effort to harness the help of the prevailing current. He was recalling almost photographically the diagram that he had studied on the desk in Toby's study. "The cox's skill at using the natural features of the course can win or lose a race" he had told Tim on many occasions during the months of training. Tim felt that he owed him and his crew to demonstrate that he was worth the trust that they had put in him. He was willing his boat to respond to his inputs. Tim could hear the rival cox exhorting his crew to give it all they had. "Stride it out! And stride it out some more" Tim called over the heads of the eight boys sitting in line before him. "We're pulling ahead" "A full bows' length ahead!" "No! You can't slack off now you lazy bastards!" Tim remembered that, in the final seconds of a race it was possible to squeeze a few last ounces of energy from a crew by insulting them. The red buoys were in sight again. It was close. Tim *thought* that David Tribble's bows were ahead of those of their rival but the distance was too small to be certain from his view point. "Easy all!" the race was over. "I think we might have done it" Tim spoke quietly to Huband, sitting facing him in Strokes' seat. "You *think* or you *know*?" "I can't be sure" said Tim simply and honestly. Seconds later they were sure. The Tannoy announcement confirmed that Barforth Under Fifteens had won. As Tim got the boat turned around and ordered the crew to row gently back to the pontoon the boys were too exhausted to react.

The entire Barforth group were waiting, cheering, on the pontoon. The First Eight knelt and caught David Tribble as Tim steered it into the side, in a gesture of respect to their success. Shortly both they and the Under Sixteens would win their respective races, causing Barforth to sweep the podium clean of all three cups.

Later, after boats had been dissembled and tied firmly onto the trailer, before the awards ceremony, The First Eight threw their cox into the river, as Tim had seen last time. "Can we throw Croy in sir?" Tim heard Huband ask Mr. Linford. "Well you really ought to be asking Croy if he minds" came the reply. "Croy doesn't mind sir" Tim answered before he could be asked. His crew gathered around him excitedly. As they had watched the First Eight do, Tim was grabbed firmly by two sets of hands on each leg and each arm and lifted horizontally into the air, as if he was laying on a bed. He was swung three times backwards and forwards and then suddenly released to fly through the air, over the river and into the water, on his back, with a heavy splosh. Tim righted himself and strode out of the water waving his fist in the air, emulating the First Eight cox. Everyone cheered.

Tim stood dripping as the Stroke of each crew was called up to receive their cup. The journey back to school was boisterous and happy. Tim's wet clothes stuck to him as they dried in the immense heat of the inside of the coach.

The Under Fifteen A's went on to win three further regattas that summer, helping to make Barforth the undisputed champion of the region.

The last Saturday of term was the day of Henley Royal Regatta. Schools could only enter their First Eights as it was such a major international event. About half of Barforth School went in a fleet of coaches to have a great day out and to cheer on their First Eight. As the boys straggled from the coach park to the main riverside event Tim and his friends were excited to see a stunning new yellow car. It looked from the front just like a Farrari but it had four doors. Upon closer inspection it proved to be a Rover 3500. Tim promised himself there and then that he would have one one day. Toby, free now from the tyranny of A levels and excited by his impending final departure from Barforth, took Tim under his wing for the last time to show him round Henley and all the famous features of the event. They had a great time together and Tim was even able to get in to the enclosure to stand proudly with the Barforth First Eight, most of whom Toby had coxed for the previous two years. Tim noticed with admiration how he was still very much one of them.

Toughing It Out

Tim's second and third years at Barforth were generally unexceptional. Beyond his surprise success in the Boat Club he remained largely unnoticed, just another boy drifting through a large school making up financial numbers on the Bursars' account sheets.

Every great Public School claims, in their prospectus, to bring out the best in the individual, to develop the strengths and iron out the weaknesses to create a "well rounded young adult". They *have* to make these kinds of promises because they are trying to sell a very costly service to clients whose children are the most important individuals in their world. For most of the parents considering a private school education for their children the high cost and long term commitment are justified for reasons of perceived high status and to assuage guilt, an attempt to compensate their children for the parents' inability to give them the time, the effort and the love that are required to raise children to become well rounded people. All the energy of these parents tends to go to achieving ever higher salaries, most of which then has to be spent with the school, which is in turn expected to faultlessly replicate the functions of "the ideal parent".

The harsh reality is that it is, almost by definition of the requirement, impossible to deliver this promise. Far from catering for, or even having any interest in, the individual, most great schools' function much more like the proverbial sausage factory than the idealised parent. The process works something like this. Over generations, often indeed centuries, each school has built, developed and refined a public perception, an image, its' unique selling point. From this the school develops a model of what the "ideal" pupil might be like by the time they finish their time at the school. Contrary to what may be suggested by their frequent use of charitable status, these schools primary aim is to make profit so that they can reinvest in more high visibility facilities with which to impress prospective parents and thus perpetuate the process. Key to this function is to select pupils for entry into the school who are likely to need the least effort of input or cost to become the schools' "ideal" leaver.

Barforth, of course, was no exception. They sold themselves on "outstanding academic and sporting success" and they maintained their charitable status, with its' tax benefits, by "supporting the sons of those engaged in Christian Service". So their ideal leaver would have been captain of the First Fifteen Rugby team, of Hockey and Cricket or the Boat Club and have won a place at Oxford or Cambridge, while having highly religious parents who had attended every Sunday Chapel service throughout their sons' five years at the school. Exception my have been made for the sons of wealthy parents who were willing to contribute generously to a major school development project.

Tim was, at best, seen as academically average. Like so many teenage boys he felt no urgency in academic matters and contented himself with doing just enough work to keep himself out of trouble. The only obvious indication of his latent intelligence was his ability to judge very accurately exactly how little he could get away with doing to satisfy each subject Master. This escaped the notice of most of his teachers so went unchallenged. For those who had any interest in Tim his whit and humour offered regular insights to his true ability and personality but these went largely unnoticed apart from those occasions when a Master or Prefect felt that he had pushed the undefined boundaries too far and issued a fitting punishment. So, through the corporate eyes of Barforth, Tim was seen as offering little potential for adding any particular value status to the school and consequently deserving of no particular effort on the part of the school.

Since Mr. and Mrs. Croy were neither especially wealthy nor at all religiously inclined Tim derived no second hand boost to his status from them. Consequently Tim remained, for the most part, an absolute nonentity.

For the Autumn Term of nineteen Seventy Six Tim had chosen, at the first opportunity, to leave the Rugby Club and had joined the small, obscure and unpopular Cross Country Club. Tim knew that, largely because of his size, he would never find success on the Rugby pitch and he found no pleasure in the game whatsoever. His decision had been made shrewdly because he knew that he needed to keep as fit and strong as possible during the long Autumn term in readiness for Boat club training sessions in the new season and he quite liked the possibility of being able to perform on his own individual merit as opposed to being lost within part of a very mediocre team. Tim knew from past experience that his strong stamina was a major benefit in the long distance demands of Cross Country running and that he could probably be quite successful without having to really put himself out too much. The Master in charge of the small club was very relaxed and laid back and would only occasionally accompany the boys on a run in person. Mostly he would meet the boys, dressed suitably for a run through muddy fields, woods and roadsides, talk them through the route that he wanted them to follow and then park on some strategic roadside half way round the course to read the newspaper in his Mini. He would then shout at any stragglers to "get your legs in gear", put his Mini in gear to drive back to Barforth and meet everyone back in his class room just to be certain that he had not lost anybody.

This lack of supervision suited the boys very well and most runs would be punctuated by a rest sitting in the Autumn sunshine on a public bench, by a visit to a village shop to buy and consume a cake or a bottle of Coke or, for some, a smoke of a cigarette hidden behind a hedge, in the hopeful assumption that the smell of smoke would be removed without trace by the panting and puffing of the last part of the run.

It was a Barforth expectation that every boy would become confirmed during their second year at the school. Boys were offered special classes in which to learn the precepts of the Christian faith and the ways in which they may be expected to implement them in their daily lives. This culminated in a special Confirmation service in Chapel in which boys would receive their first Holy Communion in front of their teary eyed parents.

At the end of the Autumn term each Fouth Former received a letter from the Reverend Pullman in the envelope containing his end of term report and the school bill, with a tear off slip that required the signature of both a parent and their son, to be returned to him on the first day of term, to confirm that they wanted to undertake the Confirmation process. Tim did not want to and his parents saw no reason to make their son do such a thing if he did not believe in it. They felt that it was a matter of personal belief and that it was not something that should be undertaken lightly in the name of school tradition. So Tim did not return the slip on the first day of the following term.

Coming out of Lunch one afternoon Tim found a letter addressed to him on the Chaplain's Notice Board. It requested Tim to visit the reverend Pullman at his "earliest convenience". Having nothing to do at that moment Tim sloped off to the Chaplains' office in the vestibule of the Chapel. The door was open so Tim tapped on the door and walked in. "You wanted to see me sir" The Reverend Pullman smiled. "Yes Tim, I don't seem to have got the signed form about your Confirmation course this term. Have you got it still or do you know if your parents posted it to me?" "No sir. We didn't send it to you because I'm not doing it sir". "Oh. Why not?" "I don't want to sir." "When I tell you that *every other boy in the Fourth Form is,* I'm

To Fight My Own Battles

sure you'll change your mind" Reverend Pullman stared hard at Tim, daring him to disagree. "No sir, I don't want to" "Sit down Tim".

Tim sat on the hard, upright chair in front of the untidy desk in the overly warm office. "What is it that you find difficult about making the right decision Tim?" "Well I just don't really believe in all that sort of thing so obviously I can't confirm it sir". "Do you mean to say that you don't believe in God Tim?" "No sir. I mean yes sir, I don't, not really no" "I'm sure you wouldn't want me to have to write to your parents telling them what you've just told me". There was a slightly menacing edge to the chaplain's voice that served merely to harden Tim's resolve. "Sir, I can't do it sir, so I'm not going to do it and my parents don't mind sir." The Reverend Pullman's face reddened "I think you'd better go. We'll try again when you're in a better frame of mind". "Ok sir. Thankyou sir".

Mrs Croy was a lady of principal and was doing her best to bring her children up in a similar vein. She was accustomed to being obeyed and did not take kindly to what she saw as insubordination from those in her employ. "So I am sure you will understand" she ended her letter, written on thick, embossed note paper with her address printed centrally at the top "that because you have failed in your duty to help Timothy to understand the teachings of the Christian Scriptures he, quite understandably, does not feel able to declare his official Confirmation of their understanding. Both my husband and I fully support his decision and we expect you to do so too". She signed the letter with a flourish of her fountain pen and, in so doing, signed away any chance of Tim ever becoming anything more than an outsider looking in at the life of Barforth.

The Reverend Pullman marched across the Head Masters' Quadrangle from the Chapel to the Head Masters' Study and knocked firmly on the door. He did not often demand instant access to the Head Master but this was a very serious matter and he knew that he would want to know about it at once. Having exchanged polite niceties the Chaplain handed the Head Master the letter and took a seat to the side of his imposing and empty green leather topped desk. "Oh my goodness! This makes it very difficult for us John, very inconvenient and possibly the start of many more such cases." "So what should we do, Head Master? Do we have a policy to deal with this kind of circumstance?" "We don't really have a choice now but to respect the wishes of the Croy family. I think that you probably made the wrong move in contacting the parents before I tried to convince the boy". He handed the letter back to its' recipient and, flustered, the Chaplain took his leave. Safely back in his office the Reverend Pullman poured and swallowed a large sweet sherry, kept in a bottle hidden behind a pile of suitably pious books in the dark oak cupboard behind his desk before he had to go to teach a Fifth Form Scripture class.

    The Head Master was not pleased. He didn't personally care whether Croy became confirmed or not. It may be mildly embarrassing when he had to explain to the governors why, for the first time in living memory, a boy had been able to avoid this important ritual in the School Year, but he could handle that. What annoyed him was that he knew that Mr. Croy did a lot of work in the Middle East and he had been planning to approach him with a view to getting some lucrative personal introductions when he attended the HMC recruitment tour to the region in the Autumn. Now that the school had ruffled the feathers of the Croy family it would make the task more awkward and less likely to be successful. There was a tap on the communicating door from his secretary's office and she brought him his morning cup of coffee and two Digestive biscuits, placing them on his desk with a discreet smile. When she had left the room and the door had clicked behind her the Head Master opened the bottom left hand drawer of his desk, retrieved a half full bottle of single malt and slopped a generous splash into his coffee.

    Tim Croy was, much to the envy of many of his fellow Fourth formers, the only boy who did not have to give up the second half of his Saturday afternoons for special Confirmation Preparation Classes.

The Boat Club continued to be a successful and enjoyable diversion from the unexceptional daily routines of Barforth life for Tim. He and his crew had morphed from being the Under Fifteens A to the Under sixteens A at the start of the Easter term, more or less by natural progression rather than with any serious competitive effort. They were being coached regularly now by Mr. Linford or another Master and, by February, they were ready to compete in the Spring round of inter school Head of River Races. Tim was unclear about the differences between a Head of River Race and a Regatta and, feeling rather lost without his special mentor Toby Philips, had sought advice from the current Cox of the First Eight, Alex Rian, who was a Fifth Former who Tim did not really know but had always seen to be a cheerful kind of guy. Tim approached Rian on the river bank outside the Boat House one afternoon as he arrived for his outing. "Hi Rian, how's it going?" "OK. You?" "OK." Tim came straight to the point. "Can you tell me about what I'm supposed to do in a Head of River Race? I haven't done one before and I don't really know what's different from a Regatta." "Nothing really". Rian was abrupt and unforthcoming. "Talk it through with old Linford, mate". I gotta go and get ready". Tim didn't like being rebuffed like that and spent the rest of the afternoon feeling sore and lamenting the absence of Toby who would certainly have given him all the help and advice that he wanted.

Drinking tea in the Senior Common Room after prep that evening with his house mates, Tim brought the matter up in conversation. "Alex Rian's a bit of a bastard isn't he?" "Why'd you say that?" Enquired Eglington "he's always seemed nice enough to me". Tim recounted his experience of cold unhelpfulness that afternoon. " Oh *derrrrr* Tim, what else do you expect?" Huband joined the conversation. "What d'you mean?" Tim felt confused, not having a clue what Huband was on about. "Well *think about it* and don't be such a der brain. What's going to happen to us all next year?" "We're going to do "O" levels?" "No, in the Boat Club I mean. We won't be Under Sixteens all the time, We'll end up in the Second Eight, waiting our turn to become the First Eight. But it's not the same for you and Alex Rian is it?" "How d'you mean?" Tim still didn't get it. "What are you hoping to do next in the Boat Club? It's obvious, isn't it? You're going to want to cox the First Eight. And whose place are you going to take?" Tim finally got it. For the oarsmen, the bigger, stronger and more muscular you were, the better you chance of rowing in the First Eight. It was, to some extent, a waiting game for age and growth to take you where you wanted to be. For a cox it was the opposite. As you grew you would simply become too large, too heavy, to be of any further value and you would be replaced by someone smaller. Alex Rian had probably felt that Tim was trying to edge him out of his coveted position before his natural time had come. Tim kept a low profile in the presence of Rian from that point on. He didn't like upsetting people and he could see that the same thing would happen to him too, in due course.

Soon it was the time of year for the inter house boat races again. School House was better placed this year, especially in the Under Sixteens and, as each heat passed and the School House crew moved up the rankings the excitement within the house grew to fever pitch. Tim, Eglington and Huband were rowing with Andrews and another boy from the Fifth Form who was still below the age of sixteen. Tim enjoyed being part of the focus of everyone's attention and looked forward to the increasingly likely possibility of winning for School House. School House Under Sixteens were in the final against Baker. Tim sat in his Four, in the Right Hand of the two lanes. He knew that he had the less favourable set of currents to contend with and this somehow sharpened his awareness of every possible opportunity to take a corner a little bit wide or of where the river widened sufficiently for him to move his boat a little further towards the middle of the water without risking clashing oars with the other boat and thus being disqualified. "Come forward to row". Mr. Linford called from his motor launch, positioned well to the rear of the two racing shells. "I'll ask you once. Are you ready? Row!" Tim's strong young crew powered their boat forward, taking clean, long strokes and rapidly moving their boat into a marginal lead. Tim concentrated on the passing land marks, waiting his opportunity to take a course closer to the centre of the river. He was confident that he had more experience, a better knowledge of the river than his rival cox and that that would help them gain a definite lead. Moving the rudder slightly "Stride it out" Tim called. The boat gained speed. "In! Out! In! Out!" The crew were giving it their all. Tim was giving them his all. The oarsmen could see now that they were a full half length ahead of their competitors. It gave them a last boost of energy. School House crossed the finishing line three quarters of a length ahead of Baker. "Easy All" Tim brought his shattered crew to a halt. They could hear cheering from both sides of the bank. Tim wondered if the boys on the farmers' side of the river would get chased by the bulls that he had often seen in that field from the safety of the river. He was glad he wasn't a spectator.

That evening the School House Under Sixteens enjoyed the traditional Chicken Chips and Coke supper in Mr. Linfords' flat. Life felt good!

Exams

In the Fifth Form boys were scheduled to sit their "O" level exams. One or two of which would be taken in the Autumn term by those boys who were considered to be ready to do so, in order to take some of the pressure off them when the main tranche came in June. Tim took English Language and Classical Civilization in November, both of which he passed. It was a good start to what Mr. and Mrs. Croy had deemed to be "a very important year, Tim."

The level and quantity of academic work was now much

more intense and demanding, meaning that Tim and most of the other boys in his year now needed to continue their work into second prep on most evenings. This new sense of urgency and feeling of pressure began to bring out new frictions between the boys of School House. Williams started to set up more pranks which lead to the whole group suffering regular mass punishments. Now that they were higher up the school the prefects did not have so much of an age or seniority advantage and so appeared less frightening and, consequently, had less natural authority. The result was frequent boisterous clashes with the prefects and more inconvenient punishments.

Tim, Andrews, Williams and Eglington were for some reason selected in November, after the "O" Level season, to represent School House in the CCF weekend challenge. They were to spend two nights camping in the Welsh hills, hiking by day and locating various items on a list. After Tea on Friday afternoon the forty selected boys assembled outside the Sargent Majors' stores to be issued with tents, utensils, sleeping bags and army rations, all of which had to be stowed in rucksacks for the boys to carry on their backs. They were to wear uncomfortable Army Issue boots, trousers, shirts and sweaters. Not a boy amongst them looked as if he was delighted to have been selected and the Sargent Major, who for some unspecified reason was "unable" to come with them could not resist the opportunity to bawl at them about their inadequacy for such a fine military exercise. After a long motorway journey on the coach, over the Severn Bridge and into the Welsh Hills the boys were disgorged in their groups at one mile intervals to ensure that they would truly manage alone. Various Masters would be driving around the area to make regular checks. The boys were to follow the precise instructions with which they had been issued so that they could complete their tasks and meet at the collection point on Sunday afternoon.

The School House contingent mooched moodily off into the Welsh darkness, struggling to get a safe foot hold on the loose slate hill side under the unaccustomed weight of their rucksacks. After an hour and a half of sliding and grumbling they believed that they had reached their allotted camp site for the first night. Sliding their burdens off their backs they set about putting up their two tents. Tired, hungry and miserable the boys went in search of suitable sticks with which to light a fire. In the dark it proved to be far from a simple task and it took the four of them a good half an hour to find and then ignite a suitable quantity of wood. Eglington went in search of water in a nearby stream to fill one of the mess tins and Andrews tore open a foil packet of sausages that proved to be floppy, pink and encased in foul smelling yellow jelly. Williams managed to snap off the pull ring from the top of the tin of baked beans without even beginning to open it. He spent an age, with the willing help of Tim, trying without success to gouge it open with pieces of slate. The boys did not eat their beans that night. Eglington set his water boiling on the fire as the sausages began to spit and split open in another mess tin beside it. Tim located a packet of "dehydrated potato powder" which he tore open and tipped in to the boiling water. Minutes later a mountain of mashed potato began to heap up in the tin, spilling over onto the fire. "What the hell are you doing Croy?" "I don't know. It's just making more and more bloody mash!"

Their meal consumed, without really satisfying their hunger, the boys had nothing better to do than to bed down for the night. Tim shared a tent with Williams. Lying on the hard Welsh mountain side with only a few millimetres of sleeping bag separating them from the rocks none of the boys were able to sleep. "It makes the crappy school mattress seem like luxury" observed Williams. "Yeah school food seems like a good choice compared to that shit. I bet it was all stale. That's why the Army gave it to the Sargent Major" Tim grumbled. "I bet he's not really doing anything. He just can't hack this kind of thing" Andrews shouted across from the other tent. The grumblings reverberated between the tents for most of the night until the boys fell, one by one, into a restless and uncomfortable sleep.

Waking early with stiff legs and sore backs the boys scurried around collecting more sticks to light another fire to make tea and porridge. It was much easier in the light of day! "Look at all that mash Croy! It's spread over half the valley during the night." Eglington teased. "I think it was supposed to feed a whole Army, not just four of us. Did you read the instructions properly?" "You know I can't read Eglington" Tim replied "I'm not a scholar like you. Anyway it was dark remember?"

Dismantling and re packing their tents proved to be far from simple and the bedraggled group began their hike late. First task on the list was to count how many houses there were along the High Street of a village. "We don't need to actually go there" Williams said "you can see each of the houses on the map look. We can save ages by not doing that and they'll never know". "Sometimes the map doesn't really show things that accurately though" Andrews demurred. "It doesn't matter. Let's do it Williams' way. If anyone ask's I'll say I counted them and must have got it wrong. Everyone knows I'm useless at maths!" Tim promised, keen not to go to too much effort for this pointless exercise. They worked their way through the list of targets bit by bit but without enthusiasm. By mid afternoon it had started to rain, intense, cold, grey Welsh drizzle that soon soaked through their Army clothes, making them even more abrasive and uncomfortable. "We'll *have* to go to this one because we've got to read the plaque on the triangulation point" Andrews said looking at the last item on the list. "What is a triangulation point?" Williams wanted to know. "It's a kind of thing on top of a hill that you stand on to look at another one somewhere else" Tim announced confidently. "We did that in Geography". "So it must be at the top of the hill" Eglington said, setting off towards the summit of the nearest hill. The other three followed him, none of them thinking of looking at their Ordnance Survey map. The miserable group had to stomp up and down two more hills before they came upon their plaque.

To Fight My Own Battles

The Music Master drove past them in his elderly Cortina and shouted at them through the open window that he had been waiting for them in the first village that they were supposed to visit but had not seen them. "We went really, really early sir because we couldn't sleep sir". Williams answered quickly.

That evening it proved easier to pitch their tents but much, much harder to light a fire with sodden sticks in the persistent drizzle. "I'm going to find a house and ask them to open those beans for us" Andrews decided and headed back towards the village through which they had passed a short time before. Tim had built a small stack of dead matches beside the pile of damp sticks that had finally, smokily, began to smoulder. Williams lay on his stomach bravely blowing on the wood, trying to bring it to life sufficiently to cook on. The three boys, engrossed in their hopeless task and alone in their misery forgot about Andrews. "That was worth it!" Andrews burst excitedly onto the scene. "The lady was really nice and she felt sorry for us and is cooking us all supper in her house. Come on and we can have a proper meal!" The four boys scrambled back towards the village and enjoyed a hearty meal in the kitchen of a kind stranger. Warmer and no longer hungry the boys slept deeply until Tim was woken by Williams shaking him. "The tents being washed away!" Disorientated Tim pulled himself out of his slumber to find that, indeed, the tent did have a veritable stream of water running through it. Both boys and their sleeping bags were drenched. Getting out of their now useless shelter they discovered that the other tent had fared no better and they set about waking their friends to the good news. By the time the boys reached their meeting point the next afternoon they were wet, cold, had blistered feet and found that they had left their list of land marks behind in the chaos of their washed out camp site.

Safely back at school the four boys soaked in the luxury of deep, hot baths in the four a sides. "I don't understand why we were chosen" grumbled Eglington. "Obviously we've dome something to piss off the Sargent Major" Tim replied. "Well now my feet are covered in blisters so I won't be able to march properly on Wednesday and he'll be even more pissed off with me" Andrews complained. I'm bloody well not going to turn up on Wednesday" Williams stated indignantly. "I'm not having him shouting at me again after this crap. He can do what he wants."

One break time in the Easter term Tim could not find his Physics exercise book on the book shelf on his desk in the Senior Common Room. He was certain that he had seen it there only the previous evening and was frustrated at the hassle that he knew he would face should he not take them to the upcoming lesson. As predicted Tim suffered a cruel and humiliating dressing down by the generally nasty Physics Master and he was still smarting when he returned from the river that afternoon. "Did we have a difficult lesson?" Slater smirked. Tim deduced at once that Slater was behind his missing books. He had never liked Slater and knew how under hand he could be. With a furious snarl Tim rounded on Slater, taking him by surprise and grasped each of his wrists with an unexpectedly iron grip. "Give my books back **now!**" "Who says I've got them?" "You just told me". "Well I haven't got them any more". Tim forced Slater roughly onto the dilapidated green sofa behind him and held him down firmly. "You'd better go get me those books *right now*" Tim had his face intimidatingly close to Slaters'. "I can't. I gave them to Lucas and he chucked them in the bin". Of all the boys in the world Lucas was the one that everybody knew Tim would not bear to be crossed by. Tim heard a kind of thumping of his own pulse in his ears. He felt slightly dizzy in his rising rage. "Lucas! You filthy little shit!" "I couldn't help it. He *made* me. You know how horrible he can be. I had to give him them". Slater grizzled, the pitch of his voice rising as he sensed Tim's fury and remembered the damage that Tim had once inflicted upon Lucas. Tim dealt the first punch, deep in his solar plexus. He heard Slater's breath sigh out of him. Tim punched several more times, hard and deliberate. Slaters' nose began to bleed. "OK!" said Tim, his rage abating as he formulated his plan. "Give me your physics book. I will keep them and you can copy out the contents in detention because I don't see why I should when you chose to do that." Slater grimaced through the dribbling blood. He knew that he had no option as he certainly did not want to experience any more of Croy's rare but renowned anger.

The School House boys began to develop a routine of extra revision together, subject by subject, over endless mugs of coffee or tea and toast. The increasing fear and pressure of impending exams at the beginning of that Summer term brought them back together as a closely knit group once more, friends supporting one another against a common enemy. They began to realise that the hopes and fears, successes and disappointments and simply the time that they had shared in such proximity to each other over the past three years really did count for something. Something which, though impossible to define with any accuracy, was proving to be very real and meaningful to each of them. If they didn't all *like* each other they did all appreciate one another, they had become melded into a kind of family, whose bonds would keep them connected in some way for the rest of their lives, whether they liked it or not.

On the river there was tension and discomfort too. The Under Sixteen A's had ceased to exist as most of the crew were now over sixteen. Most of them, Tim included, had simply moved on in name to become known as the Second Eight. But it was not the same. Huband, their Stroke for three Seasons, had been promoted to the First Eight. There was no doubt that he deserved it but it had created some envy amongst the remaining members of the crew and having to accommodate a new boy in the key position of Stroke had proved difficult for everyone. Balance, timing and the unity of the crew had all taken a turn for the worse and it was Tim's responsibility to try to mend them in time to become a race winning crew once more. It was a tall order for a young man to impose his will on eight other boys of similar age and Tim had to employ all of his considerable charisma to get anything like the result that was needed. Combined with the demands of his academic work Tim found that he had little energy or enthusiasm left over with which to enjoy life as he usually did.

One Thursday in May Tim found that he could not concentrate in the class rooms. During the History lesson his head began to ache, which may or may not have had something to do with the long list of "Essential Dates" that swam before his tired eyes. Perched in his seat at the back of the boat Tim felt cold. His fingers hurt in the cool Summer water of the river as he operated the rudder ropes. Walking back to school he could barely put one foot before the other. Tim realised gloomily that he was unwell for some reason. It was imperative that he should be fit for Saturday for the regatta. He drifted through the rest of the day in a daze. He was shouted at in Maths and again in Geography. In prep, in the relative sanctuary of the Senior Common Room, he spent most of the time dozing on one of the well used grubby sofas. He took himself to bed in the Senior Dormitory as soon as prep ended and was deeply asleep by the time that the rest of the Fifth Formers came upstairs. Tim woke with surprise to the clanging of the School Bell the next morning. Weak from his fever he moved slowly as he washed and dressed and headed for breakfast in the Dining Hall. By the time Tim had eaten a decent meal and been to Chapel he was feeling almost his usual self once more. He was pleased to be able to draw the satisfying conclusion that he had made himself ill by doing too much work. He doubted, for some reason, that either any Masters or his parents would believe him.

Getting There!

Tim sat at the Supper table at the Senior end of the Dining Hall on the first evening of the Autumn Term. He and his friends were in a state of considerable excitement that managed to override even the gloom of the start of another school year. This was the start of their time in the Sixth Forms, they would now be studying three subjects, of their own choice, no longer having to grapple with so many things about which they understood little and cared even less. They were now in the elite world, within Barforth, of Study Dwellers, shared with a selected friend, and largely free of the constant supervision of prefects during prep. They had all just entered the Dining Hall from the formal, Seniors' entrance and helped themselves to their food from the Seniors side of the servery. No longer would they have to queue for an uncomfortably long time in the dank cold of the Bogs Passage to get every meal.

Most interesting of all, however, were **girls**! For some years Barforth had admitted a dozen or so girls to each of the two Sixth Form year groups. The places were strictly rationed to the sisters of boys who were themselves pupils, or had been pupils at Barforth. The effect of a very small number of girls on a huge number of adolescent boys was always to drag untidy, lazy boys kicking and screaming towards what they believed to be a state of attractive and cool manhood. Since there would never be enough girls to "go around" the rivalry between boys to gain the attention, even a single smile, of a girl was a persistent presence in the life of a Sixth Form boy.

The friends ate their supper while unashamedly gawping at the new girls who were sitting at a separate table with the girls who had been in school the previous year. "I'm having that one with the blond hair" Williams staked his claim. "Sod off! She won't even notice a plonker like you" Tim teased him. "Well at least I *look* like a man, Titch" Williams laughed. "Girls like that go for rugged Northern guys like me" Eglington interjected somehow managing to sound as if he knew everything about this rare species.

The girls, brightly dressed in a selection of what they hoped would appear sophisticated and stylish skirts, blouses, dresses and boots, studiously maintained an appearance of abject disinterest, while covertly monitoring the effect that their hours of planning for this first encounter was having. Not only did Barforth girls have the advantage of being a highly sought after minority but they were also exempted from the restrictions of having to wear School Uniform.

The School House cohort of boys had diminished after the Fifth Form, Slater and two other boys having left for various, largely undisclosed, reasons. Rumour had it that Slater had been expelled but nobody knew exactly why. None of them were sorry to find him gone. Andrews and Tim were sharing a study in Central Block, a purpose built block of forty studies that were allocated between houses each year according to requirements. They offered the first opportunity for boys from different houses to share communal spaces and they were a popular choice amongst the boys. The less favourable aspect of these studies was that they were not residential so the School House Lower Sixth Formers would have to continue to sleep in the Senior Dormitory. The two friends set about making the anonymous, very institutional looking room their own. They lined their two trunks up beside each other against the long empty wall and covered them in a couple of blankets that Tim had brought from home for the purpose. Mike Andrews had brought two large old cushions from the back of an old sofa to add a little comfort to their improvised seat. Having planned their requirements together at the end of the Summer term, once they knew they would be sharing together, Tim produced a shiny new electric toaster and Mike brandished an equally new looking electric kettle. The comfort of the room was completed by Mikes' Fidelity music centre through which the radio, cassette or record player would blare in competition with thirty nine similar set ups, throughout most of the boys' free time.

Delighted with their efforts they boiled the kettle and made themselves the first cup of coffee in their new home. Their contentment was only fractionally diminished by the realisation that they wouldn't have any milk to put in it until the following break time when the communal Third Form fags would deliver crates of milk bottles and loaves of bread to the two kitchen areas that were located half way down the long central corridor.

Tim had done a lot of thinking, analysing, about himself, his place in the school and what he wanted from life during the course of the long Summer holidays and he had come to some understanding of things that he could change and things that were beyond his power of influence. The start of the final phase of his school career, on the edge of entering that long anticipated but never the less rather scary "adult world" seemed to him to be the right time to try to alter the future course of his life.

Barforth School had done much to demonstrate to Tim that the maxim by which his parents had raised him, to follow the rules and do as he was told, was not going to help him in life. For the past three years Tim had done exactly those things and what had he achieved as a result? He had been pushed around by his peers, bullied and abused by his seniors and over looked and largely ignored by the Masters. Although he had, so far, been unable to completely understand why, he did see clearly that he did not really fit with what Barforth wanted from its pupils. He was not exceptional academically (though he had done better than predicted by most of the Masters in his "O" levels) He was not, *could not,* be religious, having experienced first hand what he saw as the inadequacy and sheer hypocrisy of those who daily purveyed Christian indoctrination in Chapel and the Christian Union. By his own admission Tim had been very fortunate to be so successful in the Boat Club but that was only by dint of an accident of birth, because he was very small for his age. He new that it was an advantage that was unlikely to continue for much longer and that, as soon as he was too large, too heavy, he would be usurped by a younger, smaller boy and discarded. Tim had seen, experienced indeed, the fact that it was always the Stroke oarsman, the captain of the crew, who took all public recognition for successes while the cox was merely a kind of addendum, a necessary assistant who must be tolerated but should never really be recognised. It was insulting but a fact of life.

Tim's response to these musings was to return to Barforth in a rather more bullish frame of mind than he had previously demonstrated. Feeling freer and more confident now that he was near the top of the school, coupled to his awareness of his likely dominance of the Boat Club Scene for the coming season, combined with the natural hormonal changes in a maturing young man to bring about a kind of cocky insolence that Tim felt would project the image of success and maturity that he sought. Everyone began to notice the change in Tim's demeaner but not everyone considered it to be an improvement.

Academic life in the Sixth Forms at Barforth proved to be rather less focussed in the subjects that a boy had chosen to study for "A" levels than many may have been hoped. Scripture remained firmly in the weekly time table together with two periods of a subject known as "General Studies". This was a cover all term to enable a Master to teach anything that he considered to be of interest that would help to broaden the pupils' perspective on the world. The subject and the Master changed each half term so that the fortunate boy (or, now, girl) would taste the flavour of as wide a range of subjects as possible.

For the first half of that Autumn term Tim found himself in the Head Masters' group, Looking at the "effects of ancient civilizations on the world today". Tim had never been interested in History and did not much like the Head Master so he did not expect to enjoy these periods which were taught in the Reference Library, everyone sitting in brightly coloured arm chairs arranged in a semicircle, trying to appear relaxed and grown up now that they were in the Lower Sixth.

One morning, during the course of the lesson, the Head master read a passage about some king "sending down a fiat to his people". "Can anyone tell me what a fiat is?" asked Mr.

Bolton. Remembering the shiny new, red Fiat 131 that had appeared in the Head Masters' reserved parking space since the beginning of term Tim saw an opportunity to cheer himself and the class up. He put up his hand. "Ah Croy! It's good to see that you're with us in mind as well as in body for a change!" The unnecessary sarcasm stung Tim who resolved to really do the subject justice. He was good at using words as a weapon when he wanted to and the young man wanted to often. "They're a really cheap and nasty type of car sir. No one in their right mind would buy one sir. My dad says that the only good thing about them is that they rust away so fast that they never get a chance to block the hard shoulders." A snigger of poorly suppressed laughter rippled round the group as the boys realised exactly how rude Tim had managed to be. Mr. Bolton, his face now nearly as red as his Fiat, had the wisdom to take Tim's answer as a mistake. "A Fiat can indeed be a make of car Croy, but in this context fiat means a command or a decree". The lesson continued without further ado but Mr. Bolton, Tim and everyone else in that room understood who it was that had dominated the lesson.

Recounting the story to Mike in Central Study Seventeen illegally during prep the two boys rolled around their small room with mirth. "You sod Tim! Old Bolton probably saved up for years to get that car and you've ruined it for him in just thirty seconds. I bet he won't be able to get that rattle out of his brain for the rest of his life." "The really good thing about it all is that I didn't say anything that isn't true so he *couldn't* do anything about it without looking like a right idiot". "Yeah but you'd better watch it, mate, because I bet he'll hold it against you for the rest of your time here." "Yeah I guess, but I doubt it will make much difference to me really because none of the Masters think much of me anyway. All the boys who will be Prefects, Head Boys and Captains of Sport was fixed years ago and I'm not one of them" "Do you really think so" Mike sounded genuinely appalled. "Yes, **DER**! Haven't you worked it out yet? Come on, lets make a list now – all the School Prefects and captains of Sport between now and Summer Nineteen Eighty. Then we can tick off our predictions one by one as they come true. Then you'll see the truth about this place".

The two friends set about drafting a rough copy of their predictions amidst much merryment. The more they thought about the boys who were real candidates for being a Head of House or Captain of a sport the more obvious it became that, on the whole, the candidates had been clear since the Third Form. For School House they made the prediction that Richard Norton would become Head of House for the next two terms, followed by John Eglington who would be doing Oxbridge next Autumn and then it was sure to be Simon Huband after that. It was equally easy to deduce that Norton would be next Captain of the Boat Club with Huband the following year. Both of those boys were already in the First Eight. At the start of Second Prep Mike went to collect a sheet of A3 card from the Art room so that they could make a smart copy of their predictions to keep pinned on their wall. They would then wait to see just how accurate they had been.

Within six weeks they had been able to tick Norton twice as both Head of School House and Captain of the Boat Club. Of the other nine houses they got eight correct Head of Houses and the correct Head Boy. They got the Captain of Hockey wrong.

Night Out

Tim grinned a silly grin in the mirror of the School House washrooms. He splashed water on his light brown hair, which was dry and bouncy from being shampooed at least once every day in the communal Senior (HOT!) showers. It was also daringly, subversively long, potentially covering his ears which would, if clocked by Mr. Linford, trigger a demand to visit the school barber. So far Tim had managed to escape this fate by keeping it combed back from his ears. He ran his combe in a squiggling motion over the front of his head, forming a fashionable flick of hair protruding like the peak of a cap beyond his forehead. Retrieving a rectangular bottle of clear blue liquid from his red spongebag Tim applied liberal and unnecessary quantities of Clearasil to his nose, chin and cheeks. He had been fortunate to have avoided the worst plague of teenage spots but he certainly wasn't going to take any risks now that he had girls to impress. Returning the bottle to the spongebag Tim exchanged it for a can of Brut 33 which he sprayed, over enthusiastically, all over his black shirt, top button open but sleeves buttoned at the cuffs. Grinning cheerfully at the mirror once again Tim headed down stairs to the quad.

One of the many small privileges that derived from being in the Sixth Forms at Barforth was that you could seek permission from your House Master to go out on a Saturday evening for "a meal". It was widely understood and accepted by boys and Masters alike that "a meal" was a euphemism for going to one of the nearby pubs to attempt to procure an under-age pint of beer or two. While, of course, in no way condoned by the Barforth authorities, this rite of passage of boys who were close to the legal drinking age was largely overlooked, provided that it was not taken to a drunken excess. In the interests of demonstrating that he had his finger firmly on the pulse of School House senior boys, Mr. Linford would grant permission for such excursions with the proviso that the boys must report back to him upon their return to school, whereupon he would often demand that they should walk in a straight line on tip toe to demonstrate their sobriety. This evening a group of boys from the top end of the Boat Club had arranged to have some fun.

Eglington, Huband and Caldicott were already hanging around in a group beside the Library. Tim greeted them with the customary "Hi" and they waited a couple more minutes for Norton and then Rian to join them. Amidst further cheery Hi and Alright? Greetings the group set off down the Private Lane. Each boy was dressed surprisingly similarly, according to the Barforth interpretation of "cool". To any outside onlooker they would have appeared to be wearing a uniform but the boys knew that they were now privileged to be allowed to leave the school premises in their casual clothes. In high spirits they crossed the main road and headed down a country lane towards their destination.

The Lock Keepers Hotel was located in the next village, a couple of miles from Barforth. Near enough to be easily reached on foot, it was, nevertheless, far enough away from school to be considered by the boys to be safe from regular visits from any of the Masters, who generally frequented one of the two hostelries in Barforth itself. A major added bonus was that the land lady, Mrs. Mundy, was sympathetic to the needs of the young men of Barforth School, having sent her own son to the school a few years earlier. She could be relied upon to turn a blind eye to their evident youth and would willingly give them the use of the safety of her "private function" room to further protect them from the possibility of being "busted" by any contingent of keen young Masters who may feel like impressing their seniors by asserting their authority and demonstrating their diligence by catching boys drinking and reporting them to their House Master who would then be obliged to issue severe punishment.

Mrs. Mundy, busy behind the Main Bar, directed the boys down a deep red carpeted passage way to the Private Function room. It had a small hatch that opened onto the Main Bar so that drinks could be ordered and served with ease. The whole hotel smelt of years of tobacco smoke that had been absorbed by deep pile red carpets, velour covered seats and velvet curtains. To the boys this faded, rather out-dated opulence seemed like the height of sophistication. Each of them ordered a pint of Bitter, none of them having much knowledge or experience of beer drinking. They settled themselves with their heavy beer mugs around a large oak table. Tim had never drunk beer before in his life and did not like the taste at all. Assuming that all the others did like it, Tim took another large gulp of his drink to demonstrate his enthusiasm for it. Other boys began to do the same. Caldicott went to the hatch and bought four packets of crisps that they emptied into a bowl, provided helpfully by Mrs. Mundy. The saltiness of the crisps somehow made the beer taste less bitter.

The light-hearted banter about school life, Rugby, the latest pop charts moved happily around the select group. As the first pint of beer neared its' end and began to take effect the mood became more excited. Tim went to order another round of Bitter and added a large packet of Dry Roasted Peanuts to the almost empty bowl of crisps. The song "Dancing In September" was playing on the Juke Box in the main bar and the boys joined in with the chorus from time to time. John Eglington asked Mrs. Mundy for some darts and the boys began chucking them inexpertly at the darts board. None of them was much good at the game but their efforts caused them much hilarity and the second pint of beer was soon finished. Huband suggested that they should drink some Guiness next and soon each boy had an open bottle of the smooth, dark drink in front of him. Tim found it even less palatable than the Bitter but was, by now, quite able and willing to consume anything.

Talk turned, inevitably, to Rowing and to the likely composition of next seasons' First Eight. Caldicott and Huband had already been in the crew by the end of the previous season so it was assumed that they would remain in it. Eglington was widely felt to be deserving of a place. There was a sudden rather embarrassed silence as it was realised that the conversation had brought Rian and Tim into potential conflict. Despite his haze of tipsy well being Tim sensed danger, remembering clearly and with regret the hurt that he had unintentionally inflicted upon Alex Rian. To his surprise and everyone's relief it was Alex who broke the silence. "Well, obviously, I'm out of it now. I could hardly get into the cox's seat by the time we went to Henley so that's it for me. I guess it's time for the First Eight to welcome Tim!" "TIM" the group raised their glasses and swigged their beer. Tim felt his throat constrict with unexpected emotion. "Thanks" he managed to mutter.

Mrs Mundy diplomatically refused the boys' request for more beer and guided them on their way back to school. She had had four sons of her own and had been keeping an expert eye on her customers for more years than she wanted to remember so she was very good at getting the boys to feel that they had made their own decision. Walking tipsily along the narrow country lane towards school Huband announced that he needed a piss. Everyone else decided that they did too and the happy group jumped over the low dry-stone wall to relieve themselves. When they were finished one of them noticed that they were in some kind of an orchard and that there were apples strewn all over the grass. There ensued half an hour of boisterous apple fight, boys flinging the soft, rotting fruit at one another, devising different rules of conflict as the fun developed. Eventually getting back on their way to school the group traversed the main road and got onto the Private Lane. As they passed the Main Playing Field Rian suggested that they should go to sit on the veranda of the Pavilion for a bit. Excitedly they ran across the field to claim their castle. "Let's have a night cap!" Caldicott produced a flat bottle of Whiskey from his pocket, cracked open the seal and took a swig. He passed it to Eglington who did similarly and passed it to Rian who gulped a mouthful and then collapsed in a fit of coughing. Huband grabbed the bottle from him before he could spill it and helped himself. Tim drank his share of the throat burning golden liquid carefully, seeing the detrimental effect that it was still having on Alex. "Have another swig, Alex mate" Matthew Caldicott advised, handing him the bottle. "No way man!" "No, go on", Tim encouraged, banging him on his back to help him recover his composure. "It might help your throat". Seeing the reason in this idea Alex took another careful gulp. Each boy took another turn and then another until the bottle was empty.

Darting behind the Pavilion for another piss the happy

group headed back to school. Tim fell into step beside Alex. "That was really decent of you". "I've been wanting to apologise to you for what I did in the Spring. I just didn't think." "No, Tim. I didn't need to be harsh like I was. It was well tight of me. You didn't do anything wrong". "Yeah, but I didn't think about how it might look like I was trying to take the piss out of you. I do kind of understand how it must feel now that I can see that it will happen to me if I do get selected. But I didn't think about it then, not 'til Simon Huband pointed it out to me after". "Forget it man. We're mates. No need for apologies". The two boys thumped each other affectionately on the back in the Barforth gesture of friendship.

The School House boys duly reported to Mr. Linford's flat at the side of School House. "Well done. Did you have a good time?" He greeted them. Then with a frown "What's that all over your shirts?" The boys looked down at themselves and each other. Every one of them had several large circular brown splodge marks on their shirts and jeans. "Oh" laughed Eglington "they're rotten apples sir. We had an apple fight on the way back sir." "An apple fight?" Mr. Linford raised one eyebrow. Well you'd better try my straight-line test. Come on all of you. The four boys wobbled and teetered across Mr. Linford's sitting room, honking with laughter as they attempted to keep as straight a course as possible. "You should try it sir. It's impossible" Norton joked. "Off you go to bed!" was the firm reply.

Tim lay in bed, unable to sleep. Every time he closed his eyes the bed began to pitch and roll as if it was floating on a rough sea, making him feel sick.

When Tim was woken by the School Bell on Sunday morning he wished that he had not been. His head ached and his stomach was churning dangerously. Cautiously he got up, washed and dressed in his suit ready for Chapel. Despite his discomfort Tim spent considerable time knotting his tie in a fashionably wide knot and combing his thick hair into a trendy frontal wave. Sitting in Breakfast with just a cup of warm tea and a slice of dry toast in front of him, Anthony Williams came to sit opposite him. "They call it a hangover where I come from!" he shouted painfully loudly. "Thanks for that" Tim grimaced.

As Tim walked out of Chapel later that morning he was feeling cheerful. His hangover had largely receded and he knew that he had made amends with Alex Rian. The luxuriant emptiness of a Sunday, interjected with a good roast dinner lay before him.

"Timothy Croy!" Mr. Linford called as he fell into step beside Tim, half way across the quad. "Did you have a nice meal last night?" "Yes sir, thank you sir". "What did you have to eat?" "Some nuts and crisps sir" replied Tim honestly. "Well, if I may advise you, next time don't drink quite so much beer with your crisps and nuts. You nearly failed my test last night and that wouldn't do at all". "No sir". The Master and boy walked in silence for a minute or two. "I think now may be an appropriate time to tell you, off the record, obviously, that you will almost certainly be appointed as cox to the First Eight next term Tim and that will give you a very high profile around the school. You will be watched more than most boys, off the river as well as on it. Please keep that in mind". Tim felt a heady rush of excitement at the informal confirmation of the news that he had hardly dared to hope for. Simultaneously he realised that Mr. Linford was one of those rare Masters who was on his side. "Wow! Thankyou sir! Yes sir, I do understand". Tim kept on feeling bursts of excitement and anticipation about his future role for the rest of the day and, indeed, the next week. He only wished he could share his news with somebody, though he knew that that had been the widely expected outcome amongst his friends in the Boat Club already.

Rise To Fame

To Fight My Own Battles

When Tim returned to Barforth for the Easter Term and took his things up to the Senior Dorm he found, sitting hunched on one of the beds, a swarthy, dark haired young man, immediately standing out as being different because of the thick, dark stubbly beard that enveloped his face. He looked up as Tim came in and a huge, engaging white grin spread across his face. Tim had already clocked from the notice board in the washroom that this new boy went by the name of Albad. U. The boy rose to his feet, showing himself to be unexpectedly tall, and extended his hand towards Tim. Slightly taken aback by the strangely adult, formal greeting, Tim shook his hand. "I'm Tim Croy". "I am Usman Abad. I have come from Jiddah". Tim had no idea where Jiddah might be but was more concerned with getting his name right. "Abad or Albad?" Tim pronounced the boys' name as he had heard him say it and as he had seen it spelt. He had been fortunate to have grown up with a regular stream of his fathers' foreign clients visiting their house and he knew how important it was to welcome people from overseas properly. The Croy family always went to great lengths to make people feel at home in their house and many interesting family friendships had blossomed as a result.

After he had dumped his bag on his bed Tim asked Albad where his Study was. "Oh, it is in the Central Study number twenty actually". "Great, I'm in number seventeen. Let's go down there, it's better than sitting here. I can show you round a bit if you like". Albad stood and followed Tim. He took him via the Four a Sides, guessing that he would not have found that useful short cut yet. Tim noticed the look of incredulity on Albad's face as he took in the unexpected sight of eight bath tubs lining two sides of a thoroughfare. Regretting that there would be no milk or bread to be able to proffer tea and toast, Tim took him into his study, still feeling rather cold and unlived in at this premature stage of the term. Tim introduced Albad to Mike who had just arrived and, again, he proffered his hand, engendering a similar slightly confused reaction from Mike. Tim gave his new friend a quick tour of the school, explaining the important land marks and talking him through the pattern for the rest of the evening. He returned him to his own study and left him to get to know his room-mate.

Later that evening Tim knocked for Albad in Study Twenty to escort him up to the Junior Dorm for the customary House Meeting. Mr. Linford came in, accompanied by Richard Norton, the newly appointed Head of House. He welcomed Norton into his new position and then introduced Albad to the house. After the meeting the boys milled around the dormitories and washrooms, catching up with each others news from the holidays and lamenting the coming term. Tim noticed Norton in close conversation with Mr. Linford in the washroom, with much nodding of his head, clearly in agreement about whatever it was that they were discussing. After the two more junior dorms had been settled down and had their lights turned off Norton came in to the Senior room and addressed Albad. Tim was shocked as he saw him hand the young man an electric shaver. "You have to shave every day in this school. We expect everyone to look smart. Please go and get cleaned up straight away, before you go to bed." "Looking confused and, naturally, embarrassed Albad headed to the washrooms. Norton followed him immediately, together with an inquisitive entourage of boys excited to watch this unexpected spectacle. Rapidly recovering himself, Tim felt a need to support his new friend but did not want to associate himself with the crowd of nosey onlookers. He stood in the door of the washrooms as Norton stood over the lonely new boy making certain that he shaved to his complete satisfaction. Tim felt sickened to see the clumsy, bullying use of self-imposed power over a newcomer, alone in a strange school in a foreign country, by a boy not much older than himself and for whom he had always had considerable respect. He realised the he was going to have some power over Norton as his cox in the First Eight. He wondered how that dynamic was going to play out. At that moment Tim would have liked to be able to even out the odds between Norton and Albad but he was powerless to do so. He contented himself with sitting and talking to Albad about the ways in which power and control were distributed around the Masters and Senior boys, attempting to make excuses for Norton who, he explained, was new to his role and would have to do exactly as Mr. Norton bid, even if he didn't like it.

At the end of the second week it became official. Tim came out of lunch and, now out of the habit of nearly four years, was checking the cluster of notice boards. There it was, on the Boat Club Notice Board. A neatly typed sheet of paper headed simply First Eight 1979. There followed the full crew list, each in the position in which they would sit in the boat. At the bottom was typed Cox : Croy. T. Tim stared at it. He felt strangely distant and remote, as if he were watching this happening to somebody else. He had known that this was likely to happen for months, had hoped and dreamed of it for years now and Mr. Linford and Norton had invited him into Mr. Linford's flat earlier that week to confirm it but seeing it in print, made public for all the school to see, on a typed sheet signed in ink by Mr. Linford, made it suddenly real, true and undeniable. Perversely Tim felt suddenly embarrassed by the publicity and the attention that he knew it would draw on him. He could hear more boys emerging from the Dining hall and, blushing deeply now, Tim hurried away from the bard and back to the seclusion of his study.

"You really have showed them! Well done mate" Mike burst through the door of Central Study Seventeen, followed by several other excited well-wishers. "Thanks." Tim looked down at his desk shyly." I've been very lucky, that's all". "You've worked bloody hard more like" Andrews was not going to let his friend hide behind false modesty. Norton suddenly appeared, carrying a plastic case of six cans of Coke. "Come on Cox. Start pouring" he grinned. MIke scurried off to beg or borrow some clean cups from other nearby studies. Tim yanked on the ring pull of the first can, sending a massive spurt of brown foam all over himself and the crowd of cheerful boys who were now crammed into the small room. He had fallen for the oldest trick in the book. With whoops of delight the boys began shaking cans and spraying Coke everywhere and soon the excited party spilled out into the long passage way. Very little of the Coke actually remained to be drunk.

Over the next few days Tim and his new crew settled into a strict and demanding routine of daily outings on the river and circuit training in the gym in second prep three times a week. As Tim overcame his reticence towards ordering some of the most senior boys in the school around he found himself thoroughly enjoying the hard work, the feeling of being a key part of an elite group at the top of their game.

As events unfolded they actually got very little serious rowing or training done that first half of term. After less than a week there were days of heavy snowfall, rendering it impossible to get on the river. The crew were confined to more fitness training in the gym, safe behind steamed up windows during games times and along with the rest of the school, to the more discreet and subversive sport of tobogganing on plastic trays "borrowed" from the Dining Hall. So popular did this become that the Head Master was forced to issue a total ban on the activity because so many trays had been broken that there were insufficient for their intended use in the Dining Hall.

As the snow melted, the river flooded, making it unsafe to row through the swirling currents or to navigate round well known but now submerged and invisible hazards that threatened to rip a delicate racing boat open. Before the floods subsided the school, like the entire country, was enveloped in an epidemic of Flu. For ten days there were never more than three of the First Eight who were well enough to train. The Sanatorium was totally overwhelmed so boys, listless, sweating and ill, were confined to their own beds in studies and dormitories, the School Sister, supported by hastily drafted House Masters' wives, scuttled in and out, up and down, trying to administer aspirins and take and record temperatures. Tim seemed to have escaped this malady until he woke up one Saturday drenched in sweat and shivering violently in the freezing dormitory. He lay there, with two other sad boys, for two whole days, drinking occasional cups of tea brought to them by a nice, motherly, lady who they did not know. By the time Tim was well enough to venture back to lessons on Monday afternoon he was so weak from enforced starvation that he had no chance of joining his crew for training. Impatient and worried about his hard-won position, Tim forced himself to complete the crew and get out on the river on Wednesday afternoon. He had difficulty shouting loudly enough to make Bow hear his commands but he was glad to feel the water beneath him once more. It took a further week for all the boys to be back to full strength.

While all this was happening Tim quietly, and largely unnoticed, passed one of the key milestones in the climb to adulthood. He became seventeen and filled in the application form for his provisional driving licence. He had had the form and its' prepaid envelope in his desk drawer since the beginning of term and took great care in completing it, keen to ensure no delay in receiving his coveted licence. He had helped Mike complete his just the previous week so he had little difficulty and hurried down the village street to post it. Pushing the rough brown envelope into the gaping red mouth of the post box and hearing it flop onto the other letters awaiting collection inside it gave Tim a thrill of excitement. This was the first official recognition of his impending status as an adult and he and all of his friends had been keenly waiting to begin the race to drive. To have a full driving licence and, ideally, access to the use of a car, was the ultimate status symbol for every young man of seventeen. The Barforh School Rules, pinned imposingly on a board, protected by a locked glass cover, stated clearly that "No boy shall drive any motor vehicle within a five mile radius of the school." No boy had any intention of obeying this unreasonable edict.

Tim stood, once more, grinning stupidly at the washroom mirror. Having brushed his teeth, twice, he slicked his hair forward with his wet hand and smothered himself in Brut Thirty-three. Carefully knotting his tie in his customary super wide knot Tim pulled on his jacket and glanced down at his black shoes, to check one more time that they were impressively shiny. Mike's parents were driving down to take the two boys out to a meal. That was good reason enough to be in a high mood but, even better, Mike had a sister, Sarah, who was sixteen and who Tim had admired from a distance several times in the past years. It seemed obvious to Tim that since he and Mike were best mates Tim had a good chance with Sarah! He clumped down two flights of stairs and joined Mike in the Lower Library where they could wait in relative warmth with a good view of the Quad so that they would see the Andrews' car when it arrived. Tim began to feel shy. The red Peugeot Family Estate swung onto the quad and parked longways across several spaces that were designated for senior Masters. "That's my dad!" Mike laughed. "You'll like him Tim. You don't need to be shy". The two boys went out to the waiting car. It was warm inside. Mike introduced Tim to his parents, Sarah and two younger brothers who were giggling and poking each other in the third row of seats. "Do you like pizza, Tim" asked Mrs. Andrews. "Ofcourse he likes pizza" Mike's father answered for him. The car pulled out of the school gates and headed towards the nearby town.

"Michael tells me that you're a bit of a super star in the Boat Club this year" Mr. Andrews laughed as they waited for their pizzas to arrive. "I'm not sure about super star" Tim replied. "But yes, I'm cox to the First Eight". "Shame Michael didn't go for rowing. We told him it would be a nice change but he never listens to us!" Mrs. Andrews joined in warmly. "What's a cox?" Sarah asked. Tim began to explain to her, pleased for the opportunity to talk to her directly and hoping that his position might impress her.

After what proved to be a really nice evening the boys were delivered back to Barforth and they made their way to report back to Mr. Linford. Tim was pleased not only to be able to pass the "straight line on tiptoe" test but to be able to do so while looking Mr. Linford in the eye.

Princess Elizabeth

The Summer term heralded an important milestone in Tim's academic development. He had elected to study Biology as one of his three "A" Level courses for the simple reason that he enjoyed the subject and liked Mr. Dymott, the Master in charge of the department. A requirement of the course was that every candidate had to carry out a research based project of their own choosing and present it, written up correctly, in "not more than two thousand words". Tim had little concern about exceeding the stipulated number of words! He had rather more difficulty thinking about anything suitable and possible for him to research within the confines of a boarding school. After much thought, and several meetings with Mr. Dymott, Tim decided to study the optimum conditions for the growth of yeast. This was not quite as random a choice as it may appear because he already had a fair bit of experience in the subject, having been making wine at home from the excess fruit that grew in his parents' orchard for several years. It was evident to Tim that this topic would not prove too taxing and that it may actually help him to perfect his hobby further. As he planned exactly how he should set about doing the research part of the work it became clear that, because he would need to check the growth of his yeast at regular intervals of three hours in order to obtain consistent results, he would need to have access to the Biology Laboratory during evenings and weekends. Mr. Dymott, a young Master, had better things to do at these times than to sit in his place of work on the off chance that a pupil might want to come in so he readily offered Tim a copy of the key to the Biology Lab. Tim had been secretly delighted, both because he felt that he was being treated as trust worthy and because he was quick to recognise the potential benefits of having private access to a lockable room in which he would, effectively, be fermenting limitless supplies of wine with the blessing of the school.

The first time that he availed himself of this facility Tim approached the locked door with some doubt. Could this really be possible? Would the key fit? Would he have the laboratory to himself? The lock clicked open and Tim let himself in to the eerily silent room. He shut the door quietly behind him and stood for a moment, filling his lungs with the distinctive smell of the Biology Lab. The air in here was always laden with the combined smells of Ether with which Mr. Dymott killed rats from a cage for his students to dissect as part of their "O" or "A" level courses and cigarette smoke with which Mr. Dymott was gradually killing himself. Tim moved across the room, feeling a strange sense of guilt, of trespass, and let himself into the room at the back which was a kind of combined store room and office for the Biology Masters. Crucially for Tim's purposes, it contained a fridge in which he would store the product of his project. As the term progressed Tim became comfortable in his new, private world within school.

On his way out of Breakfast one morning Tim found a note addressed to Croy. T. on the "Urgent" notice board. Opening the folded paper as he headed to Central Study seventeen Tim read "Please come to see Miss Coulson in the Sowing Room for your fitting." Not at all sure what he was supposed to be having fitted, or why, Tim diverted back the way he had come and up the unfamiliar external concrete steps to the Sewing Room. He knocked brusquely on the door and waited. A lady opened the door. "I've been asked to come and see Miss Coulson" Tim explained. "A boy to see you, Brenda." She called. Miss Coulson came to the door. "Yes dear?" "You sent me a note to come for a fitting or something" Tim explained again, feeling rather stupid by now. Miss Coulson looked blankly at him for a moment. "Are you Croy?" "Yes." "Oh!" She beamed excitedly. "Come in dear. Mr Linford sent me a note asking me to get you fitted out with the Cox's uniform. You must be so pleased dear. Well done!" Tim moved shyly into the warm room, surrounded by wooden open fronted lockers containing items of clothing, fabrics, sundry tools of their trade and, bizarrely, a tall, red, tin of pilchards in tomato sauce. Three other ladies were sat at tables in front of sewing machines, each of them smiling at Tim. Miss Coulson looked at him, went and selected a white jacket with braided cuffs and lapels and held it up against him. "Try that dear" Tim pulled it on. It felt very tight. She fetched another one which was a better fit but too long. Miss Coulson fussed with safety pins and her tape measure. "You've got nice broad shoulders dear. That means you're going to grow quite tall. I wouldn't be surprised if you don't outgrow the boat before the end of the summer". Tim blushed, embarrassed to having his physique discussed by a group of old ladies who he didn't know. "Pop in there and try both these pairs of trousers dear" Miss Coulson indicated a corner of their room that was curtained off. Tim did as instructed, relieved to be free of the gaze of the ladies. He emerged, wearing the better fitting of the two, and Miss Coulson fussed once more with pins and measuring tape. Tim returned behind the curtain to change back into his own uniform trousers. "Come and collect your things tomorrow, before Chapel. I'll make you up two sets because I know that you'll get thrown in to the river so we'll be forever dry cleaning them for you dear. You have to look your best when you're representing Barforth. We'd never live it down if you didn't!"

On the river things were going well for Tim and the First Eight. The weather was fine and the river conditions were good enabling the crew to perfect their performance early in the term. Their first Regatta was to be down in the West Country, somewhere near Bristol. The crew were in a positive frame of mind as the school minibus arrived at a beautiful river side location surrounded by steep hills and green fields. The oarsmen were dressed in their new Barforth kit and Tim sported his specially tailored white Cox's blazer and trousers with a new white shirt. He felt a bit strange to be honest, feeling somewhat

Tobi Tarquin

over dressed for sport, as if he was supposed to be going to some formal event rather than coxing a boat. Once they had unloaded the trailer and assembled and checked the Brockley Jones the boys took a walk along the bank to see the course along which they would be racing. Tim had, as usual, studied a map of the course so that he was familiar with any likely currents or bends in the river that could be used to advantage. He had suggested that it would be good for the crew also to see the course before the first race so that they would have an idea of landmarks as they passed them, enabling them to pace themselves as well as relying on him.

When they got back to the boat Mr. Linford had the order of races on a printed sheet and they found that they were drawn against their old adversaries Gainswell for the first heat. Hardly had they had time to share anything that they remembered about their opponents than they were being summoned to the river by the Tannoy. Tim squatted on the pontoon, holding the boat as his crew fastened their oars in the gaiters, got themselves installed in their seats and checked each component once again. Tim jumped in lightly, pushed the long boat expertly out into the river and steered it into position in the far lane, as instructed from the idling motor launch behind him. He ordered his crew into position. "Come forward to row" came the familiar command, "I'll ask you once", "Are you ready? "Row!". The Brockley Jones positively leapt forward, Tim was still surprised at how much more smoothly this boat pulled away than anything he had previously coxed. He pulled his thoughts back to the task in hand. He felt that the Gainswell boat was pulling ahead of Barforth. This could not be allowed. "In! Out! In! Out! In! Out! Tim willed his crew to reach their peak of power quickly. Still the two boats were bow to bow. "Stride it out" he heard their cox call. Tim waited to see the result, not wanting to tire his crew without need. Barforth were holding their own, evidently finding their pace and settling to it. They were just past half way now, Tim recognised a kind of cottage on the far bank. "Stride it out" he commanded. He saw Norton in the Strokes seat in front of him stretch himself to his maximum as he slid up his runner, leading the oarsmen to give it their extra inches. Yes! Brockley Jones' bow was clear of Gainswell. "In! Out! In! Out! Tim was willing the boat to find a little more. They passed the string of red buoys. They had done it! "And it's Barforth who go through to the semi-final confirmed the Tannoy as the boat coasted to rest.

The semi-final was against a new school called Cliffeside. Barforth managed to take the lead from the start and had a full length between them by the end of the race. They were to meet Sommerton in the final.

There were two hours before the final and the First Eight enjoyed supporting the junior Barforth Eights as they relaxed and consumed the obligatory energy drinks. At last they were on the water and ready to go. They had the near side lane this time, which Tim believed would be marginally the better one. Sommerton powered a full bows length ahead almost immediately. They were visibly the taller crew which gave them an advantage in how long each stroke could be. The race would depend on the strength and stamina of the crew and on the skills of the cox! The boats were more or less level by the time Tim saw the cottage on the far bank. "Stride it out" he yelled. "And stride it out again". Brockley Jones' bow inched ahead. There couldn't be more than a couple of hundred metres left. Tim could hear the rival cox exhorting his crew to "stride it out". "Stop holding back you lazy buggers!" Tim goaded his crew, hoping that insulting these boys, most of whom were his senior, would have the intended effect. It did! "Easy all!" the crew lowered their blades onto the water and sank wearily onto their seats, too breathless to speak. "Brilliant!" Tim shouted over their drooping heads. "We've done it!" As soon as the Tannoy had confirmed their win they paddled back gently, Tim alighted and held the boat steady as the oarsmen got out and took their oars to the trailer. Together they lifted their boat out of the water, carried it on to the trestles and Tim set about washing and leathering it, almost lovingly, before the crew descended with their spanners to dismantle it once more. When everything was safely secured on the trailer the crew gathered round Tim. "Lazy buggers are we?" grinned Norton. That was the signal. Tim was expertly grabbed by eight sets of hands and tossed with consummate ease into the river. It was deeper than Tim had realised and, when he found his feet, the water reached up to his shoulders. As he raised his fists above his head in the traditional Barforth victory salute a memory of a less happy occasion when he had stood shoulder deep in water flitted through his mind. How fast time had passed.

Next morning at breakfast the crew assembled, dressed in their spare, clean Regatta finery. Richard Norton squatted down for Tim to get seated on his shoulders, brandishing the silver cup. As he stood up Tim felt decidedly unstable but, to Nortons' shout of "Barforth Boat Club's Best!" they marched into the Dining Hall to the clatter of six hundred spoons on six hundred cereal bowls, paraded once round the room and then Tim reached up and placed the cup in the centre of the shelf, beneath the portrait of the Founding Head Master. To roars of delight and pride from the school they marched back out again. Flushed with pride, excitement and a hint of his usual shyness, Tim remembered the first time he had witnessed this great Barforth tradition. He could barely believe that he was now an integral part of it.

As the term progressed Tim began to develop a tradition of his own. Most Sundays, after lunch, he would retire to the Biology lab, often with Mike or Anthony, to lounge on the easy chairs in Mr. Dymotts' office and drink his home-made wine. It became a bit like a private gentleman's club, safe from any chance of disturbance, excitingly illegal and yet almost officially sanctioned. Most of all it was a deliciously unexpected privilege. As time passed Tim widened his project from merely fermenting different concentrations of sugar solution to adding some fruit juice, ostensibly to find out if the acidity helped the yeast to grow but, in all honesty, to make the Sunday afternoon drinks taste better.

One Sunday morning, between Chapel and Lunch, Tim was sitting toying half-heartedly with an Economics essay in his study. Mike was playing squash with a group of mates so Tim was trying to make the most of the quiet time to make up for some of the study periods that he had lost through Saturday mornings away at Regattas. There was a tap on his door. "Yeah" Tim called in his usual off hand manner. The door opened and a girl, who Tim vaguely recognised, let herself in. "Hi Tim! How's the Coxing going?" She spoke confidently, as if they were old friends. Tim wasn't sure who she was or where he had met her. The answer was on the edge of his brain, he could *feel* it but he couldn't recall it. Being polite he offered her a cup of coffee, which she accepted. As Tim handed her her steaming mug he remembered. Sally Anne! She was from the girls' school in the nearby town and Anthony had been going out with her once or twice last term. Why was she here? They sat looking at each other in silence. "Mike told me you won some cups in rowing. That's brilliant Tim!" "Mike?" Tim was confused. "Yes, I was here with him yesterday and last Saturday while you were away". No wonder he's been looking so smug lately Tim thought. He felt a bit irritated for some illogical reason. "He's playing squash. Do you want me to take you up there?" Sally Anne put her mug down and moved uncomfortably closer to Tim on the makeshift sofa. Tim fidgeted away, suddenly embarrassed. "Actually I came to see you. I was so impressed when I saw your cool blazer hanging up the other day. I *love* well dressed sportsmen." To Tim's horror she leant sideways and planted a juicy kiss on his cheek. Tim felt himself blush and felt an excited stirring inside him. This had to stop now. She was Anthony's girl. Or was she Mikes girl? Now she seemed to be chasing him. Suddenly disgusted and furious Tim stood up decisively. "Come on. Let's go to find Mike. He'll be about finished by now. "No. I'm not looking for him today" she pouted. "I thought you'd like to get to know me today". With a toss of her long hair she departed as suddenly as she had come. Tim sat, shaken. He had heard stories about her spreading herself around Barforth and that she was considered "Easy". Now Tim knew for sure that they were accurate.

The First Eight experienced six further Sunday Breakfast Ceremonies, maintaining an unbroken record throughout the Summer Term. They rowed hard, daily, and trained with vigour and dedication in second prep in the gym three times a week. They developed a tight and very emotional bond, young men on a highly successful mission. They were regular visitors to Mr. Linford's flat, enjoying the privilege of his post Regatta parties and access to his television. They were known throughout the school as the greatest Boat Club success in a generation, though some of Tim's peers in the Lower Sixth felt some injustice and envy and would occasionally demonstrate their feelings via mean little comments aimed against Eglington, Tim and Huband, none of whom, in their opinion, should have access to privileges that befitted Sixth Formers only. So powerful are the tiniest nuances of status within the boarding school environment.

Tim, it must be recorded, was worried. He was growing fast. He knew it from the way in which the sleeves of his uniform jacket seemed to be moving weekly further up his arms as his fashionably flared trousers rose, far from fashionably, further from his shoes. He started weighing himself in the small office beside the gym after most training sessions and watched with dismay as ounce upon ounce began to move towards a whole stone of extra weight. Tim tried to eat less but a growing boy cannot defy nature and his efforts were in vain. He tried to exercise harder, mirroring exactly what he was asking his crew to do but, far from helping, this seemed only to speed his growth. As he squeezed himself ever more tightly and uncomfortably into his seat at the back of the boat he remembered daily Miss

Coulson's prediction about his broad shoulders indicating that he would grow tall. He hoped that his continued success and experience would be considered enough to outweigh his increasing weight disadvantage.

The end of the Summer term and the school year approached with manic speed. The First Eight had one final event in their sights. Henley Royal Regatta, the International flag ship in the rowing calendar. The School event was the Princess Elizabeth Cup. Barforth had won it once before, early in its' history and it had been every crew's dream to secure it again. The First Eight were to go to Henley on the Thursday before the Saturday of the race so that they would have the opportunity to row the course a few times before the actual event. The River Thames was by far the largest and most powerful river that they had had to row on and it was important that they had a feel for it before they had to give the performance of their lives. Tim had studied the diagrams of the course, under the experienced eye of Mr. Linford, until he felt that he knew every nuance with his eyes shut. Nothing, however, had prepared him or his crew for the sheer width, the vastness of the river at Henley. As soon as Tim pushed the Brockley Jones away from the pontoon the crew could feel the power of the current. At first this unsettled the crew, making their performance suddenly rather raged, knocking their confidence and lowering their spirits. Tim was trying hard to learn and analyse the currents in the different stages of the course and to memorise the land marks of expensive houses and pavilions and he struggled to calm and encourage his crew. They returned to the pontoon for a crew debrief with Mr. Linford and, encouraged by him and a good meal, they went out for one last time that evening. Things were better this time, each boy being more prepared for the unfamiliar effects of the fast flowing water on the behaviour of his oar.

They were staying at the vast house of an Old Barforthian, just outside the town, and, after another hearty meal they bedded down on mattresses on the floor of a huge room for an early night.

After an early breakfast on Saturday the boys got dressed in their Crew Colours and headed back to the enclosure at the site of the Regatta. They were amazed and not a little intimidated by the spectacle of so many people, the corporate entertainment marquees, acres and acres of expensive parked cars with well dressed people setting up extravagant pick nicks. Soon three coaches of Barforth boys would arrive to lend the crew their rowdy support. They set about checking the Brockley Jones and then Tim lead his crew through some mild warm up exercises on the bank of the River Thames, just relaxing and loosening up their muscles. He could see Mr. Linford standing chatting with a man with shoulder length hair who he did not know. He assumed that he was the coach of another school.

Nervously Tim steered his boat into position at the start line. There were four lanes and they were in the left hand middle. Tim could feel the tension and excitement of his crew. They were off! The Brockley Jones pranced forward with the eagerness of a living entity. They gained a small advantage early in the race and finished a full half length ahead of their nearest rival. They repeated similar success in the quarter final and then the semi final, securing Barforth a place in the final. The pressure on the young Barforth men was almost tangible. Mr. Linford understood, shared indeed, their feelings and worked hard to downplay the significance of the next race as the crew ate a light but energy rich meal in the long lunch interval.

It was nearly four O'clock before they found themselves positioned in the near lane for the race of their lives. "We're about to start final of the world famous Princess Elizabeth Cup. Barforth School versus Upper Langley." The Tannoy emphasised the significance of the moment. "Come forward to row". The River Marshall instructed from his motor launch. "I'll ask you once. Are you ready? **ROW**. The Barforth crew leapt into beautifully synchronised action. Tim could see that Upper Langley were holding level and continued to do so. He let the crew settle into their race before encouraging them with a few "In! Out!" commands. Both boats were still level. Tim couldn't remember ever having been so closely matched before. He felt slightly flustered. Why did this have to happen now, of all times? He calmed himself, obviously in such an important race they were going to be up against the best there was. It was normal. Only to be expected. They were half way along the course now, Tim recognised a particularly ornate boat house on the right hand bank. It was now or never! "Stride – it – out!" Norton obediently increased the stretch and pace of the stroke. Tim focussed his attention on maintaining as central a position as he dared, without risking clashing oars with his rival boat. He *thought* that the white ball that stood proud of the bow of the Brockley Jones was easing fractionally ahead of that of Upper Langley but it was impossible to judge such small advantages from the back of his own boat. "**Stride – it – out!**" Tim yelled, his voice suddenly beginning to tire. "*You're the laziest bastards I've ever coxed! In! Out! In! Out! In! Out! In! Out! In! Out!*" Tim was willing, begging, insulting, praying that his crew could find just an ounce or two of extra energy. He could hear the roar of the crowds as the finish approached. He thought he could hear Barforth, Barforth, Barforth on the far bank but the world was flying past in such exciting confusion that he really didn't know for certain. The red buoys! "*Eassssy all!*" Tim croaked. The oarsmen sank down in their seats, exhausted beyond their furthest limits. The Brockley Jones glided to rest, blades feathered on the surface of the Thames. Waiting. Waiting. Waiting for an eternity. "That was the closest finish so far today!" The Tannoy called across the waiting crowds. The boys sat up in their seats, the rippling water lapped on their blades, Tim could feel the rudder moving fluidly from side to side like a fish. "By barely the length of half a bow I am delighted to declare............Barforth School have won the Princess Elizabeth Cup this year!"

Tim and the crew cheered, almost capsizing the Brockley Jones with the power of their pleasure and excitement. After a few deep breaths of success Tim asked the boys if they were ready to row back to the pontoons. "Carry on Stroke Side, Back her down Bow side" Tim instructed his crew for what he knew would certainly be the last time.

The Brockley Jones safely cleaned and dismantled, the oarsmen gathered, laughing, round Tim. "The water's deep, Tim", Richard Norton warned him. "Be ready to swim, Tim. I don't want to drown you before we get the P. E. cup!" Grabbing him in well rehearsed unison, his crew lifted Tim high into the air and ran, shouting his name, along the bank before hurling him far towards the middle of the Thames. Tim sank, floated and swam, heavy in his blazer, to the bank where his crew were waiting to help him out. Tim stood, rivulets of water flowing from his trouser and blazer pockets. He saw the long haired man who he had seen that morning striding towards him, a familiar grin spread across his face. "Toby Phillips!" Tim took a few sploshing steps towards his old friend and mentor. The two young men embraced in unadulterated delight. "That was fantastic Tim!" "Only because I had the best instructor that Barforth ever knew" Detaching himself Tim looked at the now drenched Toby. "Shit! I think I always secretly wanted to get you wet to pay for all the times I've got dunked thanks to your training."

The two wet friends joined the crew and Mr. Linford who was instructing Richard Norton how to open a bottle of Champaigne to maximum effect. Tim was glad to see him become drenched in a foaming fountain as he failed to point the bottle sufficiently far from himself. The best party of their lives had begun.

After the awards ceremony the victorious crew set off back to Barforth. Toby was joining them as Mr. Linford's guest for the night. The celebration party lasted throughout the night, none of them sleeping before they had to change into clean Barforth Colours for their last Sunday Breakfast Ceremony. To mark this very special win the victorious crew made three circuits of the Dining Hall to the crashing beat of spoons on bowls, being filmed by Toby and Mr Linford, before Tim hoisted the P.E. cup into central pride of place under the Founding Father.

Money

Tim had decided that he needed to get a holiday job. He was starting to crave greater independence from his parents and to get bigger ideas about the things that he wanted. He was hoping that he would pass his driving test that summer and, if he did, it was his ambition to buy himself an old car. The plethora of possibilities that such freedom would open up seemed to Tim to be beyond his wildest dreams. He was on the cusp of adulthood!

Early on the first Monday of the holiday Tim cycled the three miles to the Home Of Gardens, a large complex of green houses in which grew flowering plants for sale to garden centres and house plants for sale directly to the public. Tim chained his bicycle to a fence post and went in to the main reception. He stood shyly at the desk. "Can I help you, love?" A middle-aged lady asked. Tim explained that he had come to start a holiday job, which he had been offered in writing a couple of weeks earlier. She consulted an open book on her desk. "Tim Croy?" "Yes, that's me" "Great, come with me." Tim followed her out through a back door into a kind of yard, "Ron, **Ron**" she yelled in a surprisingly loud voice. A thin, grey haired man dressed in a blue boiler suit appeared. "This is Tim Croy. He's going to be working for you this summer. Tim, this is Ron Lewis". Ron and Tim shook hands. Tim followed the older man into the first row of green houses. He stooped to look under the first of what appeared to Tim to be hundreds of benches on which stood thousands of pots of plants. "The floor in here is covered in coarse sand. Trouble is it's covered up the heating pipes so we're wasting shed loads of money heating the sand instead of the green houses. The heating pipes run along the edge of the green houses, on each side. Your job is to crawl along and clear the sand away from each pipe in every house. Easy!" It obviously was easy. Tim took the pointed cement trowel that Ron proffered, dropped to his hands and knees and crawled under the bench to the far wall of the green house. He scrabbled around in the sand for a bit but eventually located the heating pipe. For the next three and a half hours Tim inched his way forward clearing the sand from the pipe. As the sun rose in the sky the green houses became hotter and ever more humid. At last Ron came to find Tim and see how he was getting on. "That's impressive. I wasn't expecting you to have got that far. You've done a thorough job too!" Ron spoke gently as he crawled along inspecting Tim's efforts. "Thankyou Mr. Lewis." "No, no, no he tutted. Please call me Ron. You're not at school now". "Thankyou Ron" Tim felt odd calling a man, who not only was his boss but probably old enough to be his grandfather, by his Christian name. He had never done that before. "It's lunch hour now. They've set up your card for you now so I'll show you how to use the clock". Tim wondered what these strange terms meant but didn't want to appear stupid by asking. Ron showed Tim where to find the brown card with his name on it in a kind of letter rack on the wall. He put it in a slot in a big wooden box with a clock on the front and pulled a handle on the side. With a loud click the card sprang out again with a hole punched in it. "That keeps a record of the times you start and finish work. If you start late your pay will be docked. If you start early you won't get anything extra though, so keep an eye on your time keeping". Tim was warming to Ron, he seemed both interesting and kind. Tim went for a walk, ate his sandwich and returned to work, rather enjoying the feeling of clocking on. This was the "real world" that his father had so often talked about. And this became the daily Routine for Tim for the next eight weeks.

    Mrs. Croy had booked and paid for driving lessons for Tim with Len Jarvis, a local retired police officer who had become a driving instructor for his second career. Local opinion held him to be the best driving instructor in the area. He arrived in his orange Mini outside the Croys' house at Six O'clock on Tuesday evening. Tim was waiting nervously, not at all sure what to expect. Len Jarvis told Tim to get into the passenger seat. He drove a little way up the lane and stopped in a layby. "It's always better to get out of sight of spying parents and sisters!" Tim liked Len for that understanding comment. "Have you tried a car before?" "No" "A tractor?" "No" "A Lawn mower?" "Yes" "Great!" They changed seats and Len showed Tim how to get the driving seat into the correct position and explained what each of the pedals was used for and which foot he should use to operate them. Tim felt confused immediately. "Ok, turn the key!" Tim started the car. Len talked him through finding the biting point of the clutch and how much accelerator to apply. He helped him by means of the dual controls and the car crept forward. "Turn into the road" Tim turned the wheel a very little, imagining that the car would respond in a similar way to a boat. "You need to turn it a lot more than that Tim". Tim did so and the car swerved into the lane. "You need to change into second" Tim pushed the lever. The engine began to scream. "Back off the accelerator when you dip the clutch". Surprisingly quickly Tim began to relax and get the hang of the basic functions of the car. By the end of the hour Tim was enjoying himself and starting to dream of being able to drive by himself.

Tim's sister, Annabelle, had been doing badly in French at school and Mrs. Croy, in desperation, had contacted Tim's old French teacher from his prep school, who lived in the next village, to arrange for him to give her some extra lessons in the Summer holidays. Annabelle, understandably, had not been delighted and each visit entailed a battle of wills between mother and daughter. One day in conversation the French teacher had told Mrs. Croy that he could do with some help in his large garden. She in turn had told him that she was sure that Timothy would be glad of an opportunity to earn a bit of pocket money so Tim found himself working on a Saturday morning as well as all week, obediently digging the vegetable garden, walking up and down behind the lawn mower for miles at a time or kneeling weeding between bedding plants. At first he had felt rather awkward, being at his old French Masters' house but he had always liked him and the feeling was mutual. Soon Tim felt relaxed in this new situation, though he still could not help himself from calling him "Sir". One of the French teachers' neighbours saw the results of Tim's efforts and asked him to work for him too. Mr. Reid was a retired businessman of some kind and Tim immediately found that he enjoyed talking to him and felt that he could learn a lot from him. Mr. Reid was delighted and impressed at the thoroughness and efficiency of Tim's work and very soon increased his pay in an effort to retain his services in future holidays.

So it was that Tim found himself working almost all day, every day and, in the process, earning more money than he had previously seen in his life. Tim needed a bank account! He cycled into the local town and went into a bank to ask about opening an account. He was surprised when the manager invited him into his office and showed him round the works of his branch. He was very keen to show Tim a large, beige plastic box in the corner of one room, which he explained was a computer that they had recently acquired and on which they would keep all their customers details. This, he told Tim, was the beginning of the future. Tim had never seen a computer before and he was impressed and interested. By the time Tim came out of the bank, clutching his new bank account details, he felt that he had made another large step into the "real world".

At the Home of Gardens Tim continued to burrow daily like a mole, piling mounds of sand as he cleared space around the warm heating pipes in the hot and humid world of green houses. Tim was content to work alone, thinking his own thoughts and dreaming dreams. From time to time he would find himself being sprayed with a mixture of water and plant food by the automatic irrigation system but he did not see this as any kind of problem, rather a refreshing diversion to his mundane routine.

Len Jarvis was pleased with Tim's progress and booked him in for his driving test in the middle of August. He told Tim that it might be a good idea to get additional practice outside of his formal lessons in his parents' car. Mr. Croy refused point blank. His Ford Granada was a company car so could not be used for driving tuition and his wife's Citroen was much too big and expensive to let a learner (or inexperienced driver) loose on. Tim felt rather cheated because he knew very well that most of his friends' parents were letting their sons learn to drive in the family car. He was fully appeased when his father offered to help him to choose a car to buy for himself and his mother promised to pay for insurance and tax for it. Excitedly, for bot were very interested in cars, father and son sat down after dinner that evening to comb through the advertisements in the local free paper. They rapidly discovered that their ideas of the ideal old banger for a young man were starkly different. Tim had dreams of something that might go fast and impress his mates, having no notion about the way in which insurance was designed to force young drivers into safely under powered cars or of the likely cost of petrol and repairs. Mr. Croy, being an engineer and having no concept of the need to impress anyone, kept suggesting "technically interesting" cars that would be cheap to run and easy to repair. Tim could not imagine himself driving any of his father's ideas but he did have the sense to understand the need to be able to afford the petrol to use the car and to find something that would be simple to work on so that he could learn to repair it himself. They would spend the following Sunday driving round looking at cars. Both men felt excited at the prospect.

At lunch time on Thursday Tim went to find Ron to tell him that he had finished his work in the green houses. "You done all of them Tim? *Properly?*" "Yes" "That's amazing. I seen that you've been making a good job of it. Come and find me when you get back from lunch and I'll show you your next task". When Tim came back Ron lead him through a gate at the back of the yard to a field. They went over to a large tub, built of what appeared to Tim to be railway sleepers, and lined with black plastic sheet. It was filled with a strong smelling liquid that, even in the open air, made Tim's eyes water. Ron introduced Tim to a sallow looking youth of about his own age. "Tim, this is Sid. He's just started here full time." "Hi" the two boys greeted each other. "As you can see, those two old stables are full to the roof with old black plastic flower pots. You're going to be cleaning them in this here tank. It's Formaldehyde in it so you don't want to be getting it on your hands so you need to wear these gloves." With that Ron left them to start what was evidently going to be another never ending job. The two young men found very quickly that they had little in common to talk about and they were both glad when Ron returned brandishing an old radio. This would become their constant companion, all day, every day, blaring the latest Top Twenty hits repeatedly through each new show. Tim was starting to appreciate the mindlessness of his work, which gave him endless opportunity to enjoy his own thoughts.

Sunday morning saw Tim and his father setting off in the Granada, with a map and the newspaper, to look at old cars. Tim had telephoned several "private sellers" to arrange a time to look at their car and get their address and there were a few garages offering "sold as seen" cars that they were going to check. As the morning progressed the two men's hands became blacker with grease and engine oil, Tim's brain became fuller and fuller with an understanding of the dangers of structural rust, the evidence of repeated over heating and the sounds of a newly started engine that rattled worryingly. Both men were beginning to think that possibly there weren't any cars worth buying for under £250. They stopped at a country pub for a "Ploughman's" lunch and to avail themselves of the public telephone to call some more sellers of slightly more expensive cars who may be persuaded to reduce their price. Despite Mr. Croy's assertion that Fords were too popular and therefor over priced they arranged to look at a Ford Escort, a Hillman Avenger and an Austin Allegro. By mid afternoon they were sitting in their car discussing the costs and benefits of the Escort and Avenger. Eventually the decided to return to take a second look at the Avenger which was languishing at the rear of a Honda dealership. It had evidently been there for some time and Mr. Croy felt certain that he could negotiate a good price. And so it was that Tim became the proud owner of a bright yellow Hillman Avenger Super saloon.

In whatever spare time Tim had between his three jobs and his driving lessons he would enthusiastically polish the paintwork, shine the chrome and hoover the carpets or apply "Super Shine" to the plastic seats and dashboard of his pride and joy. From time to time he would persuade his mother to sit, terrified, in the front passenger seat while Tim demonstrated his growing skill to her on the quiet rural roads.

Tim took the morning off work on the day of his driving test. Len Jarvis collected Tim at the arranged time and Tim drove to the local city, being verbally tested about the meanings of road signs and reminded how to reverse around a corner accurately. "Just remember that this is a Mini and not a racing boat, so you need to steer it properly! You'll be fine".

As the test progressed Tim's mouth became dryer and dryer and he began to sweat. He didn't dare to try to wind the window down for fear of swerving as he did so. Tim carried out a successful "three-point turn" and reversed safely around a corner on a quiet housing estate road. It had probably been easier, he reflected, to get a feel for the car than it had been to do so for the old clinker four years earlier. A short drive along the dual carriageway and they returned to the driving test centre where Tim's last task was to "parallel park" the Mini without scraping the curb. After being tested on three road signs from the Highway Code book, the examiner rustled and fumbled interminably with the paper work on his clipboard. Tim sat, becoming more and more uncomfortable in the heat of the car and the pressure of the occasion.

"It is my duty, Mr. Croy, to advise you that you have demonstrated the required competence in operating a motor car and adequate knowledge of the rules of the road. Congratulations! You have passed your driving test. You must send this completed form to DVLA in Swansea with the necessary fee in order to be issued with your full driving licence. You may drive independently, using your provisional licence in the meantime".

Tim couldn't believe it. He had done it! He was free, independent. And he didn't think that anyone had ever addressed him as Mr. Croy before. Did that mean that he really was a man in the eyes of the world?

After a celebratory lunch with his mother and sister at home Tim took Annabelle into the court yard to triumphantly cut the red L plates off his car and Tim cautiously reversed it out of the confines of the court yard, turned around and drove down the crunchy gravel drive. Indicating unnecessarily Tim turned out into the road and drove himself to work. Tim felt very uncomfortable alone in his car, without the reassurance of Len Jarvis' advisory commentary or his mothers' rigid, frightened presence in the passenger seat beside him. It was down to him from now on. He was fully responsible for whatever happened to him in the car now.

Fighting From Within

Tim returned for his final year at Barforth triumphantly. He unloaded his mother's car and engaged a younger boy to help him carry his trunk and tuck box up to Top Study three, which he was to share Anthony Williams. Returning to the car on the Private Lane Tim bid his mother farewell and, having stood politely to watch the tail lights recede into the distance, he returned to his new home. The door of Study Two was open and he dropped in to greet Usman. The friends talked about their holidays. Tim was surprised, when he told Usman about having passed his driving test, to learn that in Saudi Arabia Usman had been free to drive since he was twelve years old. Tim found this information incredible. He had been wearing shorts at prep school when he was twelve. He began to understand why it was that Usman always appeared to be much more grown up and confident than English boys of the same age.

Later that evening, after the customary House meeting, Tim caught up with John Eglington, who had now been promoted, as predicted by Mike and Tim a year earlier, to Head of House. "D'you have a good holiday John?" "Yeah, you?" "Yep. Great thanks". "You're not going to lead the initiation ceremony tonight are you?" Tim had watched this ceremony with unabated dismay three times now, unable to stop it and too cowardly to be seen to abstain from it, half-heartedly flicking his towel, making sure that it never made contact. Now that the Head of House was in the same year as Tim, had been his friend for four years and had worked with him in the First Eight last year he had some reason to hope that he might be able to influence a change. "Yes, of course I am. Why wouldn't I?" "Well, it's pretty brutal isn't it? Fifty boys humiliating and hurting helpless new boys on their first night, when they're already probably feeling horrible". "It's a house tradition. Probably been happening for more than a hundred years. It's certainly not for me to stop it". "But somebody has to stop it one day. Come on John, you remember how horrible it was when they did it to us. I remember you ended up being cut by someone. I think you were nearly crying that night". "It didn't do us any real harm though, did it? And Tim Moor saw what a great year we were going to make and we did, didn't we?" Tim couldn't deny that observation and he realised that he was not going to manage to change this event.

At ten thirty Everyone cascaded up the long passage way to the Junior Dorm. Tim followed, reluctantly, with Usman, warning him that he was about to witness the English at their most barbaric. Tim had another reason to be there this evening because he was the Dorm Senior and he felt a particular responsibility to make sure that his young charges survived the ordeal. The lights were already on as Usman and Tim entered the room and John was explaining the rules of the "game". Tim watched from the back row as the young boys clambered from the chest of drawers up to the beams in the roof space. Some of them looked *so small*. He supposed he had looked like that four years ago. His stomach lurched as he remembered other things that had happened to him that year. At least that bastard Lucas had left now, so these kids would be safe from the worst that Tim had experienced. The signal was made by Eglington and the room full of youths closed in like a pack of hungry wolves, flicking, flailing, bullying the shocked new boys as they hung helplessly suspended from the beams. Tim saw Usman's mouth drop open in shock. The frenzy of flailing towels and dressing gown cords reached its' crescendo and then, at Eglington's signal, stopped as suddenly as it had started. The boys flooded out of the room and back down the passage. John told the Third Years to get down and get back to bed and then he, too, stalked off, leaving Tim and Usman standing watching the young boys limping back to their beds. Tim felt embarrassed, ashamed that these small boys should have had to endure such injustice. "Tim, look! He is badly hurt I think" Usman interrupted his thoughts. Quite a tall boy with a dishevelled mop of brown hair was sitting on his bed trying to stem a fast flow of blood from his ankle. Tim went over to him and knelt down. "Usman! Go and get some bog paper, quickly". "I'm sorry." Tim looked the boy in the eyes. Usman returned with a roll of paper and the two older boys started wiping and dabbing at the young man's leg. He winced but said nothing. Tim guessed that he was trying very hard not to let any of his peers see how much it was hurting. Usman seemed to know what to do and was keeping a wad of paper pressed hard on the wound. At last it stopped bleeding. "Thanks for that". The boys voice had a wobble to it that confirmed what

Tim had been thinking. He got into bed. Tim glanced round to see if everyone else was OK. "I'm Tim Croy. I'm Dorm Senior so you'll be seeing me every day! Now try to get to sleep because tomorrow will be a very busy day."

A few days later the Sixth Formers were summoned to a meeting to be told how they had to fill in their UCCA forms, the official forms that had to be sent to a central clearing house in order to apply for a place at university. Tim knew that the school did not think that he was likely to get a place but his parents had told him that he should apply in order to keep his options open. "Just try dear" his mother had advised. "If you don't try you certainly won't get in but if you do try you *might*." Tim was not sure that he wanted to go to university. He had little idea of what it would be like but he had developed a fear, based on the logic of experience, that it would prove to be every bit as harsh as Barforth had been to a new boy but because everyone would be older, even more so. He was certain that he could not endure a repeat of his first year at school. The following weeks were filled with reading colourful prospectuses, collected from the Careers Room. All of them were crammed with pictures of smiling young men and women engaged in exciting looking activities and promises of "The time of your life, opportunities to build life long friendships, enjoy learning with like minded people." Tim doubted that any of it was true, he knew that they were trying to sell themselves and he had seen a copy of the latest Barforth prospectus which definitely bore no relation to his experience of the school.

Not being very confident academically Tim decided that he didn't want to risk experimenting with subjects that he had never heard of. He applied for courses in joint Economics and Geography, the two subjects that he was really enjoying at school and that his tutor told him they thought he was most likely to do sufficiently well at in the summer. He applied to Northern universities because he had a kind of romantic notion that the North would be somehow more real, more down to earth than the south where he had lived all his life. Tim wanted a change, an adventure and to be far away from home, parents and Barforth when he was having it!

After prep one evening Anthony and Tim were talking in their study. Anthony was lamenting the fact that whatever went wrong was somehow pinned on him. "Just because I used to piss about all the time when I was in the Third Form doesn't mean I still do". "Yeah but it wasn't *only* in the Third Form was it? And you still like to take the mick now". Tim pointed out reasonably. "You do it worse than me now Tim. Remember when you ripped into the Head Master's Fiat in front of the whole class last year". Yeah, I suppose. But they've made you a House Prefect, look, and they haven't done that for me" Tim brought up the topic that had been rankling with him for some while. He didn't think he was jealous of his friend and he trusted him and enjoyed their friendship very much but he was feeling sore that he was now the only one of his year group who had not been appointed as a prefect. He could not see any concrete reason why that should be and he was half hoping that Anthony would point out something that he had missed. He didn't. "I was expecting them to make you one straight away this term after what you did in the First Eight". Anthony was telling the truth and intended that Tim should feel encouraged and supported but the comment only served to make Tim feel even more hard done by. Both feeling completely hacked off now the boys made themselves a mug of tea and stood watching the Fourth Formers washing for bed through the fire door window.

Tim was still feeling tetchy the next day. He had a general feeling of dissatisfied malaise about him without being conscious of any specific reason for it. On his way back from lunch he passed the Chapel and saw that the door was open and that a sign was advertising the Chapel book sale. On an impulse Tim went in. He didn't like the Reverend Pullman, perceiving him as being simultaneously dishonest and inadequate. He looked disinterestedly at the array of books about "Finding Salvation

Through Prayer" "How God helped me revise" and Ten Rules for Communion". Tim was formulating a plan. He selected a book titled "Ten Scientific Truths from The Old Testament" which didn't sound too obnoxiously self-congratulatory. He checked the price, which was the most important criteria of choice for Tim on this occasion. "It's a nice surprise to see you here Timothy" The Reverend Pullman commented. "Well I wasn't going to come sir but I was passing by and I saw your sign up sir". "Ah, the guidance of the Good Lord" he smiled. "Yes sir. I suppose so sir. Sir, would you let me take this book on credit sir – Mr. Linford only does House Bank on Saturdays and Mondays sir" "Of course Croy. We're always here to encourage learning about our wonderful faith!" "Thanks sir!" Tim left, book in hand. As soon as he got to his study Tim pushed the book to the back of one of his desk drawers. He had no intention of reading it and didn't want anybody seeing it in his possession. He had a plan, the idea for which he had read in a philosophy book some time before, and now he needed only to wait for time to take its' course.

Half term was fast approaching and on Saturday, on the way out of the Dining Hall after Tea, there was a new notice on the Head Masters Notice Board. A new tranche of House prefects had been appointed. Tim read it with growing rage. Three boys in School House, from the year below Tim, had been appointed. Tim, yet again, had not.

Tim stood at the window of the Junior Dorm, watching the school hurrying up and down the terrace two stories below. Everyone seemed to be excited, happy, heading purposefully towards whatever it was that they were supposed to be doing on that Saturday afternoon in October. Tim was not. He had nothing really to do. Nothing left to offer. After reading that announcement he felt as if he had been hit in the chest by a great force. Winded. He hadn't felt like going to his study, where he would be required to appear boisterous, cheerful, fun. He didn't feel any of those things and didn't see why he should have to pretend to. He stood alone wrestling with a flood of emotions and feelings that he couldn't control and didn't want to acknowledge.

What had he done that was so wrong that he deserved this massive humiliation, this shattering of any remnants of self-esteem that four years at Barforth had left him with? He remembered the casual conversation with Anthony earlier that term. It was true that Tim had always played by the rules, behaved himself, done what he was told and where had that got him? precisely nowhere! Anthony had had fun, done whatever he wanted, pushed boundaries and rocked boats but he had been rewarded. Whatever way Tim looked at it it didn't seem fair. The problem was that Mike and Anthony were Tim's friends and this injustice obviously wasn't their fault. Tim really didn't blame them, wasn't angry with them and didn't want it to affect their friendship but he did feel hurt, made to appear inferior to his peers. Barforth was trying to, and beginning to succeed in, ruining his very friendships. *But why?* How was he supposed to move forward from this moment of despair? He wished he could simply melt away, never have to face anybody from Barforth ever again. He had eight, no nine more months to survive and he didn't feel as if he could get through one afternoon.

Tim began to think through the few possibilities that sprang to his mind, rather numbed by the misery of his plight. He could simply ignore the situation. Pretend that he hadn't noticed, didn't care. He was well practiced at that kind of approach and had been killing his feelings and emotions for the best part of ten years. But he didn't feel up to it. He was hurt and upset and he had started to believe that there was a genuine conspiracy to make a final concerted effort to break him. Barforth was not going to let Timothy Croy leave after five years within it's moulding, crushing shaping forces, unscathed and unbent. How about fighting it? He could march into Mr. Linford's flat right now, confront him, demand to know why, insist on a change. He had the confidence and the audacity to do that now. But that approach would certainly lead to further humiliation. If he failed to get what he wanted he would be exposed as a spoilt, immature boy who was evidently not up to the job of Prefect, thus confirming the wisdom of Barforth. If he did get what he wanted his appointment would be confirmed separately, an evident afterthought, a laughing stock. He could run away, which felt like the most attractive choice right now but that was obviously a non-starter. Tim couldn't think of any more scenarios to consider so he just watched the people far below him, wishing that he was anyone of them in preference to being Tim Croy.

He couldn't stay in the Junior Dorm forever. The floor evidently wasn't going to swallow him up so he was going to have to cope with it. Squaring his shoulders determinedly Tim clumped down the long passage and turned left up to the Top Studies. Anthony was sitting at his desk writing an essay. He looked up as Tim came in. "You OK? You look kind of rough mate". "Yeah I'm fine, just been working too hard!" The friends grinned, Anthony stopped his work and they put on some loud music to cheer on their afternoon.

That evening Mike had invited Tim to a meal out with his parents. Tim prepared himself carefully, wanting to appear smart and cool. Hair washed to a dry, crumpled bounce in an over hot shower, combed forward in his customary flick, white T shirt hanging out of his blue, slightly flared jeans and a generous spray of Brut 33 to complete the effect. Waiting in the Library with Mike he found himself looking forward to chatting to the Andrews' family again. They seemed to Tim to be much more open and relaxed than his own parents. When the Peugeot swung into the Quad the two friends went to meet it. Mr. and Mrs. Andrews got out of their car and Tim was surprised to see them get straight back in to it, but in the back seats. "You're my passenger tonight" Mike grinned as he got into the drivers' seat. Tim was amazed. Not so much because Mike was driving, the two boys had celebrated their Summer Holiday driving test successes together at The Lock Keeper's Hotel on the first Saturday night of term, but because he was allowed to drive such a big car. Tim remembered how his father had dismissed, out of hand, any possibility of letting him drive their family car which was the same sort of size as theirs. It did feel strange, sitting in the front seat next to one of his friends driving a car.

The Sixth Formers had spent a morning having a series of films, lectures and "question and answer" sessions about recruitment to the Armed Forces, either directly after leaving school or to be sponsored through university. Tim had no idea what he wanted to do for a job and liked the idea of being paid to go to university. He had had two or three flying lessons while still in the CCF in a Chipmunk training plane and had enjoyed it. He picked up a brochure and application form from the table at the back of the hall as he left. Back in their study he found that Anthony had a booklet for the Army. "Are you serious about it Tim?" "I dunno. I doubt I'd get in anyway, but it would be good to get that money at university."" But think of all the training shit you'd have to get through. Remember that silly camping we had to do in Wales?" "mmm But I quite fancy shooting around flying a fighter jet at Mach One." Both boys decided to fill in their forms for a laugh anyway.

The expected note appeared, addressed to Croy. T. on the Chapel Notice Board. Tim didn't need to bother reading it. He swaggered cheerfully over to the Reverend Pullman's office and tapped on the door. "Come in!" He looked up from a pile of half marked Latin books. "Oh Tim! I do like the way you're always so quick to respond!" "Thanks sir! I really hadn't forgotten, things have just been busy sir." Tim handed the Master his one pound note. He opened his note book to cross off the young man's debt. He looked up. "I need three pounds from you Tim." "No sir, you said one pound would do." "No, the book cost three pounds, I wrote it clearly in here". "Yes sir, it did sir. But you said that three is the same as one and that one is the same as three sir, so here's one pound sir." Reverend Pullman stared at Tim, his face reddening as it displayed, in rapid succession, perplexion, recognition, insult and, finally, unsuppressed rage. "Tim! You may think that you are very clever but you're not. That is an insult to me and it's an insult to God. Get out of my room now. The Head Master will be dealing with this. You've gone far to far this time." Tim left, delighted to have had the planned effect. He was sick of Barforth, it was they who had pushed things too far with Tim and now he was going to let them see who he really was.

"I don't understand what's got into you Croy." Tim was sitting in the subdued plushness of the Head Master's Study. "You were always so polite and helpful but recently you seem to have gone off the rails seriously. I think you need to explain yourself." This was going much better than Tim could have imagined! "Well to be honest sir" The Head Master looked at Tim with a flicker of interest. "I don't think that you've treated me fairly sir. Well, no, not *you* really sir, I mean Barforth. Like you said I've always tried really hard to follow the rules and do things as they should be done but it hasn't got me anywhere sir. Other people who have behaved much worse than me have all been made prefects and now boys from the year below me are being made prefects and I'm just left to be laughed at and humiliated sir." Mr. Bolton was, at heart, a fair and just man and Tim's words were making some sense to him. "Is there anything else you need to say?" "Well you know that I coxed the First Eight last year sir? It doesn't seem fair that that doesn't count for anything sir. Stroke is always made Captain of the Boat Club and usually a School Prefect too sir but the cox just gets forgotten about. I mean if they didn't have a cox they couldn't row at all could they sir?" "No, you're absolutely right there Timothy!" "Well that's all really sir". The unexpected agreement had taken the wind out of Tim's sails. There was silence for a moment. Mr. Bolton had worked all his life in Public Schools and Barforth was his second Headship. As he rapidly approached retirement he had been increasingly questioning the truths on which he believed the great schools to be founded and he often found things within the system that he didn't like. Young Croy, with so much ahead of him and so little behind him had just summarized, most succinctly, the essence of many of his musings. He warmed to Croy, had started to do so when he had tried to insult him about his car in such a well contrived opportunity. Yes! Timothy Croy seemed to Mr. Bolton to encapsulate potential and success, though definitely not in the very specific Barforth mould.

"If that's all, I think we'd better go to get our lunch before it's all gone." The Head Master rose, ending the conversation. Tim felt dazed, a little dizzy and very surprised. He had come in to the room expecting a thorough reprimand and a good beating but now he was leaving as if he had been chatting to a friend. "Thankyou sir!" Tim meant that.

Community Service

In January, excitingly for the boys, a new decade, Tim began his new and final role in the Boat club as the trainer in chief of the Third Form novice coxes. Tim was conscientious and wanted to make a good job of it. He had what he believed to be an excellent example in his own coach, Toby Phillips and decided that he would try to do as he had done with the addition of any improvements that came to his mind. In a strange way Tim found that he was ready for this new challenge and that he really didn't feel as disappointed at no longer being part of the First Eight as he had feared that he would. Determined that there should not be the friction between him and his successor, William Smith, that had built up between him and Alex Rian, Tim had sought Smith out to offer his support in any way that he needed. Very soon Tim was fully immersed in the task of teaching the skills of the cox to the next generation. Nobody understood better than he did the significance of his task.

One afternoon when Tim was luxuriating in a long, hot shower to try to defrost himself after a long session standing at The Tank, Mike joined him in the communal Senior Showers. They greeted each other with the customary "Hi" and Tim shut his eyes as he smothered his hair in Head and Shoulders shampoo. Suddenly he felt something brushing against his back. No! Not brushing. Distinctly stroking, caressing even. Tim recoiled, shocked. Rapidly swilling the shampoo from his hair and face he opened his eyes. Mike was smiling at him. "What the hell are you doing?" Tim was appalled, stunned, as the full meaning of what had just happened sank in. "Oh my God! You filthy fucking queer!" Tim jumped out of the shower, still bubbly with soap, grabbed his towel and hurried out to the changing room. He sat huddled in his towel, shaken and shaking. He wanted to get dressed, get out, get away but he felt strangely listless and unable to move. At length he got himself dressed, put away his games kit and went up to his study. He couldn't settle to anything. He was shocked, disgusted even, quite naturally. But much worse was the way in which this sudden turn of events had snatched one of his very best friends away from him forever, without warning and with no chance to sort things out between them. It was distressing and it hurt.

The next day Tim sat, pointedly, at a different table from the one which he had shared with Mike in Economics lessons every day since they had started the subject in the Lower Sixth, eighteen months earlier. He did the same thing in their Geography lesson later that day and this chilly situation between the two boys persisted until it became the norm. It wasn't what Tim wanted, he wouldn't have dreamed that things could turn out like that between them, but what else could Tim do after the incident in the showers?

A year earlier, when he had first entered the Sixth Forms, Tim had taken the earliest opportunity to quit the Wednesday Afternoon Combined Cadet Force and had enrolled, instead, with the Community Service group. He had had a rapid succession of different activities, cutting hedges for old people in Council houses, playing games with children in an orphanage, collecting litter from local beauty spots and even digging snow from paths around the school. Since September Tim had been paired with Usman, working in the garden of a rather grand old lady in the local Town. Mrs. Quinn was very old, had once evidently been very tall but was now stooped and shrivelled and always supported their toils with hot tea and home made cakes. She lived in a big house with once beautiful grounds and Tim, who loved gardening, was really giving the task of reclaiming her garden his best shot. As the Easter Term progressed a profusion of bulbs began to emerge, Snowdrops, Aconites, Crocus, Daffodils, Hyacinths. Mrs Quinn would sit on her terrace and talk of her husband, children and happy family days in the garden. Tim found her fascinating.

One afternoon, as Usman and Tim walked up the road towards Mrs. Quinn's house they heard the clattering of high heels running along the pavement behind them. "Tim! Tim! It is you, isn't it?" Tim turned, embarrassed. A girl was approaching, head long, towards the two young men. "Don't you remember me Tim? I'm Sally Anne!" The girl introduced herself, not waiting to find out if Tim did remember her or not. "How could I forget you?" Tim's voice was thick with double meaning. "Oh I know. We *did* have good times together, didn't we?" Usman was watching this emotional reunion with considerable amusement. He knew nothing of Tim's history with this girl but it was obvious that they had been very close and, judging by the kind of girl she appeared to be, he could easily imagine exactly what their good times must have involved. "And who's your Friend? Aren't you going to introduce us?" Without waiting for her introduction Sally Ann stepped forward, put one hand on the back of Usman's head and kissed him, deep and full, on his mouth. "I *love* tall dark foreigners like you!" Sally Ann filled the stunned silence.

"Oh my God! How do you know that girl?" Usman asked Tim later, as they chopped and dug their way deeper into Mrs. Quinn's wilderness. Tim laughed. "I don't really know her. She used to come up to school every weekend last year and try to get off with a different boy each time. To be honest, when it was my turn, I told her to piss off". "She is very rude. In Saudi she would be imprisoned for doing that to me in the street. She made me feel sick." "I think she made every Sixth Form boy in Barforth feel sick last year. I suppose that's why we don't see her any more". Both boys laughed as they joined Mrs. Quinn on her sunny terrace for tea.

Bored and needing a change of scenery one Sunday afternoon Tim had set off for a walk into the local town. On an impulse he had marched up the long path to Mrs. Quinn's front door and rang the bell. He heard it tinkling somewhere deep inside the big house. After a minute there was the sound of sliding bolts and rasping locks and the big door creaked open. Mrs. Quinn looked at him, appearing confused, as if she had been sleeping. "Tim, dear. I wasn't expecting you today." "It's such a nice afternoon, and I was fed up with work so I thought maybe you'd let me come and get on with your garden for a bit" "Well nobody could refuse an offer like that!" The old lady laughed. Tim thus became a regular weekend visitor to the house and the overgrown garden rapidly began to display its design and symmetry once more. On these visits gardening would be regularly interspersed with tea, cakes and conversation. The young man was fascinated by the stories about a life well before the Second World War and he began to seek her perspective on anything that might be concerning him at the time. The old lady was genuinely flattered that such a nice young man should want to help her and seemed to like her company. Her own children were both living overseas with their families and she missed them and her grandchildren. Tim was a cheerful diversion from a lonely life in her old house full of memories.

One evening during prep Tim had popped over to the Library to find a book to help him with a diagram of the formation of a temperature inversion for a Geography "A" level practice question. Taking a short cut back to his study through the Junior Changing Room to reduce the chance of being intercepted by a Master or, worse, a prefect more junior than Tim, he experienced a strong feeling that he was not alone in the dark room. He flicked on the light and looked around him. He was just coming to the conclusion that he was imagining things when he saw a movement in the far corner. Focussing he made out the outline of a boy, half covered in several string bags of sports kit. "Who's that?" Tim asked sharply. A couple of the bags parted to reveal a small, dark haired Third Former called Ford. "What are you doing? You're supposed to be in prep". Ford just stared at Tim. Some kind of sixth sense told Tim that there was something wrong. He moved across the dirty room and sat down beside the young boy. "Why aren't you in prep?" Tim asked very quietly and gently. Ford continued to stare straight ahead, seeming not to hear Tim. He was about to react with irritation when he saw tears running silently down Fords' cheek. "What's happened?" Tim tried again. "I don't want to be here any more. I can't do it. I just want to go home." "Why? What's happened to make you feel like this?" Tim persisted, his sense of responsibility for the young boy increasing by the minute. Ford shook his head. "Listen, the most important thing that I've learnt at Barforth is that it can really, really help to talk to someone when things feel like they're too hot to handle". He tried a different tack. He needed to help this boy sort things out because he was clearly overwhelmed by whatever it was that had befallen him. "I don't want to tell you". "No! You need to tell me. Look I'm not a Master or a Prefect or anything so I can't do anything to you whatever it is that you've done." Ford took a deep breath. "I was attacked". "What do you mean attacked?" Ford's lip began to tremble and he started to cry properly. Flustered and concerned Tim put his arm round the small boy's shoulders in an attempt to comfort him. "I'm not queer or anything mate, I promise". Tim heard himself say. He remembered an occasion four years earlier when James Long had said similar words to Tim. Like a flash of lightening the connection was made. "Please God, no!" Tim prayed silently. "Ford, is it something that makes you feel too ashamed to talk about?" The desolate boy nodded. "Was it an older boy?" Another nod. "A prefect?" Another affirmative nod.

"OK, Ford. You can't just stay here all through prep. Williams will have noticed that you're not there and he will have to report it. Come up to my study for now and I'll sort things out with Williams". Tim took control of his feelings and the small boy. Installing Ford in his study, pleased that at least his room mate was safely out the way, Tim instructed him to help himself to any of the motoring and football magazines that the two study mates had stacked on the floor. Tim sprinted down the two flights of stairs to the Junior Common Room and walked in. The boys looked up from their prep. Anthony stood and came out of the room in response to Tim's signal. "I've got Ford up in our room. He's very upset about something and I'm trying to sort him out". "Ok, cool. I don't need to do anything about him then". That was one of the qualities that Tim most liked in his friend, he was always relaxed and easy going. "Cheers mate! Have fun!" and Tim went on his way. He made some coffee for himself in the dirty communal kitchen and, on an impulse, remembering, he helped himself to a spoonful of somebody's Hot Chocolate mix and made a hot, sweet drink for Ford.

At the end of prep Tim left Ford under Anthony's watchful eye and went in search of Andrews. He found him in his study with his room-mate, listening to a Super Tramp LP. Mike was visibly surprised to see Tim visiting him and set about making coffee and toast. Once the three boys were settled down Tim began. "I'm so pissed off! This place really get's me down. Every year the Third Form get bullied or worse. Nobody ever does anything to stop it". The boys agreed, reminding each other of past atrocities that they had seen, heard about or experienced. "I just found poor little Ford in a real state. Some bastard's hurt him really, really seriously. I tell you what." Tim fixed Mike with a hard stare firmly in his eyes. "When I find out who it was, you remember how I put Lucas in hospital that time? Well when I find this guy I'll do worse to him. If I get my way he'll never have children!"

If he hadn't been in a position to do what he wanted to do,

Tim had, at least, done the best that he could do, given his total lack of evidence and authority. He finished his coffee and left.

When Tim got back to his study Ford had had to go to bed. Anthony was waiting for Tim. "What's happening Tim? I haven't seen you like this before. What happened to Ford? He's really upset, I can see, but he wouldn't talk to me". "He wouldn't tell me much either. I had to fit tiny clues together and I'm not at all sure that I really know anything but I think I might be onto something." Tim appreciated his friend's concern for the young Third Former and his willingness to bend the rules to support Tim just because he trusted him.

That Sunday Tim was keen to talk to Mrs. Quinn about his worries. "It's weird really. Because I'm not important and don't have any power in the school I get told things, I'm kind of easier to talk to for the younger boys, so then I get this kind of responsibility to help them dumped on my shoulders but I don't have any of the authority that I need to do anything about anything." Mrs. Quinn sat looking at the earnest young man for a moment. "Well dear, there are a number of things in what you've just told me. I don't think the younger boys come to you because you're not a prefect. They trust you because you're a very kind and patient young man. That's a very valuable trait which everybody will always appreciate. Responsibility is a difficult thing. I think that you *feel* responsible because you *want to be able to change things* but, because you are not in a position to be able to do anything you cannot really be held responsible." Tim felt some relief of the tension that had been building up in his mind. Mrs. Quinn made things seem so much clearer. He guessed that this was something to do with what his father called "experience of life". "Thank you. It's been going round and round inside my head and you make it seem so simple". "Tim, dear, please try to remember that you have probably done more to help that poor boy just by talking to him than you would by somehow punishing the perpetrator."

Much to his surprise Tim was invited to an Officer Cadet

appraisal session with the RAF. It involved three days of intensive training and assessment and, best of all, three days away from school. Tim set off in high spirits. He was not really bothered whether he ended up being selected or not so he didn't feel under any pressure. There were lots of other hopeful young men there and Tim sensed that it might become very competitive. He knew he was as good as anyone else. After a tough afternoon of physical activity, which Tim did not find as gruelling as he had feared, they were enjoying relaxing in the "mess" before dinner. A tall guy with black hair and a very white face came and introduced himself to Tim. "Hi! I'm Andy. I think I recognise you. Were you the cox of Barforth First Eight last Summer?" "Yes, I was. I guess you must have been in one of the crews we raced against?" "Yes. Sommerton. Barforth were really impressive! You always looked so much more relaxed than we did. As if you were all having fun. Barforth must be a great school." "The Boat Club's great. Not so sure about anything else though." It amused and surprised Tim to hear the perceptions about Barforth of a boy from another school. Evidently Andy didn't have a very high regard for Sommerton. Or was it a classic case of the grass always being greener somewhere else?

Last Laugh

It was the start of the Summer Term nineteen Eighty. The last time Tim would return to Barforth and, indeed, the last time that Tim would have to return to any school. Ever. Sitting through the familiar routine of the "First Evening" Chapel service the congregation were kneeling in prayer on the hard and dusty floor, squashed into tight rows of pews that, for the Senior boys at the back of the Chapel, were almost too cramped to bear. Tim's mind was wondering back to his first service in that Chapel, when he was sitting at the front and had been taken by surprise by the thunder of the organ. His mind was suddenly snapped into sharp, shocked focus. "Let us pray for Michael Andrews and his family at this very distressing time." "Let us pray for all of us who will be taking exams this term and let us pray……..." The reverend Pullman's voice faded back out of Tim's consciousness. Why were they praying for Mike? What had happened? Did anyone else know what he was on about? Tim tried to look at the faces of the boys around him, to try to see any indication of understanding, but he saw only blank faces, with one boy, two along from him, visibly praying, hands clasped, evidently a "Bible Basher" Tim thought disparagingly.

"What happened to Mike" Tim asked Anthony as soon as they got back to their study. *"Didn't you know?* You must be the only one who doesn't. He crashed his mum's car, really badly apparently, and he's in hospital in a bad way. They thought he was going to die but it seems that he didn't." Tim felt a bit shaky. Like most young men, he had always assumed that he and his friends were indestructible, would somehow all live forever. "Shit, that's rough." He said simply. He couldn't get his imagined picture of Mike, nearly dead, out of his mind.

The 'phone was ringing. "Hello" Tim pushed his ten pence coin into the call box outside the Dining Hall. "Hello. Mrs. Andrews?" "Yes, speaking." "Oh, hi. It's Tim Croy, Mike's friend from School. Do you remember me?" "Tim! Yes of course." "I was wondering if it would be OK for me to come to visit Mike on Saturday afternoon?" "Oh. I know he'd like that. Do you want me to come to collect you from school?" "I'm not sure what time I'll be finished. I'll come on the train, probably about four O'clock, I'll call when I get there". "I'll meet you at the station then Tim. See you then."

As Tim ran along the river bank, coaching one of the Third Form crews, he began to worry about his forthcoming visit. Suppose Mrs. Andrews thought he was being nosey? Maybe she knew that he had been thoroughly nasty to Mike. He could always just not go. Pretend he forgot or that he couldn't get away. That would be easier. But he couldn't do that. He had told Mrs. Andrews that he was going to go and she would have told Mike. Maybe Mike didn't want him to go. He might think Tim had come to laugh at him, another opportunity for him to be nasty to him. *To bully him.* Tim felt that he needed to say that phrase to himself because that was the truth about what he had been doing to Mike. *Bullying.* The very thing that he hated most in other people. That he had tried so hard to fight against at Barforth for so long and he had started doing it himself. If there was really any justice and love, as the Reverend Pullman kept promising, relentlessly, in Chapel, every day, then surely it should be Tim lying, nearly dead, in hospital, divine retribution for his hypocrisy.

Tim ran harder up and down the river bank, trying, almost, to run away from his distress. He had been to see Mr. Linford after lunch to get some money out of House Bank and to seek permission to go out. When he had heard where Tim was going he had handed Tim a crisp five pound note. "I'm paying for your ticket, Tim, and buy some sweets and magazines for Mike with the change. Send him all our best wishes." Tim had been taken aback at this decency. There were some good Masters at Barforth. He had looked forward to telling Mike the story. That would cheer him up a bit.

Tim was peering out of the dirty window, watching the nondescript countryside clattering past. He saw black and white cows in fields of long, lush grass. There was a queue of cars waiting at a level crossing and a man in his garden, chasing his lawnmower. Tim liked mowing lawns, the smell of cut grass and of exhaust smoke were both a pleasure for Tim.

The train was slowing down. The straggle of houses became denser, turning into red brick factories and the neglected backs of shops. Tim's chest felt constricted. He had to go through with it now! When he alighted, seemingly the only person wanting to visit this unremarkable town late on a Saturday afternoon, he was surprised to hear his name being called. Looking around him he saw Mrs. Andrews, smartly dressed as she always seemed to be. "Good! I guessed right! I thought I'd save you having to 'phone me. Shall we go straight to the hospital?" She led the way past the ticket inspector, who made no effort to check Tim's ticket, to the small car park. He was surprised when she unlocked a new, silver, Citroen Familiale. "We needed eight seats and there was a long waiting list for another Peugeot because they've stopped making the 504 and the new one hasn't come out yet" Mrs. Andrews explained, as if she had read Tim's mind. "We've got one of these, but just the ordinary estate version. In fact my mum just got another one. They seem to be quite good." Tim was glad to be able to talk about anything except that which needed to be talked about. They drove in silence for a while. "Tim" Mrs. Andrews broke the silence, glancing at him as she did so. "Do you know what happened to Michael? Because I think I need to tell you before you see for yourself". This was it! Mike had told her what a bastard he had been to him. Tim felt shame and regret flood through him, he really shouldn't have come. "He was out in the car, in the middle of the morning. Nobody really knows how it happened but he pulled out in front of a lorry which hit the car. The car was a wright off, of course, and poor Michael was very badly hurt. They told us he was lucky to be alive." Her voice trailed off. Tim wasn't sure if she was upset or having to concentrate on driving for a moment. "Tim, they couldn't save his leg. They had to amputate it." Tim's head filled with a dull, hopeless horror. His shoulders ached, as if an elephant was sitting on them. They were passing blue signs now, directing them to the different areas of the hospital. There was no escape for Tim. He realised that his discomfort was nothing to what Mike must be feeling but the guilt that was swirling around his mind, maybe that was the Divine Retribution that he had prayed for earlier.

 Mrs Andrews led the way confidently into the hospital. Tim supposed that she must come here several times every day. The hospital smell of ether and disinfectant made Tim feel queasy. They walked into a ward, and nurses greeted them. "Mike's in that side room" Mrs Andrews indicated a door. "I'm going to go and talk to the nurses. Leave you boys to talk boys talk for a bit!" Tim felt as if he was rooted to the floor. Heavily he moved towards the door of the side room. He peered shyly round the door. Mike was sitting up in the bed, propped against a pile of pillows. His left leg was encased in a plaster cast and suspended by a kind of miniature crane. Tim's eyes moved to where his right leg should, by rights, have been. It was covered in a blanket but Tim could see that it stopped short at about where his knee should have been. He thought maybe he was going to be sick. He wanted to run away, run and run and run forever. The huge, familiar grin spread across Mike's face. "**Tim!**" Tim walked over to the bedside. Dropping the magazines and Fruit and Nut bar that he had bought with Mr. Linford's money onto Mike's bed he held his outstretched hand for a moment. Letting that go, Tim dropped onto his knees beside the bed and hugged Mike as tightly as his position would let him. "Mike! Oh shit Mike! I'm so fucking sorry. I've been such a bastard to you. You're the best friend I've ever had and I've buggered it all up. I'm just so sorry." Tim was crying now. Unable to control himself. Crying as he had been wanting to cry since that day in the shower. He could feel that mike was crying too. That made him feel a little less stupid. "No Tim. *I'm the one who's sorry*. What I did was wrong. I know you're not queer. And I know what Lucas did to you that time so I should have known how much it would hurt you." Suddenly there was a sense of relief, of peace between them. Tears turned to heart felt laughter. "And now look at us" continued Mike. "Two wankers crying like a bunch of girls!".

Mrs Andrews came in at that moment and the boys reverted to a more formal, stilted kind of talk, the freedom of youth constrained by the presence of an adult. They talked mainly about school, the things that boys had been doing, the latest rumours and speculations. He told Mike of Mr. Linford's kindness and that reminded them to start to share the chocolate. Tim tried hard to keep the conversation away from Mike, his injuries and what he was going to do next. He really wanted to know, to be there to encourage and support the friend who he had neglected and opressed so cruelly these past few months, but he felt shy to do so, especially in front of Mrs. Andrews.

All too quickly it was time to go. "I need to get Tim home so we've got time for some supper before he has to get back to school" I'll be in first thing tomorrow Michael." The two visitors got up and took their leave. "You don't need to give me supper" Tim said as they got into the car. "I can make something for myself when I get back." "Now you're putting yourself at risk of making me angry! You boys never get enough decent food as it is. I've already cooked and Michael would never forgive me if I didn't look after you as I would look after him." Tim recognised from her tone of voice that there would be no dissuading this formidable and kind lady.

The lasagne was excellent, and the family had red wine with the meal. The twin brothers were boarding at prep school but Sarah was at home and Tim enjoyed the opportunity to talk to her and to get to know her better. Tim felt really welcome and started to feel glad that he had come. "I think you'd better drive Tim back, Ed." Mrs Andrews told her husband. "I was just thinking that Tim might as well stay the night now, then he can see Michael again tomorrow." "I haven't got permission to stay out, thank you. You know what Barforth rules are like!" "Don't worry about that. I'll 'phone them." So Tim stayed the night. He slept in Mikes' bed which he found strangely comforting. He lay thinking about ways in which he could try to make amends to Mike. He still felt devastated from the ups and downs of the day. At last sleep claimed the young man.

After breakfast Mike's parents drove Tim with them and Sarah to the hospital again. The four sat with Mike in his room, talking and laughing as if they were at some kind of a party rather than in a hospital. "Let's go and get some nice food for us all" Mr. Andrews steered his wife and daughter. "I know the boys need some time to themselves." The Andrews family left.

"What are you going to do now Mike?" Tim thought it best to broach the subject directly. "They're going to fit a prosthetic leg to me tomorrow. Then I'm going to learn to walk again and then I'm going to get back to school." Mike was equally direct, matter of fact, with his reply. Tim felt kind of intimidated, unsure how to respond. Mike was so brave. So cool and calm about this catastrophe. "Mike I'm going to say this because I mean it and I want it. But I'm not sure if it's going to come out how I mean it. However long it takes and whatever you need from me, I will be there for you. It sounds kind of silly, saying it out loud, but I do mean it mate. I want to help you when you get back to school." "I wish you hadn't said that mate. You're going to make me cry again" The boys hugged, each of them managing not to cry this time. Both knew that their friendship was repaired, that there was a new strength to it. Mikes' parents returned, brandishing the pizzas that had now become something of a tradition when they were all together. Mr. Andrews drove Tim back to Barforth later, promising to come to collect him again the following Saturday.

"It was really decent of them, having me to stay like that, when you think of all the hassle they've got at the moment". Tim was recounting his visit to Anthony and some other boys in their study later that day. Nobody had been aware of the extent or seriousness of Mikes' injuries and all of them were stunned by the news. Each of them, secretly, was glad that it had been Tim and not they who had had to endure the embarrassment of finding out. None of them was sure how they would have to behave towards Mike when he returned. Each was feeling awkward, embarrassed, uncertain of what should be expected of a friend in this unimaginable situation.

When Tim saw the big Citroen pull on to the quad the following Saturday and park, as usual, across several parking spaces he was taken aback to find Mike sitting in the front seat. "Shit! It's good to see you in the real world!" Tim blushed and apologised to Mr. Andrews for his language. "A good welcome from the heart! You can't better that!" Mr. Andrews put Tim at ease adeptly. "I'm going to spend the next two weeks learning to walk then I'm back to school after half term". Tim felt overjoyed. Once again Tim was welcomed into the midst of the Andrews family and enjoyed great company and good food before being driven back to school.

Two days before half term was due to begin Mr. Linford caught up with Tim on his way to lunch. "Tim, I've been meaning to see you. I think it must be about time to make you a House Prefect. Come and see me after half term and we'll sort it out". "No thankyou sir. It's not worth it now. I've got my A levels coming up so I don't need any extra hassle sir and then I'll be leaving. It's too late for that now". Tim quite surprised himself at the ease with which he answered. He didn't even feel angry. It had happened, for whatever reason, and Mr. Linford was a good guy. Tim hadn't forgotten about the train ticket. "I must say I'm a bit surprised, Croy." "Yes sir, but I guess you can get my point sir." "Yes, I think I do." "Oh sir, there's something I wanted to ask you sir. You know Mike Andrews is coming back after half term sir, well If I can get Anthony Williams to agree, can he and Mike swap studies so that Mike shares Top Three with me sir. I think it would be easier for him because it's nearer the washrooms and things and I promised him I'd look after him a bit because things are sure to be difficult for him". "I think that sounds like a great idea Tim. Well done!"

Adiew

Tim had a busy half term. In the Easter holidays he had spent a lot of time working in Mr. Reid's gardens, while he and his family were away. Mr. Reid had walked around with him talking Tim through the kind of thing that he had in mind and had then left Tim to interpret and execute the work as he saw fit. Tim was a confident and competent gardener, having grown up helping his father in their own large gardens. He had felt simultaneously pleased that Mr. Reid should trust him to that extent and responsible for ensuring that the extensive work should be completed to the best of his ability.

On the way home from school Mrs. Croy told Tim that Mr. Reid had telephoned her upon his return to his house to tell her how impressed he had been with Tim's work and to ask her to ask Tim to call him at half term. "He said such positive things about you. I felt very proud of you indeed."

Tim drove over to Mr. Reid's on Monday afternoon. As he drove his mind turned to Mike. He imagined the screeching of brakes, the lorry thundering towards the red Peugeot, the crunching of metal, the tinkling of glass and the fear and pain. He realised that he hadn't driven since hearing about Mike's accident and it filled him with a sudden fear, the first true realization of mortality and the possible dangers of the road. His leg felt suddenly weak, almost unable to press the pedals. Tim told himself not to be so silly. He turned on the radio, loudly, and wound down the window to feel the warm, sweet smelling country air swirling around his head in an effort to dispel such morbid thoughts. Parking his car in the large gravelled parking area in front of the house Tim pulled on the Victorian door bell lever. He could hear the genteel tinkling of a bell somewhere in the depths of the large house. Minutes later Mr. Reid appeared at the door, pulling on his dark green waxed jacket. "Tim!" Tim shook his outstretched hand. He had the feeling that he was being treated like a man, part of the adult world. It reminded him that he would soon be leaving the boys' world of school. Tim looked forward to that day. "I was so pleased when I got home. You did things exactly as I had hoped. The way that I would have done them myself. Let's go and see how they're looking now that everything's in full growth." The two enthusiasts set off on a winding tour of the great gardens. They passed the potting sheds, climbed the stepped slope up to the orchard and soft fruit garden. Tim admired the sprouting raspberries, the swelling gooseberries the fragrant black currents. They moved on to the sweeping herbaceous boarder that Tim had dug up and replanted. It was now looking full with the early summer growth, fading giant poppies and budding pink flocks and deep blue delphiniums. "This has been heavenly, Tim. I think about you every time I come out to the garage." "I really enjoyed doing it. I'm so glad it actually worked out properly." They headed back towards the house and then sat at a stone topped table on the terrace outside the sitting room doors.

"Tim I don't know what your plans are for when you finish school but I feel that I should stick my oar in." Tim smiled. He liked the easy way in which this man always spoke. "I don't really know what I'm going to do to be honest. I'm not that good so I may or may not get into university, fifty fifty at best." "Would you consider gardening as a career? Because I'm a Fellow of the RHS and I know that they offer excellent apprenticeships at their gardens at Wisley. I've taken the liberty of getting a prospectus and application form if your interested. I would be more than happy to act as a referee for you." Tim was taken aback. He hadn't expected this. "Thankyou. That does sound very interesting. I really wouldn't have thought of that." "You clearly have so much talent and you evidently know a lot already. It could prove to be a really good career for you."

They wondered towards the house once more and Mr Reid asked Tim about his car. Tim knew that he was some kind of engineer and that he had several exciting vintage cars that he kept in the huge garage block that was hidden behind the original coach houses of the large property. Tim took the prospectus and application form with him, placing them carefully on the front passenger seat. He promised Mr. Reid that he would fill it in and send it off that evening.

The return to Barforth was one of mixed feelings. Pleasure that this was to be his final return to School. Dread for the impending finality of "A" levels. Uncertainty about what the future, beyond Barforth, may actually hold. Excitement at the opportunity to try to help Mike in a practical way, to demonstrate his regret for the nastiness that he had built up between them. Shyness about how best to support his friend without being insulting or over bearing. It felt almost as if Tim's brain enjoyed searching for things to worry about. He toyed with the idea of verbalising his thoughts to his mother as they drove to school but he didn't feel really able to do so. There had developed a strange kind of barrier, a kind of reserve and distance between mother and son that neither felt able to bridge. Misunderstanding, each having the desire to help and protect the other from difficult truths, secrets that were kept by one and felt by the other but which could never be talked about.

There was a tap at the door of Top Study Three and it opened. Mike swung his way in on his crutches, followed by his parents. There was a moment of slightly embarrassed awkwardness. Tim pulled the chair from under the desk and positioned it so that Mike could easily lower himself into it. He offered his chair to Mrs. Andrews and indicated a seat on the bed for her husband. "I got Anthony to swap studs with you, Mike because I thought this one would be easier, with the washrooms beside it and that kind of thing". "You're obviously in good hands Michael" Mrs. Andrews laughed. They sat chatting, laughing, settling in. Tim apologised for being unable to offer them a drink as there would be no milk before the next morning. Mikes' parents declined his offer of biscuits and, reminding their son of the necessity of putting the prescribed cream on his severed leg at the correct intervals, they made their departure, promising to come to check up on him at the weekend. Tim stood to shake their hands and was embarrassed when Mrs. Andrews hugged him and whispered "thankyou Tim".

"It's great to have you back mate." "I never thought I'd say it, but it's great to be back!" "Mike" Tim decided to broach the subject that had been worrying him for the past month. "You know that I'm here to help you in any, and I mean any, way that you might need me to. I've been trying to guess the sort of things you might need but I'm not you and so I want you to promise to ask."" I do know Tim. And it's because my parents know too that they let me come back." There was a knock at the door and Huband and Williams burst in, exuberantly welcoming Mike back to Barforth. The rest of the evening was spent laughing, eating biscuits and celebrating the return of Mike.

Tim jumped out of bed the next morning and was washed and dressed before most of the boys in the Junior Dorm had even finished brushing their teeth. He hurried down to the Dining Hall. Ten minutes later he was clomping back up the stairs to Top Study Three bearing a tray loaded with bread, butter, a jar of marmalade, milk, eggs, bacon and a full packet of Rice Krispies. He kicked open the door, Surprising Mike who was getting himself dressed in his uniform. "It feels like an age since I wore any of this crap. I've obviously grown because my trousers don't fit my left leg properly now." Mike made it easy for Tim to talk about the missing right leg. "Have you put that cream on?" "Yes, Mum!" Mike laughed. "Do you need help putting your new one on?" Tim still felt shy of talking about it, as if, by raising the issue, he was somehow being insensitive. "No, I'm fine Tim. What's all that?" Mike was looking at the tray that Tim had put on the desk. "I went to see the Gnome before half term and told him how difficult it would be for you to get to breakfast in time. So he agreed to give us the stuff to make our own every day. It was really decent of him. Now we're going to have a party every morning!" "You scrounger! How did you wangle that? I'd never have thought he'd do that." The friends laughed and Tim headed out to the dingy kitchenette to concoct a full English Breakfast.

The next few days were busy with fussing for Tim. He was overly concerned for the welfare of his friend and underestimated the extent to which Mike had recovered his independence. Mike, in turn, did not want to appear ungrateful despite feeling almost smothered by Tim's effusion of unneeded assistance. Both young men were so relieved that their friendship had been rebuilt that neither dared to take even the slightest risk with it. The first short week felt, for each of them, as if they were juggling with expensive plates so keen were they that the relationship should never be damaged again. As time passed both felt relief as they fell into their old relaxed normality, insulting, teasing and laughing at one another as mercilessly as they ever had.

"Usman's been busted!" Anthony burst in to Tim and Mike's study. "Why?" "Caught smoking". "That's nothing new. He's always smoked since he came here". "Well he's busted now." Tim went down to look for himself. There on the Head Master's Notice Board was pinned the simple statement, intended as a warning, almost a threat, to other boys who may have been doing similar things.

Internal Suspension

Albad U. (School House) has been suspended for three days and stripped of his status as a House Prefect with immediate effect having been apprehended while smoking. Barforth School will not tolerate such reprehensible behaviour from any boy.

Tim felt that some kind of injustice had been committed against his friend but could not quite work out what it was. It was true and well known that smoking was against the school rules and it was generally accepted, even amongst those who did smoke that, if you were caught, it was fair enough that you should suffer a severe punishment. And yet….somehow it seemed to Tim that Usman should have some level of special status. He was much more grown up than other boys in his year, he came from a very foreign country where everybody behaved differently and it had been normal and considered quite right that he should smoke regularly and openly since he was twelve. You couldn't really expect him just to stop. Tim also happened to know that Usman's parents had to pay about twice the fees that English parents were asked to pay in order that the school could provide for the special requirements of an overseas pupil. Shouldn't making some exceptions to the normal expectations of the school be a part of those costly "special requirements"? Tim remembered the bullying, publicly humiliating shaving incident on Usman's first night and the way in which he was often unable to eat the food that the school provided because of his religious beliefs. And, anyway, Usman was a visitor to England and it was important, and, surely, only Christian to try to make a visitor welcome.

Tim and Mike grappled with these ideas together later. They started to speculate about who might have set out to catch him. "I bet it was Huband" stated Tim. "He loves throwing his weight around". "Yeah but we can't prove that so you can't just go and accuse him Tim". Mike pointed out reasonably. "Yeah I know but that doesn't make it right, whoever it was."

Mikes' fag brought the boys' post up one morning along with their ration of bread and milk. They no longer had such an urgent need for this source of sustenance with their special supplies of breakfast provisions but they were happy to take it none the less. Boys of eighteen have limitless appetites. Tim had a thick brown envelope, his address typed on the front and it was franked rather than having a stamp stuck on. Tim read the contents with some surprise, followed rapidly with a feeling of the winds of uncertainty about his future. "They've offered me a cadetship, with five thousand a year for three years if I get to university." "Who have?" "The RAF." "That's about a hundred pounds every week. You'd be well minted!" "I've got to get in to university first" "Yeah, but just think what you could do with that much money."

Exams were upon them! The Third Formers of nineteen seventy-five were now the Sixth Formers of nineteen eighty. Tim had six exams spread over seven week days. On one of those days he had two exams. This was it! Make or break! On the Sunday before "A" levels began Tim saw the School Fags setting up the desks and the signs that read "Silence! Exams in progress" in the passage way outside the Hall. He had seen this many times before but this time it made him feel kind of chilled inside. Mike and Tim had their first exam on Tuesday morning. Neither boy felt much like eating their home cooked breakfast that morning. "At least it will be over by lunch so we'll be able to eat properly then" Mike observed. Tim didn't feel that he was likely to want lunch either but he refrained from verbalising the thought.

It was all over! The candidates had done their best and the examiners had done their worst. The contest had been completed and futures had been sealed. Nothing to be done now until August when the results would be sent to each boy at home in a self-addressed envelope that he had deposited with the Head Masters' Secretary. Three more weeks of term during which boys were expected to undertake a "Leavers' Project" of their choice and to make two or three "Careers visits" to local companies that they had selected from a list published earlier in the term. Because he hadn't been there and had made no selection, Mike was excused this latter activity.

Tim had elected to do a Geography project with his old accomplice Alex. Both had been studying the subject for their "A" levels and both had thought that there was some fun to be had from "studying" the brook, in which they had suffered so many frozen hours in their first term at Barforth as "Brook Ball Boys". The fact that Mr. Harding, the Geography Master, was easy going and unlikely to chase or check their activities too thoroughly and that simply skulking around beside the brook and around the pavilion throughout long sunny days didn't seem dauntingly strenuous may have influenced their selection too.

One morning, after Chapel, all leavers were summoned to the classroom of the Master who was supervising their "Leavers' Project". Tim duly headed for the Geography Room where he was handed a two-sided printed form titled rather pompously "Barforth School Leavers Achievement Record". They were to fill in their full name and their House. Below that were printed various things that a boy might have been expected to achieve with a box next to it to be ticked. Followed by a large box in which to write "Any Other Achievement" Tim filled in his name. Timothy Croy. School House. 1975 to 1980. His eye roved, with increasing dismay, down the long list of potential achievements. Scholarship. Captain of Rugby, Captain of Hockey, Captain of Cricket, Captain of Boat Club, President of Christian Union, Chorister, House Prefect, School Prefect, Head of House, Head Boy. Tim found not a single box that he was entitled to tick. Suddenly he felt wave after wave of humiliation and a sense of injustice sweeping over him. A lump developed in his throat. How could it be that, after five long years of trying Timothy Croy could be leaving the school without having achieved anything that they recognised as being of any value? Not a single thing! He could see everyone else cheerfully ticking boxes. He felt sure that everyone else would be seeing that he had nothing to tick. Tim was worthless. Of no value. Somebody who deserved only to be ignored and overlooked. He felt the stinging of tears of self-pity forming at the back of his eyes. No! He was not going to dissolve in this way. He had not let Barforth crush him for all these years and he would not let it finish him off in the last two weeks! "Fight your own battles." Resolutely Tim began to write in the large "Any Other Achievements" box.

"I have been cox to the Under Fifteen A crew, the Under Sixteen A crew and the First Eight. You have not provided any boxes for these important achievements. I have managed to survive nearly five years of bullying and oppression. I have been nearly drowned in the brook as a fag, been punished because I didn't get confirmed, Ignored and overlooked for all positions of responsibility. I have always tried to follow the rules and behave in a decent way but this is not considered of any value at Barforth. I have helped, encouraged and supported other boys who have been hurt or lonely and who the school has not bothered with. Most of all I am still Tim Croy and I will never be Tim Barforth."

Tim signed the bottom of the form, clicked his biro shut with an air of finality, and took a deep breath of relief. He felt as if, in writing the truth, in a final act of defiance, he had relieved his soul of a great weight of hurt. I kind of emetic for the heart. Tim fully expected there to be some kind of come back for this written, signed, deliberate act of insult, which could not be claimed to have been misunderstood or misinterpreted, but he didn't care. In fact he positively relished the prospect of the opportunity to put forward his perspective on Barforth to the authorities one last time. He handed the form back in and went on his way.

"Are you alright?" Mike demanded in their study at break time. "You look really ill Tim." "I feel sick! Sick of this bloody school, sick of being humiliated and sick of being ignored." "Woah! I can guess what's brought that on. Don't take it to heart Tim. Lots of the best things are never counted. That's what my dad says." Tim was sitting on the bed now, feeling tired, weak and deflated. Mike eased himself onto the bed beside him. "Tim, I know you're thinking that it's easy for me and Anthony and Simon because we're all prefects and captains and crap like that. We fit into Barforth boxes! But, don't you see, it's because you *don't* tick those pointless boxes that you're such a good mate. You wouldn't be Tim if you did and then you wouldn't be such a special kind of guy." For the second time in as many hours Tim felt near to tears. "That means a lot Mike. You'll never know how much." "I've been waiting, hoping, for the chance to cheer you up like you helped me Tim." Mike told him quietly. The two young men sat in amicable silence, enjoying the special feeling of mutual care and understanding. "Let's have our coffee" Mike got himself to his feet. He flicked the kettle on and hobbled out to wash their mugs. "Do you want toast?" he called from out in the kitchenette. "Yeah go on then." It wasn't until the two of them were half way through their toast and coffee that Tim realised that Mike had made it, carried it, stood buttering the toast, by himself. Without his crutches, which were lying on the floor beside the bed. "Mike!" "I know Tim. Things have suddenly got easier this last couple of days. My physio said they would one day. I didn't believe her but she was right." "Do you think, if we got a taxi, you're up to a pint or two down the Lock Keepers' tonight?" "Let's do it man!" "I'll go and get permission."

Tim's careers visit to a chocolate factory was cancelled.

That was the only visit he had really wanted to get on, in the hope of being given lots of free chocolate at the end. He had to go through with his visit to a rubber processing plant. Tim and a couple of other boys spent the day walking round with a man in a white coat and a clipboard being shown heaps of raw rubber sheets, vats in which they were melted, moulds in which the rubber was shaped and climbing a cooling tower to see just how high it was. The only effects of the day on Tim were to convince him that he certainly didn't want to end up working with a clipboard in a factory and to make his clothes reek of melting rubber.

Thursday July tenth nineteen eighty

The end of term and the end of Tim's life at Barforth careered towards him with relentless speed and determination. How could five years, five years that had so often felt like they were a life sentence, have passed so quickly? The last few days held strange feelings for the Sixth Form boys. Excitement and relief for having reached the end of their school days. Trepidation because nobody could really make certain plans for their future until the "A" level results were published in August and provisional university places confirmed or denied. Sadness at the feeling of finality of the parting of friends. A feeling of detachment, of irrelevance, as information for the following September was published on the Head Masters' Notice Board. School Prefects, Captain of Rugby, Head Boy. None of these things, so important within the community of Barforth, held any significance for the leavers. All at once they had become the past. Yesterday's news, a tiny part in the great history of the school. This is what the ending felt like.

On the last evening of term Barforth tradition held that the Head Master had a drinks party for the Sixth Form Leavers in his private garden. Simon, Mike, Anthony, Usman and Tim, meeting in Simons' School Study One, discussed, in a state of some hope, exactly what they might be offered. "We've almost left Barforth now, so maybe he'll let his hair down a bit and hand out some decent beer and stuff" Anthony suggested. "He hasn't got much hair to let down" Tim laughed. "That's not very respectful." Simon reprimanded. "Oh sod off! Can't you snap out of your succerish Head of House mode now?" Mike dug Simon in the ribs as he spoke. Simon had always tended to say the right thing at the wrong time, infuriating his peers and making himself appear to be trying to endear himself to the school authorities, which he probably was. "Well let's find out!" said Tim, getting off the bed and stretching luxuriantly. The School House boys set off up the village street towards the Head Masters' House.

As they progressed up the street they fell in with groups of boys from other houses. They turned off the street and through the white painted gates of the Head Masters' House. None of them had been there before and they all felt a bit uneasy. The Head Master was standing behind a table covered in a white cloth that flapped in the light evening breeze. About twenty boys were already there, standing awkwardly in the contrived situation. Mr. Bolton handed each newcomer a small, twisted flute of sherry. It tasted very sweet and sticky, more like cough mixture than a nice drink. Tim helped himself to a handful of ready salted peanuts. "It's just about all I'd expected" Alex laughed to Tim. After a few more long minutes of standing around and not being offered any more drinks Mr. Bolton Stood on his terrace above the throng of boys and began a speech.

" Congratulations on reaching the end of your wonderful years at Barforth. I know that many of you will be feeling sad at this significant point in your life. Do remember, if I may offer one last piece of advice for your future, that whatever life presents you with you will always be an Old Barforthian! That alone will make you welcome wherever you go. So if your "A" levels don't work out as you hope just go knocking on doors, look people in the eye and say "Here I am. I've had the best education possible and I'm ready to give you my best, in the way that Barforth School has taught me to". Well done and best of luck to all of you!"

"Do you think that he *really* believes all that crap about the whole world knowing how wonderful Barforth is?" Tim scoffed as they headed back to School House. "Nobody ever heard of this place in Jiddah" laughed Usman. "That's what he's *paid* to think. But, obviously, Barforth is his world so he probably does think it's true" Mike added.

The School congregated in the Chapel for the final service. There was the usual sense of bubbling optimism of the last act of the school term. Freedom beckoned. Tim stood with his School House friends to belt out the traditional Hymn. They slammed their hymn books into the tray in front of them and walked out of the Chapel onto the Head Masters' Quadrangle and into their futures. For longer than usual Tim and his peers wondered about, thumping friends between the shoulders in good natured parting, occasionally shaking a well liked Masters' hand. Then, suddenly it really was over. The crowd of people swarming around the quad thinned. Tim headed, for the last time, down the private lane to find his mothers' car already parked beside his waiting trunk. He felt a little embarrassed to find Mrs. Andrews standing chatting to her. "I hadn't realised that your mother was one of the people we met on that dreadful tea party!" she laughed. "I've been telling your mother what a hero you've been to Michael these past months." Tim blushed, looking at the ground. She didn't know the truth about him. He excused himself and went over to Mike beside his car to help him get his stuff loaded. He was sure it would be difficult for him with his false leg. The two friends hugged, both unable to think of the right thing to say. "see you!" they finally said, simultaneously, as Mrs Andrews approached.

Tim helped his mother load his belongings into the gaping boot, slammed the lid shut, belted himself into the front passenger seat and the car pulled smoothly away. Barforth disgorged Tim, without ceremony and largely unaltered, as it had attempted to swallow him almost five years earlier.

Epilogue

There remains no lasting evidence that Timothy Croy ever attended Barforth School. No gold leafed name on an honours board outside the Dining Hall recording him as having been Captain of Boat Club 1979, Head of School 1980 or having been awarded a place at Oxford 1980. Within four years no boy would remember him and after twenty years there would remain no Master who knew him either.

The lasting legacy remains with Tim. The crippling self doubt, borne of five years of being crushed, squeezed and moulded by the mighty rollers of tradition and expectation of one of the great British public schools. The constant fear of rejection and the need to feel part of a group that results from five years of ostracism, of being in a state of looking in from the outside, of somehow not belonging to the community that claims you. The strength that comes from total self reliance and the vulnerability of feeling unable to trust or to rely on another person. A kind of eternal reprimand for refusing to succumb to the will of Barforth.

But wait a moment! Head, if you will, up the steep, winding staircase to School Study One. Fling open the leaded window and look closely at the lead flashing around the base of the dormer. You will discern, prodded into the soft grey metal, with the point of a pair of compasses, forming a kind of inverted Braille, the defiant message "Tim Croy. 1980" staking his lasting claim to the top job.

Printed in Great Britain
by Amazon